BAD APPLE

ALSO BY MATT WHYMAN

The Savages
American Savage
Boy Kills Man

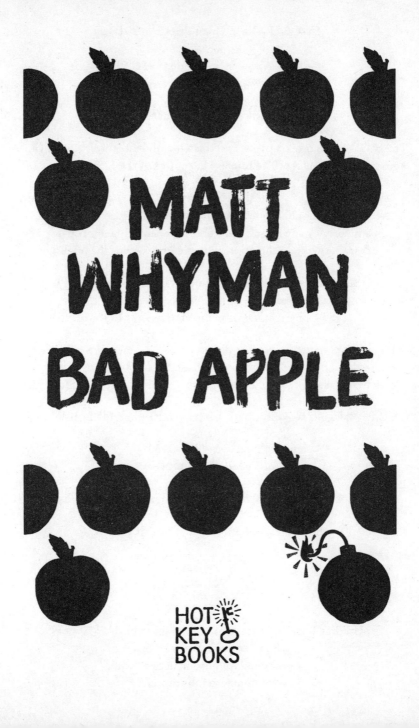

MATT WHYMAN

BAD APPLE

HOT
KEY
BOOKS

First published in Great Britain in 2016 by
HOT KEY BOOKS
80–81 Wimpole St, London W1G 9RE
www.hotkeybooks.com

A CIP catalogue record for this book is available from the British Library.

ISBN: 978-1-4714-0420-7
also available as an ebook

This book is typeset in 10.5 Berling LT Std using Atomik ePublisher

Printed and bound by Clays Ltd, St Ives Plc

Hot Key Books is an imprint of Bonnier Publishing Fiction,
a Bonnier Publishing company
www.bonnierpublishingfiction.co.uk
www.bonnierpublishing.co.uk

For Ethel Honey Rose,
the baddest apple of my eye

Ages ago, thousands of generations ago, man had thrust his brother man out of the ease and the sunshine. And now that brother was coming back changed!

H. G. Wells, *The Time Machine*

MIDDLE ENGLAND

Five years ago

'Why can't they just go back where they came from?' The man addressed the television as if he expected a direct answer. 'There should be laws!'

On the screen, the reporter stood before a crater. It spanned the complete width of a freeway, sixty kilometres south of Dallas according to the sliding news ticker. Judging by the way several vehicles teetered over the edge, a catastrophic event had occurred without warning.

'This is the largest known sinkhole to appear since the crisis began,' said the reporter, who struggled to stop her hair from blowing across her face. 'One eyewitness claims the freeway "just dropped out of sight". Several drivers are being treated for shock, but with no fatalities, this has been one lucky escape.'

'You can say that again,' the man grumbled. 'No doubt the low lives who caused this vanished without trace.'

'You can't say *low lives*.' A little girl sat at the man's feet with her legs crossed and hands in her lap. 'We're not allowed to call them that. We had an assembly on it this week.'

'She's right.' The child's mother sat beside her husband on the sofa. She looked at him disapprovingly, and not just because he'd just flopped beside her in sweaty jogging gear. 'She'll only repeat it at school.'

'Emergency crews are assessing the tunnels exposed by the collapse,' the reporter continued, 'but once again safety is an issue.'

'What did I tell you?' The man looked around at his family, which included his mother-in-law who was snoozing on a recliner with the footrest extended. 'They dig wherever they please, undermine everything and get away with it! If I were in charge, things would be different. No low life would go to ground on my watch!'

'They're *not* called *low lives*!' The little girl glared over her shoulder this time. 'They're trolls.'

'Whatever.' The man waved away the correction. 'They still spell trouble.'

As if to support his claim, the news bulletin cut to a digital globe. It revolved on a tilted axis, slowly revealing a world dotted with red spots.

'At least they haven't come over here,' the woman commented, glancing briefly at her mother as she began to snore.

'They wouldn't dare.' The man lifted the neck of his running vest, as if to release some heat. He frowned as the snoring grew louder, and then sucked the air between his teeth. 'What she needs is a wake-up call,' he said. 'I'm struggling to hear myself think here!'

The little girl had been watching an art show for children before her father sat down and assumed control of the remote.

With the channel switched, she would've left the room had it not been for the news item. Like so many people, she was gripped by the discovery of a subterranean race of reclusive – some said primitive – creatures that had previously been confined to myth and legend. With every sinkhole that appeared, a result of centuries of secret tunnelling which could no longer be supported at ground level, the existence of trolls had become undeniable.

'But when will we *see* one?' she pleaded. 'I want to know what they look like.'

'Oh, they can't keep retreating into the rat runs they call home,' her father answered with contempt. 'One day soon we're going to come face to face with these idiots. Then they'll be sorry!'

As he spoke, the man was forced to raise his voice. He scowled at his mother-in-law, only for his expression to regroup in surprise on seeing that she was now wide awake and no longer the cause of the noise. For the rumble had become more persistent than a snore. In fact, it swiftly approached a level that seemed to creep up the walls of the house. A vase on the mantelpiece began to shake before toppling to the hearth, which prompted the little girl to whimper and clamber into her mum's arms.

A moment later, the spot where she had been sitting on the floor just sank away.

Then, to the sound of splintering timbers, the carpet began to follow it down. When the recliner glided forward, like a ship leaving berth, the startled old lady shrieked and grasped the armrests. The man on the sofa, along with his wife and child, simply looked on with slackened mouths. It was with hammering hearts that they witnessed the chair come to a halt before them, with barely enough time for the passenger to look in their direction before both plunged out of sight.

'Granny!' The little girl scrambled to the edge of the hole that had just opened up between the foot of the sofa and the TV. As she did so, a frail hand snapped up through the dust and grasped the man's ankle. His first instinct was to attempt to kick loose. Then a voice cried out, which brought him to his senses along with his wife.

'Help! Save me!'

Grasping the stricken geriatric by her wrist and cardigan scruff, the pair peered into the abyss. Below, with both legs flailing, she appealed once again for someone to haul her out. What seized their attention, however, was the sight some way further down. For several pairs of eyes blinked up at them, close set and filled with surprise, fear and astonishment, as if this was the first time that they had witnessed the searching light of day.

OVER HERE

Just now

'This is not a prison. It's a living, breathing settlement. The citizens may not be permitted beyond the perimeter walls, but life here is just the same as it is for us on the outside.'

The teacher with the microphone faced the students from the front of the coach. Mr Wallace possessed a voice so monotone it seemed incapable of carrying enthusiasm. Even now on a tour through the urban sprawl they had come to see, he made it sound as dangerous as a retirement community. In his carefully knotted tie and wire-frame glasses, he looked at odds with the view through the windscreen behind him. The road was in a state of some disrepair, as were the buildings, while youths in hooded tops warmed themselves around braziers on every corner. As the bus passed them by, crawling through one rundown district after another, they eyed the passengers with muted hostility.

It didn't help that many of the pupils on board were pulling faces.

'Greetings, losers!' crowed one boy at the back, before baring his buttocks at the window. 'Don't forget us in a hurry, will you?'

'Remember we are ambassadors for the school!' Mr Wallace held the microphone so close to his mouth that his words distorted. 'Now, as we progress you'll note that the majority of inhabitants are in their teens and early twenties. Can anyone tell me why?'

A hand shot up near the front.

'Because that's when the antisocial hormone kicks in.' The girl who answered the question ignored the catcalls from the rear. 'A troll might look human, but at puberty they can't hold back their true nature.'

'That's correct, Olivia.' Mr Wallace beamed at the girl. 'We're talking about the urge to pursue feral, disruptive activities. Now, who can give me an example?'

'Theft!' offered another girl near the back, before quietly flicking a V-sign at the figures outside. 'I blame the parents.'

'Well, yes Stacey. You have a point.'

Mr Wallace sighed at the upswing in noise as the pupils sounded their agreement. He couldn't argue with her comment, even if it had come across a little bluntly. Ever since the existence of trolls was uncovered, and following the realisation that generations had been secretly switching their offspring with human babies at birth, people came to regard them with anything from suspicion to outright hatred. Yes, these wretched underground dwellers were only hoping to give their flesh and blood a better start in life on the surface, but nobody knew what fate befell the little ones they spirited away. That there was no way to determine if a child was in fact a troll imposter until adolescence just made things worse. Only then did a tell-tale hormone go live that immediately prompted a profound and damning failure to be civil. The riots just proved how widespread the switching of offspring had become. Thankfully, advances in genetics enabled the first trolls to be identified and cast out from society, which certainly made life easier for teachers like Mr Wallace.

'But let's just imagine how these youths must be feeling,' he pressed on. 'One day they're enjoying life in a stable and happy environment, growing up just like you guys. The next thing they know, some deterioration in their behaviour leads to a simple swab test and they find themselves here. The families that raised them so unwittingly as their own can no longer even bring themselves to say their names. As *changelings*, they're abandoned, unloved –'

'And untrustworthy.'

This was the boy at the back once again. He was no longer mooning, but his comment provoked a cheer. Mr Wallace flattened his lips. The aim of this trip was to promote understanding and insight, not prejudice and bigotry. The paperwork alone had taken up enough of his time. This wasn't like an away day to a war memorial or natural wetlands. Like every school that took the tour, security clearance was required in advance and the forms he'd sent home with each pupil were obliged to disclose a full risk assessment. Judging by the antics of the fools in the back seats, he thought to himself just then, it was the low lives that were being exposed to all the abuse.

'Settle down!' he ordered crossly, causing the coach speakers to crackle once again. 'If we can't show the trolls how to behave nicely, what hope do they have?'

'Nothing will change them, sir.' This was Olivia. She appeared to be alone in devoting her full attention to him. 'Trolls are a lost cause.'

'They're a menace to society!' A boy just behind her drew the teacher's attention. He too broke free from sneering through the window before making his contribution. 'Natural-born vandals. That's what they are.'

'Which is why, once discovered, they're contained in settlements like this one.' Mr Wallace noted that a hum of chatter had begun to accompany each answer.

'Sir!'

The girl raised her hand once again. Mr Wallace tried hard not to appear pressed.

'Olivia?'

'All these low lives,' she said. 'They look a bit . . . Neanderthal?'

Mr Wallace could sense control of the coach slipping from his grasp. He waited for a moment for the chatter to subside before clapping his hands.

'Let's not be discriminatory,' he said, well aware that over time most changeling kids developed the same close-knit brow, sloping shoulders and tendency to mumble when speaking. 'Studies show the trolls share ninety-nine per cent of our DNA.'

'And are one per cent pure thug,' said the clown behind Olivia.

'That one per cent remains a mystery!' snapped Mr Wallace, his patience now down to the bone. 'And can we *stop* calling them *trolls*?' he asked, reminding himself as much as everyone else. 'Somewhere in the mists of time, many thousands of years ago, a tribe belonging to our ancestors went underground. For whatever reason, that's where these hidden people chose to remain. Evolving out of sight from the rest of the world. Now our paths have joined once more. As cousins, of sorts, it's down to us to understand and embrace them.'

A groan rose up from every seat in the bus, as if each pupil had just opened their packed lunch to find egg and cress sandwiches. The fact was nobody called them the *hidden people*. In the same way, very few teenagers who tested positive were referred to as changelings. It was the media that had branded them trolls when the cause of the sinkholes was confirmed, while *low lives* was a term often heard at rallies and on marches. Just then, Mr Wallace told himself that he really should lead by example, despite the time in recent weeks when he found his car door had been keyed. Then, the social sciences teacher hadn't just used the unofficial term out loud but preceded it with several expletives.

'Sir.' It was the clown behind Olivia once again, who gestured at the boy in the aisle seat beside him. 'Maurice really needs to pee.'

Mr Wallace levelled his gaze at the kid in question with the dark, curly hair and thick-rimmed glasses, and tutted for the benefit of everyone in earshot. The kid just looked unhappy at being the focus of so much attention.

'I'm fine,' he said quietly, but clearly in some discomfort. 'It can wait.'

'You all had the opportunity back at the security area,' Mr Wallace reminded everyone. 'I said expressly that there would be no further opportunity until the tour was over.'

'Maurice didn't like the look of the patrol dogs,' explained the joker with a smirk. 'He wouldn't get off the coach.'

Mr Wallace waited for the laughter to subside. Maurice continued to look pained, and not just because of his full bladder. Still, the teacher figured he was used to being the subject of mockery and mirth.

'Just hold on,' Mr Wallace told the kid. 'I don't think I need to spell out why we're forbidden from getting out and wandering around.'

The joker glanced side on at the boy.

'You could always tie a knot in it,' he said. 'If only it was long enough.'

Mr Wallace closed his eyes as yet more laughter filled the coach. He expected better from his sixth formers. They had been fully briefed beforehand, in assembly and before the gates opened up for the coach. The first few minutes inside the settlement had reminded him of visiting a safari park as a child. The kids had crowded to one side of the coach when the first young trolls were spotted, but the novelty quickly faded and their interest had turned to antagonism. He checked his watch. They had been touring the streets for half an hour now. Another fifteen minutes and the coach would reach the gates on the south side. Then, following a stop for the restroom, the settlement would be behind them. Even if his pupils failed to calm down, he could safely ignore them for the duration of the journey back to school.

'Can we please have some respect for our surroundings?' he asked, sounding strained now and not a little half-hearted. 'You wouldn't behave like this at home.'

With the volume only growing, Mr Wallace opted to fall silent. Where some of his colleagues would tackle the level of noise and disruption head on, he preferred his kids to pick up on his displeasure and calm themselves accordingly. As the academic years went by, however, he found he had to wait a little longer for them to read his mind. Just then, amid the chatter and squeals, the beleaguered teacher grasped the top of the seat rests on each side of the aisle and focused on the landscape outside. It really was a desperate and derelict environment. Weeds flourished from every fissure in the pavements. Billboards sported torn and sun-bleached advertisements. One offer for a holiday in paradise looked more like a taunt from another world. As for the buildings, most of the windows were so badly cracked or smashed it could've been mistaken for a blast site. They passed makeshift junk stalls and hawkers touting lethal-looking homebrew. In Mr Wallace's view, those shops that had been reclaimed were stocked with household goods that must've been scavenged when the trolls first arrived here.

'A bomb might not be a bad thing,' he muttered to himself, only to turn away from the coach window when one of the low lives out there locked eyes on him.

In the twilight, with shadows at full stretch, the figures visible to the coach party assumed a sinister quality. The street lamps remained dormant, which only suggested that some gang or other had diverted the power for their own illegal gain. Crime was the central currency inside the settlement, and the authorities tolerated that. In dealing with such inveterate troublemakers, they provided the troll population with the basics to survive and just allowed them to get on with it. Welfare workers were assigned to their care, of course, but like most people Mr Wallace wondered why anyone bothered when ultimately the perimeter wall kept these reprobates in check. The distant band, visible between tower blocks, was like a steel horizon. Ultimately, it served as a means of security and protection for those on the other side, which is where he set his sights as the coach trundled through the central district. He barely noticed they had slowed down until the driver started yelling.

'Hurry up, pal. We don't have time to waste like you!'

The sound of the vehicle's horn prompted Mr Wallace to glance back at the driver – some guy with ash-coloured hair slicked tight to the crown of his head and nicotine embedded into the pores of his skin. This was the first time the man behind the wheel had done anything but sigh since they'd set off from school. Now he was exchanging an angry glare with some troll who was deliberately dragging his heels as he crossed the road. Mr Wallace winced at the second blast of the horn, but at least it forced the troll out of the way. The driver was just doing his job, Mr Wallace decided, which focused his attention on the purpose of their visit.

'Now, you all have projects to complete by the end of term,' he reminded the group over the catcalls as the coach rolled onwards. 'If anyone is hoping to shine in their final exam, I suggest you make full use of this opportunity. It's time for you to observe and enquire. Don't just sit back and enjoy the ride. This is social management in the making. Challenge *everything*!'

Bracing himself for questions, Mr Wallace took a step back to steady himself as the coach braked yet again. He looked across at Olivia, expecting her to strike up with something, only to see her staring straight ahead with some concern.

12

'Sir.' This time it was the boy, Maurice, who called for his attention.

'There's no way we're stopping for a wee!' snapped Mr Wallace. 'Man up, lad!'

For a moment, in the wake of his outburst, the harassed teacher believed that he had at last found a level of authority in his voice to bring silence to the coach.

'Seriously, sir.' Maurice sat up straight with his eyes widening. 'What's going on out there?'

Mr Wallace turned to face the front, just as the driver punched the horn once more. This time, he saw not one troll but a whole knot standing directly in the path of the vehicle. By now, figures could be seen loping from the side alleys and the surrounding buildings. When one of the pupils stood and shrieked, it was enough to provoke an air of panic.

'Stay in your seats,' demanded Mr Wallace, upon which several more students rose to their feet. 'We're quite safe here.'

He had barely completed his sentence when something heavy hit the top of the coach. Such was the impact that the overhead light casing lost several screws. A second later, a mechanical roar struck up from above. Mr Wallace looked up with a gasp, just as the teeth of a buzz saw bit through the roof.

'Keep calm!' he yelled, as kids screamed and scrambled to distance themselves from the shower of sparks. Within seconds, the trolls surrounding the coach began to hammer the sides with their fists. '*I said keep calm!*'

By now, the buzz saw had cut three sides of a square directly overhead. Only when the blade disappeared did Mr Wallace think to move away, but by then it was too late. With tremendous force from above, the metal roof peeled upwards to reveal several hooded figures in silhouette against the sky. When a pair of hands reached down and grabbed the teacher by the collar of his jacket, it happened at such speed that he appeared to just lift right out of the coach. The driver and the passengers simply looked on in horror, and did nothing to help the one boy who had jumped from his seat to grab the man by his trousers.

'Let him go!' cried Maurice, his feet swinging clear of the ground. 'Hands off! Give him back!'

To the sound of a collective gasp, and with the coach now rocking dangerously, the last of the teacher and his pupil ascended through the square in the ceiling. A tearing sound followed, along with a startled cry. A moment later, the mob surrounding the coach melted into the shadows before a body crashed back into the aisle. Mr Wallace hit the floor so hard it left him winded. Muted by the trauma and with the hem of his trousers in ribbons, all he could do was raise one frail hand and point at the ragged hole.

High overhead, the vapour trail from a plane turned silver in the last light of the day. Mr Wallace found the aircraft, focusing hard, and watched it promptly slip from his sight.

PART ONE

1

Maurice always woke just ahead of his alarm. Like clockwork, he would spring from his dreams into the first worries of the day. So it came as no surprise when he surfaced with his heart racing. As ever, despite the adrenalin rush, he was determined not to open his eyes until the bedside buzzer went off.

Within seconds, lying on his side, the profound silence tested his resolve.

Normally, Maurice would register his mother downstairs, signalled by the sound of the toaster popping. Ever since he could remember, she always prepared him two slices with a thin spread of butter and a generous layer of jam. He had given up trying to persuade her that he was quite capable of fixing his own breakfast, but she insisted. *You might burn yourself*, she would say, as if the toaster was some kind of open forge. His dad didn't help matters. Whenever Maurice suggested that most sixteen year olds were equipped to make a cup of tea, he'd simply shrug and make out that it would be easier all round if he just let her carry on managing the kettle like she did their lives.

Just then, however, Maurice heard nothing. All the noises that usually marked the start of his day – from the kitchen radio to the dog whining for a walk – were missing. Despite it all, he told himself not to give in to his anxieties. At his age, it was only normal to lie in. Just another minute of dozing, he decided, would be a small victory.

There were times when Maurice wondered if he might be more relaxed if his parents just stopped treating him like a toddler. The quiet downstairs didn't necessarily mean they were lying on the tiles with the bloody footprints of an axe man leading towards the back door. Nor did the damp, clammy sensation in his crotch area automatically mean that somehow he had wet himself overnight. Assuming the worst was just second nature nowadays, and he hated it.

Then the odour of stale urine reached his nostrils.

Maurice snapped open his eyes, and realised with a start that he had been blindfolded. He took a sharp breath, which promptly brought the fabric of the gag around his mouth to his attention. Panicking now, he attempted to move, and that's when the full extent of his confinement became apparent. Bound at the ankles and with his wrists tied behind his back, it took a moment for Maurice to haul himself upright. For someone prone to a little fretting, this wasn't a good start to the day.

'Help!' he called out. 'I can't breathe!'

When the gag snapped away, Maurice gasped and then froze. Someone was close by. An unwashed presence, judging by the sour funk that hit his nostrils. Then he felt fingers fumbling with the knot at the back of his blindfold, which promptly fell away from his face. In desperation he struggled to focus, sensing also that someone had just taken a step away from him.

'My glasses,' he croaked. 'I can't see without them.'

Whoever crouched before him didn't respond. Maurice blinked fiercely in a bid to clear his vision. All he could make out was a figure in silhouette framed by the dim, early light from a window. His head still spinning from shock, the boy had a vague memory of being dragged from the school coach. What had happened after that was beyond him, though the side of his head throbbed madly now he was upright, which suggested something bad. Quite suddenly, the figure advanced towards him. Maurice shrunk away on instinct, and then reminded himself to breathe on feeling the arms of his glasses slip over his ears.

'Thanks,' he said, as the figure retreated once more.

Straight away, with his focus restored, Maurice knew that he was face to face with a troll. Generally it was tough to tell. In the years since the discovery that many had been hiding in plain sight, planted with new parents in place of their natural offspring, it was their adolescent actions that betrayed them. The suspect would be caught in possession of a bag of weed, a can of aerosol paint or some social media account responsible for a barrage of monstrously offensive posts, and suddenly it all made sense. Just like the underground dwellers themselves, however, the hormone responsible proved impossible to detect before the damage was done. As a result, families with kids considered to be a handful could do nothing but simply hold their breath when puberty kicked in and hope they'd settle down. Facing the youth crouched on his haunches, Maurice needed no test results to know what he was dealing with here. Even though the hoodie cast the figure's face in shadow, that sullen glare was unmistakable.

'They'll be looking for me.' Maurice glanced around at the state of the room. It comprised of a mattress, a sink with a mirror covered in toothpaste spots, a portable gas cooker with a pan and a plastic storage tub containing some clothing. 'You and your friends can't just snatch people from coaches,' he pressed on, and noted how the figure before him now avoided eye contact. 'Not without consequences.'

The troll turned his attention to the window, flinched as if some abseiling commando was set to come crashing in, and then seemingly resigned himself to facing the boy again.

'Do you speak?' asked Maurice, addressing him slowly and a little bit louder now. 'Can you understand what I'm saying?'

From inside his hood, the troll's eyes widened. Judging by the way he rocked back and forth, making a strange squeak every now and then, the boy's captor seemed to be struggling with himself internally. It was enough for Maurice to experience a flash of anger. Nobody expected to wind up in this situation, after all. On a school trip, the worst thing you would expect was to find yourself sitting next to someone who suffered from travel sickness.

'Listen, if this is supposed to be part of the tour, then you've done a great job. I won't forget the experience in a hurry, but it's time I went home.'

Still the troll didn't respond, just carried on beading him with barely a blink.

'Is there someone less stupid I can speak to?' Maurice attempted to roll his shoulders, feeling more assertive all of a sudden despite having urinated in his pants. 'Hello?' he called out, which caused the troll to spring to his feet with one finger pressed to his lips. '*Anybody?* An idiot is holding me hostage! I need some assistance here!'

Seeing his captor jump up only prompted Maurice to shout louder. Frantically, the troll waved his hands in a bid to shut him up, but the boy just carried on yelling, and that's when he reached for the pan.

'Someone please do something!'

It all happened so quickly that Maurice failed to register the cooking utensil until the flat bottom connected with his temple. The impact served not just to silence him but also to return him to an all-consuming darkness that needed no blindfold.

2

Bonita Shores grimaced as she attempted to shift up a gear. Why it always made that terrible noise was beyond her.

'It's not me,' she told her father, who had drawn breath sharply. 'It's your car.'

'Just focus on the road,' he told her. 'Good driving comes with practice.'

'I *am* a good driver,' she insisted, and sped up just a little to beat the lights at the pedestrian crossing. 'If you had a better model I would've passed my test first time.'

Governor Randall Shores quietly pressed the imaginary brake pedal beneath his foot, and wondered what his day had in store. For the last eight months, ever since she'd turned seventeen, Bonita had driven to college each morning while he held his breath in the seat beside her. In that time, the streaks of grey through his hair had multiplied considerably. It had come as a disappointment to Randall that she wasn't a natural behind the wheel. Nevertheless, as a father it was his role to be as supportive as he was instructive. Right now, that meant not reminding her of the fact that she was driving a company-owned BMW 6 Series. One that reflected his role as the man in charge of the country's largest troll settlement.

With work in mind, he glanced down at his mobile. Randall had slotted it into the charger when they set off from home. On seeing that Bonita had switched it to power her own phone, he tutted pointedly.

'Why does everyone unplug me?' he muttered, and swapped over the phones. 'Your mother did it while I was in the shower and now you.'

'Stop distracting me, Daddy!' Bonita glared at her father, and then snapped her attention back at the road to prevent the car from veering. 'If we have an accident because you're moaning then it'll be your fault. Just be quiet and let me concentrate!'

She took after his wife in lots of ways, the Governor reflected, but mostly in her cast-iron confidence and the sense that at any moment he was about to displease her. Randall Shores cradled the mobile in his hand, waiting for it to power up.

'I use my phone for work,' he reminded her. 'It ran out of juice last night, but every time I try to charge it, someone else decides that their social life is more important.'

'I need my phone for college,' protested Bonita, who realised her indicator was still flashing from a turn she'd made over a minute earlier. 'What if I'm mugged?'

'Who's going to mug you?' her father asked. 'Any mugger round here is under my watch.'

'You'll be sorry if something happens to me today,' Bonita complained. 'If I have to go to the secretary's office to reach you by landline, they're going to think I'm neglected.'

Randall drew breath to respond, only for his phone to alert him to several missed calls and a string of alerts from the settlement's control centre. He cursed to himself, ignoring the fact that Bonita also offered more choice words at a bus she'd decided to overtake on a corner.

'I need to get to work,' he told her. 'Stop the car and let me drive.'

'But we're nearly there,' said Bonita, squeezing in front of the bus to avoid the oncoming motorbike. 'If you take over we'll both be late.'

'This is important!'

'And so is this.' Without warning, Bonita pulled in alongside two boys who looked to Randall as if they had dressed for college that day by pulling clothes blind out of a charity sack. 'Hey, Ryan!' she called. 'What's up, Benny? Why don't you guys jump in?'

All of a sudden Randall found his daughter leaning across him to his nearside window with a playful look at the pair.

The boys glanced at one another with a smirk.

'I'm always up for a ride with you,' said one, and swung his manbag over his shoulder.

'What about your dad?' asked his mate, looking both wary and highly amused.

Randall clenched his phone tightly, well aware that he didn't have time to remind these two gutter hound dogs that they were facing a man who should command their respect. Things would be different from the moment he arrived at work, he promised himself. After what he had just learned, today the changeling youths within the perimeter wall would be reminded of just who was in charge. For all the innuendo going on here, however, Randall felt sure that Bonita wasn't the sort of girl who would play fast and loose with boys. She

24

could still look him in the eye when he asked and swear that she always behaved nicely around them.

'Daddy is just the passenger here,' Bonita told Ryan and Benny as they climbed into the back and slammed the doors in unison. Randall winced at the lack of consideration for his vehicle, and then glanced at his daughter in the hope that she wouldn't be tempted to show off behind the wheel. In response, before shifting the car into gear, she gestured dismissively at his mobile phone. 'Haven't you got some calls to make?'

*

As ever, Candy Lau had dressed by the light from the landing. If she switched on the bedside lamp, Greg always pointedly placed a pillow over his head. It didn't matter if he was already awake at the time. Even now, as she crouched beside the bed, Candy's boyfriend eyed her unhappily.

'I'm going now,' she whispered, and leaned over to kiss him on the forehead. 'Don't forget to put the bins out.'

With a groan, Greg reached up and gently pulled her into his embrace.

'Take the day off,' he mumbled. 'If the only thing I have to look forward to is the bins, it's your duty to keep me company.'

Candy pressed her palms against his chest and raised her head to address him.

'The bins won't take all day,' she said. 'I thought you had a paper to write?'

Since graduating the year before, Candy and Greg had seen their lives take different paths. While Greg stayed on at university to study for a doctorate, which seemed to involve spending a great deal of time in front of daytime television,

Candy had placed her foot on the first rung of her career ladder. Her job with the settlement welfare team wasn't easy, but she loved it. Greg failed to understand why anyone would want to work with a bunch of antisocial delinquents. Candy considered it her calling.

Aware that time was not on her side, the young social worker rolled off the bed and tied back her hair in the mirror. With her fringe cut short, it fell naturally to frame her face. She smoothed her skirt, straightened her blouse collar and lifted her chin to inspect her final appearance. It was a stance that reminded Candy of her old grandmother back in Kowloon. On market day, whenever a trader proposed a high price, she would adopt the same upright posture and haggle until they agreed on something more reasonable. Even now, she felt it was a look she could grow into over the years.

'It must be torture for those guys,' said Greg, sitting up as Candy applied a blood-red lipstick. 'You breeze into the settlement each morning, looking hot to trot, and expect a bunch of sex offenders to behave themselves.'

'They're not sex offenders,' she said crossly. 'The residents might have many undesirable qualities, but I've yet to encounter one who didn't recognise the concept of respect. Even if they choose to challenge me, there has always been a line.'

'It's only a matter of time.' Greg scratched himself under the duvet, before devoting his efforts to a long yawn. 'My point is should you dress so provocatively?'

Candy turned to face him.

'I dress smartly to please myself, as I always have done.'

'You mean you don't do it to please me?'

'I thought you loved me for my personality.' Candy took a step towards the door. 'Have a good day, now.'

'One thing,' said Greg, who waited until she had turned full circle. 'No sweets in the car, OK? Sweets mean wrappers. And wrappers mean Greg gets angry.'

'You mean sulky,' she said with a smile. 'I've never seen you get angry. You just go quiet until I realise something has upset you.'

Greg grinned, though Candy knew full well that he was being deadly serious about eating in the car. They'd gone halves on the vehicle, but often if felt as if he was loaning her the keys.

'Just don't trash it,' he said to finish. 'And take care of yourself, OK?'

'You say that every day, like something bad will happen.'

'You spend your day with *trolls*,' he said, and hauled the duvet up to his ears. 'Something bad is bound to happen.'

Candy stopped herself from smiling.

'I wish you wouldn't speak like that.'

'Are you about to tell me we can't call them trolls now?' Greg pretended to look affronted. 'Everyone calls them trolls, including you! Mincing around with words isn't going to make the problem go away.'

'None of us is perfect,' she said plainly. 'But what I mean is do you have to say it with such contempt?'

Candy reached for the door, facing her boyfriend as she took a step out under the landing lights. Greg settled deeper into the bed.

'You might think you have their measure,' he grumbled. 'Just don't drop your guard.'

'Trust me,' she told him, smiling as she finally closed the door behind her. 'I'll take good care of the car.'

At the interview, shortly after picking up a degree in Psychology and Social Work, Candy Lau had set herself apart from the other candidates by remaining quite calm when a fight broke out between two young changelings. They had been eating lunch in the canteen when the fists and trays went flying. Rather than back away like everyone else, she had been the first to intervene and negotiate the return of the bread roll that first caused them to come to blows. The Governor had warned her never to place herself in such danger again, of course, but even at the time she knew her handling of the situation quietly impressed him.

'You've got some balls,' she said to herself just then, smiling as she tucked in her chin to mimic the way the man had addressed her. 'I like that in a lady.'

In her view, the guy was like all the security staff at the settlement. The only difference was he had more stripes. Having spent the best part of a year in their company, Candy could honestly say she favoured her time with the changelings more than her colleagues. Both could be rude and abusive, but with patience, trust and hard work, one group did at least show some small improvement.

Grabbing the car keys from the kitchen counter, as ever with no time for breakfast, Candy headed out into the street. Rain had begun to fall. Judging by the clotted clouds, the day looked set to be a stormy one. With the collar of her coat turned up, Candy hurried for her car. Once inside, she gunned the engine, waved at Greg who always spied on her from behind the curtains, and then reached for the glove compartment. She would grab some fruit before her first assignment. Until then, she could stem her appetite on the journey in by sucking on some travel sweets from the bag she had stowed in there. With the end of one wrapper wedged between her teeth, she twisted the first sweet free and popped it in her mouth. Then, having pulled away out of sight from her boyfriend, Candy Lau took great delight in flicking the wrapper onto the floor well of the car. She would clean up before her return home, of course. Until then, the day belonged to her.

3

Opening his eyes for a second time that morning, Maurice found the room's troll count had increased considerably.

'Something tells me this isn't room service,' he muttered, and winced on locating another angry bump on his head. The boy sought to sit up, noting that at least his school trousers had dried, though it did nothing to stop his stomach from knotting. 'I don't want any trouble,' he went on. 'Just let me go home.'

Instead of one hooded individual observing him intently, Maurice counted more than a dozen. Collectively they looked like urban druids. All of them regarded him in silence, differing from one another in just height and frame. It prompted him to look around with a sense of rising panic, for it felt as if they were close to using up all the air in the room. Two girls were among their number. One wore a plastic pink clip to pin her fringe to one side. The other chewed gum furiously. Both had plucked and shaped their eyebrows so savagely they looked like quotation marks. It did little to soften the way they stared at him. Looking away smartly, Maurice recognised the little troll who had assaulted him with the pan. He was standing back from the others, and dropped his gaze to the floor just as soon as the boy laid eyes on him. As Maurice struggled to process the situation, it struck him that the low life almost seemed to be ashamed of himself.

'Can you tell me the difference between a human and a troll?'

Maurice's attention shot across to the individual who had just addressed him. The troll pushed his hood back as he spoke. It revealed a youth with a head that looked like it had been squashed at the sides. With hair receding sharply at the temples, it left him with a stripe at the front, effectively pointing at the scowl across his face. Nervously, having dubbed him 'Long Skull' in his mind, Maurice cleared his throat.

'Do you want me to answer that?'

'It's why I asked the question.'

The troll spoke with a voice that was gruff but calm. He also made it sound as if an incorrect response might have consequences. At school, thought Maurice, a question like the one he'd just been asked would invite all kinds of put downs. So what *was* the difference between a human and a troll? he asked himself. You only had to leave them alone in a shop for ten minutes and then empty their pockets to find out. Not that he had any intention of sharing such an observation with the degenerates in front of him.

'I've done nothing,' he said instead. 'Let me go.'

'The answer,' said Long Skull, seemingly deaf to his protest, 'is one per cent. Genetically we're identical but for this tiny fraction, and yet you choose to cage us here like stray dogs. Now tell me, is that fair?'

Maurice was well aware of the close similarity in biological make-up. That difference in DNA between the low lives and people like him was indeed minuscule. Even so, leading experts had declared it to be responsible for all manner of mayhem and antisocial offences. Without the establishment of a settlement like this one, and every country had several like it, the world would be in anarchy. Given his predicament, however, the last thing Maurice wanted right now was a debate.

'I'm not in charge,' was all he could think to say. 'I don't make up the rules.'

'Just as my brothers and sisters here didn't make the decision to be raised among you.' The troll addressed Maurice without once blinking, gesturing left and then right at the figures alongside him. 'Is it fair that we're punished for a decision made by our blood parents?'

Like all kids his age, Maurice had grown up at a time when the world's response to the existence of the hidden people had turned from shock and awe to borderline panic and outright resentment. The moment proof surfaced that many had been secretly planting their progenies into society like cuckoos in a nest, nobody considered them as underground cousins any more but child snatchers and bringers of grief. For such apparently simple creatures, and with estimates that the practice extended back centuries, they had learned to sneak into maternity wards and stage the exchange with stealth and cunning. As most newborns arrived with puce and knotted faces, it left exhausted new mums and dads with no idea that the bundle of joy blinking up at them from the crib the next morning was anything other than their flesh and blood. Even with security measures raised, these subterranean dwellers knew just how to seize that moment when nobody was looking.

As for the changelings, they might've had no say in being swapped at birth, but on finally testing positive – following some unforgivable act that went far beyond the natural exuberance of adolescence – they were simply regarded as aliens in need of containment. Nowadays, almost everyone knew a parent who had disowned the imposter they'd unwittingly raised. It changed them. Some swore that they would not rest until the fate of their true children was uncovered. Others withdrew from life to become as reclusive as the creatures who had spirited away their sons and daughters. To date, their underground domain had proven so vast, treacherous, multilayered and seemingly mined without logic that it remained largely uncharted. Military squads on every continent, emergency rescue teams, amateur potholers and a string of attention-seekers had made numerous attempts only to surface looking grubby, disorientated and dejected. It left a world that existed on two levels, only one continued to undermine the other.

'You're hardly doing yourselves any favours here,' said Maurice, irritated by the troll's apparent bid to portray himself as a victim. 'This is kidnap and assault.'

'What choice do we have?'

'Well, how about you stage a peaceful protest?' Maurice suggested.

Long Skull's expression tightened as if he had just undergone an increase in internal pressure.

'How about you shut your face?'

Maurice didn't argue. He knew how quickly trolls could deviate from acceptable social conduct, and this one looked capable of violence. It was easy now, looking back through history at the tyrants and hell raisers, to recognise their subterranean roots. People widely accepted that the very worst cases were down to changelings who had made it through to adulthood undetected. Only recently, the bad boy exploits of several global rock stars had led to tests and a spectacular fall from grace. The trolls, it seemed to an increasingly alarmed general public, were everywhere.

Briefly, Maurice thought of the Jacksons who ran the florist shop on the high street. He had taken to crossing the road to avoid their boy long before he embarked upon the trolley rampage through the supermarket when Mrs Jackson refused to buy him a four pack of extra-strength lager. There was just something about his loping stride and the sideways look that unsettled Maurice, and rightly so as it had turned out. Still, his parents, neighbours and friends of the family had rallied around the couple after the swab results proved positive, and nobody had seen the kid since.

Maurice looked around at the slovenly gang congregated in front of him. He didn't recognise any of them.

'If you set me free,' he ventured quietly, 'I can talk to the people in charge.'

His offer was met by a chuckle. First from the troll who had done all the talking, and then from the others.

'If we cut you loose they'll come for us,' said Long Skull, which killed the laughter. 'If we keep you in our care they'll have to negotiate.'

'What if they don't?' he asked.

'They will.' The troll paused to examine his knuckles. 'Even if they need a little persuading.'

Maurice sensed his heart rate quicken.

'People won't care about me,' he offered, hoping for a break.

'You're a schoolkid,' said Long Skull. 'Schoolkids make headlines when their lives are in danger.'

Just then, perhaps in some subconscious bid to feel safe, Maurice pictured himself in class. At this time, first thing in the morning, he would be listening to his teacher while ignoring mashed-up balls of paper as they bounced off the yoke of his jacket. He had long since accepted his status as an easy target. Every class needed a kid who made everyone else feel normal. Nobody bullied Maurice. They just laughed at every aspect of his life, from the kiss his mother planted on his forehead when she dropped him off in the morning to the fuss she made of his appearance on picking him up. He had learned to brush off the put-downs and focus on working hard, but this was different. Ignoring his tormentors here was not an option. As he sat trying not to hyperventilate, one of the trolls produced a phone from the pouch of his hoodie. Maurice recognised the casing immediately.

'That's mine!' he protested. 'At least let me call home. My parents will be frantic.'

A smile played across the lips of the troll with the phone.

'The perimeter wall doesn't just stop us from getting out,' he said. 'It blocks the signal, too.'

'I miss the internet.' A faraway look crossed Long Skull's face, as if he was relishing a memory. Knowing how a troll behaved online, Maurice figured it involved pornography or reducing someone to tears.

'What's the security code?' asked the one with his mobile.

'Mind your own business,' said Maurice.

The troll looked up at him, not smiling any more.

'The code?' he growled, narrowing his eyes.

Maurice told him the code. Long Skull nodded in approval.

'That's a good boy,' he said. 'If you cooperate then bad things won't happen. Now, we're not monsters. Of course you can speak to your parents. In fact, you can address anyone with an interest in your situation just by looking into the camera here and setting out our demands.'

The troll with the phone held it up with the lens facing outwards. The little red light told Maurice he had begun filming.

'Go ahead,' said Long Skull. 'Tell them you'll be freed once they've opened the settlement gates for us.'

Without blinking, as if facing strengthening headlights, Maurice simply stared at them both.

'They'll never do that.'

'It would be rude not to ask.' Long Skull offered him a loaded smile. 'Especially now we have a hostage.'

Maurice drew breath to respond, only to find a catch in his throat. For the first time in years, he felt like crying. He pressed his lips together and swallowed hard. He had no choice, he thought, but to do as they ordered and just hope for the best.

'What do I call you guys?' he asked next. 'As a group, you must have a name.' The two female trolls responded by glancing at one another uncertainly. For the first time, Maurice sensed they weren't in complete control of the situation. 'You haven't really thought this through, have you?'

36

Long Skull refocused his attention, his brow lowering.

'What do you suggest?'

'You're asking me?' Maurice touched his chest with one thumb. Then he laughed out loud – just briefly, at such a ridiculous turn of events – only to fall silent on registering that his captors were awaiting a response. 'The Trolliban?' he offered, to no reaction. 'How about the Troll Liberation Front?'

Long Skull ran a hand through his arrowhead of hair. By the time he reached the crown of his head, he was grinning broadly.

'I like it,' he said. 'The TFL.'

'No, that's Transport for London,' Maurice pointed out. 'The TFL provide travel advice for the capital's commuters. The Troll Liberation Front would be TLF.'

The jittery figure that had earlier hit the boy chuckled at this, and then froze when Long Skull glared at him.

'Get out,' he growled at the little troll. 'Now.'

'You heard the boss,' muttered the one holding the phone. 'And don't breathe a word, understood?'

For a second, it looked as if the troll who had tittered out of turn was too scared to move. Then, with a blink, he pulled his hood low over his brow and hurried for the door behind them. Long Skull watched him go, and then turned to Maurice once more.

'Just do your thing for the camera,' he muttered. 'We don't need a name. By the time we've finished with you, *everyone* will know who we are.'

'What if I refuse?' asked Maurice, who had gained a degree of confidence from this apparent fracture in the gang. It was only to last a moment, however, for that's when Long Skull stepped up so close that the boy could smell meat on his breath.

'Then we film the moment you meet a sticky end,' he said with relish.

*

As soon as Governor Randall Shores registered the figure in the plastic seat outside his office, he knew the guy was from the government. This was no man in a black suit and shades, however. In Randall's experience, the officials dispatched to the settlement were civil servant minions with a message from their masters. Usually it was about cutting costs. As the junior with the gelled sweep of hair jumped to his feet, Randall knew this one was here about 'the situation'. That's what everyone had called it just as soon as he passed through security.

'Kyle Trasker. From the Social Order Programme.' The young man offered a confident handshake that couldn't possibly reflect whatever work experience position he was in, thought Randall. He took one look at the guy in his tailored suit, carefully open at the throat, and took an instant dislike to him. 'Good to see you at last.'

'You mean I'm late,' said Randall, who was in no mood for diplomacy since Bonita had parked at an angle outside the college and handed him back his keys. At home, his wife and daughter knew just how to play him. In the workplace, however, things were different. If some of the trolls had taken it upon themselves to host an involuntary sleepover for some tour coach kid then Randall would just have to remind them who was in charge around here. Settling into his swivel chair, he watched the government geek fumbling with a notebook. Finally, he found a page for reference, and then ran his finger along a line of scrawled handwriting.

'The boy snatched from the coach is a first year A-level student.'

'What's he studying?' asked the Governor, which invited Trasker to look up in surprise.

'Does it matter?'

'My girl is doing the sciences,' he said before yelling at his secretary for coffee. 'When she qualifies as a doctor, I'll be the proudest father on earth.'

Kyle Trasker looked a little lost for words. Then he went back to his notes as if seeking a prompt.

'Modern history,' he confirmed after a moment, before checking his notes once more. 'That's one of the subjects he's studying. It's the reason for the coach trip.'

'Not a proper subject,' muttered the Governor, and then directed his irritation into a less personal point. 'When the instruction came down to open the gates to educational tours, I just knew one day something like this would happen. You can't trust a troll, son, and feel free to quote me on that.'

Trasker closed the notebook.

'Sir, I'm not a journalist,' he said. 'But in the interests of the boy's welfare, we've established a press blackout. Any media attention could provoke the perpetrators. The parents and the school are cooperating, though frankly those who were on board the bus are too traumatised to speak about it at this moment in time.'

'Silence is good,' said the Governor, well aware how important it was to present settlements such as this one as a model solution to the troll problem. Faced with strong opposition from civil liberties, they had taken a great deal of political manoeuvring to establish. No doubt those liberal douchebags had never come home to find the widescreen missing and excrement steaming on the carpet. Trolls were capable of exactly that kind of domestic horror show. Now they were safely contained behind perimeter walls, however, Randall considered life to be much calmer, more ordered and downright *polite*. Kids reported that they could go online to enjoy video games without risk of being verbally abused by other players. The comments section on news sites had actually become a civilised forum for debate. Used chewing gum became less prevalent on pavements. Posting personal status updates was no longer an open invitation for bullying and mindless insults. Even some supermarkets had removed the coin device from their trolleys, knowing they would always be returned and not parked in the nearest waterway. It was the Governor's conviction that the settlement system worked. Encouraging field trips here as some kind of progressive educational opportunity had undoubtedly led to this crisis. Reminding the low lives who was in charge would resolve it. Randall could be relied upon to close down this situation, and he would do so old-school style.

'So, what do you propose?' asked Trasker, clutching his notebook to his chest. 'We can't contain this thing indefinitely.'

Governor Randall Shores grinned confidently, and then barked at his secretary to enter when he saw her at the glass door with the coffee on a tray.

'When I find out who is responsible,' he said, gesturing for her to set it on the table, 'I'll personally tear them a new ear hole.'

The man from the government looked set to correct him on something, but evidently judged the moment to be wrong.

'I've already spoken to your chief of security,' he offered instead. 'He has squads poised to lock down every block and sweep it clean.'

'Not going to happen,' said the Governor, who promptly stopped to focus on pouring the coffee. Trasker nodded at the offer of milk while Randall made a vague effort to hide his contempt when the guy opted for the sweetener. Taking his black, the Governor sat back with his cup and saucer resting on his paunch. 'Son, do you know the first rule of staying on top of a zoo like this? You don't panic. That's a sign of weakness. Now if I sound the alarm and flood the streets with enforcement officers, the low lives would think they've got quite a prize on their hands.'

'We prefer to call them residents,' Trasker said quietly, who had found his coffee too hot to handle. 'And we have hostage negotiators on standby.'

'Will you stop turning a drama into a crisis?' The Governor took a sip of coffee, which he rolled around his tongue like a wine-taster before promptly knocking back the whole cup. 'I can handle this in my own way. Whatever you want to call them, the trolls respect my authority, and that runs to a fear of the consequences if they dare to cross my path.'

Kyle Trasker tried his cup one more time, and elected to just leave it.

'So, you're going in there single-handed?'

'Single-handed and fully caffeinated.' The Governor slammed his cup back on the table. 'Every troll knows not to mess with me, and that's how I'm going to find your boy,' he promised. 'By the end of today, your situation will be paperwork.'

4

The rain had strengthened considerably when Candy Lau pulled up at the checkpoint into the settlement. She knew every guard who manned the barrier. Even with her identity badge in hand, a smile was usually sufficient for them to see her through. So it came as a surprise to the young social worker when she was asked to wind down her window.

'Morning, Jeffrey,' she said as the uniformed figure with the waterproof cape over his shoulders peered into her little hatchback. 'Is there an issue?'

'Not on this side of the fence, Miss Lau,' he said, but offered nothing more as he scanned the interior. Candy glanced at the sweet wrappers in the passenger footwell. She wished she had been a little tidier. 'Just be careful in there today, OK?'

'You sound like my boyfriend,' said Candy.

Jeffrey stood back, smiling now. His weathered face seemed at odds with the pure white gleam of his dentures, but the warmth in his expression was for real.

'I'm old enough to be your father,' he said. 'Whatever the case, I'd have never let you take this job in the first place.'

'So many people worry too much,' she told him. 'Things might be a little more civil since the settlement program, but

43

we hardly live in a crime-free world.' Candy reached for the volume control on her car radio, silencing the breakfast news. 'Who kidnaps cops?' she asked.

Jeffrey pressed his lips together, evidently sharing her feeling about the item she had just switched off. It wasn't a fresh story, but one that resurfaced whenever another officer vanished from the beat. Just then, facing the guard, Candy hoped he recognised that at least it wasn't something that could be blamed on the individuals she was here to nurture and support.

'I mean it about watching your back,' he told her all the same.

Candy rolled her eyes, wished him a good day, and waited for the barrier to lift. Like Greg, even her friends had fussed when she'd applied for her first job here. Why would anyone want to work with low lives? they had asked. Those thieving, foul-mouthed deviants would take one look at a good-looking young woman and see nothing but a victim-in-waiting. Well, following her belief that nobody was beyond help, Candy reminded herself on following the service road towards the staff car park, she had proven them wrong. It had been almost thirteen months since she started here. In that time, she had worked with young trolls who had proven as enlightening as they were infuriating. In her opinion, they just had a different way of making their mark on the world, which was no surprise in view of their heritage.

Just then, Candy slowed behind a sanitation tanker, crinkling her nose on seeing fluid dripping from underneath. Anxious not to let any splash over the car bonnet – something Greg would be sure to note and moan about – she pulled back a little before turning off at the car park. If everyone she knew could see what

44

kind of jobs people carried out at the settlement, she thought, they'd realise she was doing pretty well for herself. Talking to changelings every day was a far cry from cleaning out toilet cesspits, though no less vital for their welfare. Candy often wished something could be done to improve living standards within the perimeter walls. As those decisions were taken at the top, however, for now her focus was on improving the space inside their minds.

The entrance here on the west side of the perimeter wall would take her into the secure compound that housed the administrative, medical, catering and educational facilities. The wall itself consisted of a ten-metre high ring of steel, topped with razor wire and studded with sentry posts and searchlights. Candy had been at school when governments throughout the world established the settlements as a means of safely containing known trolls. For practical, political and financial reasons, rundown urban landscapes were first to be reclaimed, and that began with the ghost towns. This one, just beyond the orbital ring road, had suffered terribly during the recession. Bankrupt and largely abandoned, with empty shops, crumbling estates and untended parks, those citizens who remained were quickly rehoused before the wall went up around it and the first of the new residents escorted inside. By the time she arrived for her first day in the job, Candy found the settlement was practically full to capacity. To her eyes, however, she didn't encounter a disruptive breed that had been cast out by shocked and grief-stricken families. The young social worker saw only potential.

'Hey, Candy! Keep your eyes open today, OK?'

The voice, which came from an office just off the corridor, belonged to the unit secretary. Candy paused at the door and smiled at the woman in the blouse with the pictures of her kids facing outwards on the desk. Serena acted like a mother, friend and counsellor to the small band of social workers here. She recognised how tough it could be, working with trolls, though never had a bad word to say about them.

'What's going on?' asked Candy, unbuttoning her coat. 'Even Jeffrey told me to stay alert.'

Serena beckoned her inside, and gestured to close the door.

'There was an incident yesterday,' she said, speaking low, 'but it's been played down while they deal with it.'

'An incident?'

'That's all they're saying.' Serena shrugged, and then referred to a clipboard on her desk. 'So, who have you got today?'

'I haven't looked at my schedule yet.' Candy switched her bag from one shoulder to the next. 'But I'm ready for anything.'

Serena ran her finger down the list and paused at a name. Candy watched her shoulders slump.

'Do you want me to break it to you?' The unit secretary looked up at the young social worker, and offered a brave smile.

'Is it who I think?' asked Candy.

Serena responded by nodding solemnly.

5

Ignoring the advice from his chief of security, Governor Randall Shores chose to walk the settlement streets without guards or body armour. Wearing a dark-leather bush hat and tactical jacket, boot-cut jeans and aviators, his presence quickly drew attention.

'Stop slouching,' he barked at a group of trolls on a corner, who quickly melted from his path. 'You! Those trousers are intended to be belted firmly around the waist, not slung halfway around the back of your thighs. Sort it out before you break your nose on the pavement!'

Despite the sweeping rain, the Governor walked with his shoulders square and head upright. He carried a can of pepper spray in a holster, but that was just for show. In Randall's experience, it was his reputation that served to remind the low lives not to mess with him. At every block he hoped that someone would see him and squeal all about the missing schoolkid. They could be like that, the trolls. Most would rat on their best friends for the slightest reward or privilege, which is why he had packed his lapel pockets with sticks of chewing gum. Such a simple pleasure would pretty much guarantee that someone with information would share it. With this in mind, he kept the pockets open so they could see what he was packing. And if that didn't work, well, if they really chose to push him then Randall would find a way to make them talk.

Just south of the old church now daubed in graffiti tags, as if someone had thrown spaghetti at the walls, Randall became aware that several trolls were tailing him. In a job like this it was compulsory to have eyes in the back of your head. The slightest glance over his shoulder confirmed that the pair on the other side of the street seemed close to breaking from their saunter in a bid to keep up. If they had got it into their heads to attempt a mugging, he thought, then they wouldn't just be surprised by his identity but by the force of his response. Randall didn't much like himself when his anger got the better of him, but he knew it inspired a level of caution inside the settlement. As the low lives didn't know the meaning of respect, he thought, it served the same purpose. The idea of taking out the duo behind him caused his heartbeat to quicken. It would also send a clear message to whoever had the missing kid, he decided, which fired him up all the more.

'Let's do this,' he muttered to himself, sidestepping a pothole filled with rainwater at the mouth of an alley. As he did so, Governor Randall Shores caught sight of his reflection. He paused to admire this portrait of composure and authority, only to yelp in surprise when a little figure barrelled from the alley and crashed right into him.

'*Freeze!*' he yelled a split second later, having got a grip on his response as well as the troll's shoulders. 'What's the rush?'

With a grunt, the creature in the hoodie looked up at him. The Governor peered into his eyes and immediately recognised why they pinched at the corners in sheer terror. This one had crossed him before, which instantly left him feeling both empowered and a little uncomfortable.

'Name?' he asked, as if this was the first time the toerag had crossed his path.

The little troll drew breath to answer, only to slip into a stutter. 'R-r-r-r—'

Randall looked around. It was painful waiting for him to spit it out. The two potential muggers had retreated under an old store awning, he noted. As the low life in his grip continued to sound like a struggling car ignition, he almost wished they'd stepped up to him earlier. It would've been more rewarding dealing with those grunts than it was listening to this one trying to squeeze a word from his lips.

'OK, whatever,' he said, as rain dripped from the brim of his hat. 'Now, a pupil was snatched from a coach yesterday. I'm sure every last one of you knows about that, right? I mean, it isn't every day you guys have the street smarts to stage a hijack. I'm guessing you got lucky, but we can settle this. I just want to know who's behind it.'

The troll simply blinked at him. Then his teeth began to chatter. Randall exhaled through his nostrils, feeling only pity at the lack of backbone here.

'Pull yourself together, friend. It's just a question. I'm not saying you're involved. All I want is some information.' The Governor pulled a stick of gum from his pocket. 'I'll make it worth your while.'

The little troll's gaze fixed on the stick. Slowly his whole body began to tremble.

'Come on, son. Where do I find the kid?'

The troll was making no effort to speak, which began to irritate. Still clasping him with one hand, the Governor used the other to brush back his hood. The jagged mop of hair that sprung out reminded him of a jack-in-the-box, while the terrified expression was about right for a low life under pressure. The most notable thing about his pasty, freckled face wasn't the wiry monobrow but the snub nose and pale blue eyes. Most trolls didn't look this delicate, and in fact the majority would've responded by now with a string of filthy curses. Randall narrowed his gaze. Maybe this one genuinely had nothing to hide.

'Are you late for something?' he asked instead, which finally drew an answer in the form of furious nodding.

Randall glanced at his wristwatch. At this time, the social services facility was due to open its doors. In his opinion, the kind of hand-holding they provided was a complete waste of time. Still, he reminded himself that such pointless pussyfooting kept the critics at bay.

'Who are you seeing today?' he asked, and then rather wished he hadn't when the little troll made a verbal attempt to answer him.

'C-C-C-C-C-C—' he stuttered. 'Ca-Ca—'

'Never mind.' Cutting him off, Randall released his grip on his shoulders. 'Get out of here.'

Instead of slipping away, as the Governor had expected, the troll's attention lingered on the gum peeping from his pocket.

'You want some?' Randall asked.

The troll nodded.

'Then give me some names!'

If he knew something, Randall decided, this would surely break his silence. It was clear that some internal struggle was going on inside the calcified sponge that functioned as a brain. A moment later, the low life glanced one more time at the Governor. As he did so, a noise formed in the back of his throat. It was one that quickly turned to a cry before he broke away at a sprint. Randall watched him tear off under the downpour, and felt sure the object of his search was close at hand.

*

By the third take, Maurice sensed his captors growing impatient.

'I'm sorry,' he said, as the troll with the camera deleted the last attempt. 'It's just you guys are making me really, *really* nervous.'

Earlier, several of the gang had followed in the footsteps of the jittery troll and left the room. It was Long Skull who had dismissed them. He insisted that everyone do their own thing to avoid attracting suspicion, and had promised to follow suit once they had the footage of their captive. As far as Maurice was concerned, the moment that they left him to his own devices he would be singing from the window. Someone out there had to be looking for him. All he'd have to do is shout from the rooftops and they'd surely come running.

'Do it again,' growled the troll with the phone, one of three who remained with their cranially challenged ringleader. 'And remember to say your name this time.'

Ever since they had allowed him to stand up, Maurice felt as if his knees had turned to butter curls. The headache from when the little troll had hit him with the pan was nothing to the sense of dread that churned inside his guts. At any moment, he kept telling himself, this gang would fall about laughing, confess to one massive wind up and even slap him on the back as they let him leave. Maurice glanced around, desperate for some sign that this really was all a joke.

'Come on, guys,' he said, and spread his hands. 'It's not funny any more.'

Long Skull stepped forward, mirrored his expression for a second before scowling hard. Then he punched the boy squarely in the stomach, stepping back to give him room to double up.

'You have one last chance,' he said. 'Or there'll be consequences.'

Grimacing and breathless, Maurice picked himself up. He straightened his glasses, and found the trolls staring balefully at him.

'Action,' said the one with the phone.

Maurice breathed out slowly, struggling to hold on to his composure. Then he moistened his lips and addressed the lens. He gave his full name, as instructed, and then stressed that he was being treated well by the group holding him. As he spoke, outlining the conditions for his release, Maurice felt sure that anyone who knew him could tell that he had just been assaulted. It could only double the efforts being made to find him, he decided, and finished by assuring his mother that he was nowhere in the vicinity of a hot drink.

'That wasn't in the script,' said the troll with the camera as he checked the footage. 'You got an allergy to coffee or something?'

Maurice sensed himself flushing. Having been staring hard into the lens, imagining himself to be directly addressing those closest to him, he had momentarily forgotten his surroundings.

'My mum likes to look out for me,' he confessed quietly.

Long Skull nodded, reflecting on this for a moment.

'My mum used to look out for me, too,' he said. 'Until she found out that I wasn't her real son.' Just then, the troll with the phone confirmed they had the footage they needed. Long Skull motioned at Maurice to sit on the edge of the bed. 'Do you have any idea how it feels to be kicked out of the home you grew up in? To be told that your family are not your own? That you're an imposter? A *fraud*?'

Long Skull was becoming increasingly fired up with every utterance. Maurice looked to the floorboards, terrified the troll might hit him again.

'I've done everything you asked me,' he said quietly. 'Give me a break.'

Long Skull squatted on his haunches in front of the boy.

'Have you had enough?' he asked, with what sounded like a note of concern. A moment later, the troll's expression darkened considerably. 'Welcome to our world, friend.'

'Can't you just be nice?' Maurice rose to his feet, forcing Long Skull to stand and take a step back. Having a changeling call all the shots just wasn't right. They were lesser beings, locked up so the rest of the world didn't have to deal with their appalling conduct. That's just how it was. Maurice didn't create this situation, so why he had to suffer for it was beyond him. 'Let's face it,' he continued, forgetting himself for a moment, 'if you guys had just minded your manners in the first place you'd still be living your lives and nobody would be any the wiser. Now, I can see you don't have much going for yourselves here,' he added, gesturing at the peeling walls, 'but do you really think kidnapping me is going to make things better?'

'What have we got to lose?' The troll with the gum blew a bubble and let it pop. 'A lot less than you, for sure.'

Maurice faced Long Skull once more. The punch to the gut had come as a surprise, but also served to adrenalise him. Now that feeling was beginning to recede, revealing raw fear for his safety.

'They could find me at any moment, you know.' Maurice turned to address the group as a whole. As he did so, Long Skull grabbed him by the collar of his school jacket and dragged him towards the window.

'Let's see, shall we?' he yelled, thrusting the boy against the ledge. With his cheek pressed against the pane, Maurice gasped on feeling the cold edge of a blade touch his jugular. 'If anyone comes to your rescue, then mark my words it'll be the *death* of you.'

The light from outside dazzled the boy as much as the sense of sheer panic. After a night in a blindfold and hours in the gloom, it took a moment for the skyline to stop flaring in his vision. Slowly, as he fought not to react against the sting of the weapon at his neck, the streets and buildings came into focus. They were several storeys up, with a view between two tower blocks and a jumble of rooftops to the perimeter in the distance. From what he could see of ground level, without daring to move his head in any way, figures were seeking shelter from the rain or milling about around makeshift shops and food stalls. As he had seen on the coach trip before it all went wrong, the trolls here were free to scratch a living in any way they could.

It meant if they weren't thieving from one another they were bartering, which Maurice would've found fascinating at any other time. Just then, knowing that one wrong move could leave him with a severed windpipe, all he wanted to see was some sign that people were out searching for him. Instead, overlooking this sprawling slum, he felt as far from home as he had ever been before.

'You've made your point,' Maurice dared to whisper, and gasped when the pressure of the blade against his neck dropped away. Breathing out long and hard, he turned to see Long Skull face the others.

'Kill the security lock on that phone and leave it outside the Governor's compound,' he growled at the troll who had shot the video clip. 'The sooner Shores knows our demands, the quicker we can all get out of here. And if that fails to persuade him,' he added, returning his attention to Maurice, 'then we'll have to let you go –'

'Thank you!' breathed Maurice.

'– starting with your fingers, my friend, and then your toes . . .'

6

The troll was ten minutes late for his session. This came as no surprise to Candy Lau. As a rule of thumb, they made terrible timekeepers. Still, on seeing the individual in question crash breathlessly into his seat across from her, she marked it down as a small victory. Often, they just failed to show up at all.

'Everything OK today?' Candy smiled as she gestured at the plastic water jug on the side. Glass was banned from rooms where interactivity with the residents took place. 'Would you like a cup of squash first?'

The troll shook his head, the hood revealing just a vertical band of his face, until Candy gestured for him to remove it.

'There are regulations,' she reminded him, and figured he must've pulled it up just as soon as he'd passed through the security check. 'But setting aside the rules for a moment, it would be lovely to see you.'

The troll sat on his hands, just a little slip of a thing, and stared intently at the floor. He looked up, briefly, which is when Candy noticed his nostrils twitching. From experience, she knew what had caught his attention, especially when he offered what sounded like a purr of pleasure. As discreetly as she could, the young social worker closed the neck of her blouse a little. Given that these curious souls had come from generations of underground dwellers shuffling around in the dark, they possessed an extraordinary sense of smell. Candy didn't wear perfume, but was in no doubt that he had picked up on the scent of fresh shower gel and deodorant. For a sub-species of human that were also known for their poor eyesight, however, this one had been drawn by the aroma to then brazenly stare at her chest.

'Your hoodie,' said Candy to remind him.

Having been caught looking, the little troll dropped his gaze to the floor once more.

'Don't think of it as an order,' she pressed on, well aware that they didn't take kindly to being told what to do. 'I'm just asking nicely, and for the record I'm not cross about what happened at our last session.' Candy paused there, braced for the little troll to deny that he'd been responsible for quietly removing the bolts from the table legs at his end. The consequences of his actions had only become apparent in the debrief that followed, when his supervisor sat down and the solid beech top collapsed into his lap. 'Thankfully, the bruising will heal,' she told him. 'Once he regains the feeling in his groin I'm sure he'll agree that forgiveness is an important life lesson . . . Hello?'

The troll glanced up as she tapped the table to attract his attention. Candy could at least make out his eyes, which reminded her of a young bear in a cave. She gestured at his head, then, with an audible sigh, he reached for the hood and dropped it around his shoulders.

'There you are!' she said, beaming across the table as a

dramatic head of hair sprung out into the daylight. 'It's nice to see you, Richard.'

The little troll's ears reddened, which was striking as they stuck out like plates. It was at this moment that Candy wanted to climb from her chair and offer him a hug. They were always like this. Often, they would swagger in with attitude and suggestive looks, only to revert to awkward kids just as soon as the hood came off. Already this one was struggling to find something in the room to look at that wasn't Candy.

'Let's start again,' she said, aware that he had winced at the mention of his name. 'You prefer to be called Wretch, right?'

Nodding intently, with his gaze back on his scruffy trainers, the troll slipped one hand free and began to fiddle with the string of his hoodie. A lot of them went by street names, she reminded herself. It was as if they were purposely trying to distance themselves from their former lives, before it all went wrong. In a bid to let Wretch reclaim his composure, she left the table to pour them both a drink anyway. A moment later, setting the plastic cups on the table, she noted he had switched from blushing to scratching at the cuticles of his thumbs.

'You seem agitated,' Candy pressed on. 'Would you like to talk about it?'

She asked this in the loosest sense of the word. After three sessions, the troll had barely uttered a word. He wasn't mute, but at times that felt like his default mode. One glance at the file in front of her reminded Candy that he possessed a quick mind. It was during the last session that he'd suddenly drawn her attention to a fly in the room in a bid to steer away from the subject of his upbringing. Wretch's notes also flagged up his stutter at times of high anxiety. In her mind, it explained his tendency towards selective communication.

'Before you moved in here,' she said, pitching it like the residents had been given the choice, 'how did you deal with stress and tension in your life?'

The little troll shrugged, which was something.

'Personally, I like to get some fresh air,' Candy prompted, drawing upon her training in encouraging constructive, non-confrontational conversation. 'When things get too much, I just find some space to breathe.'

'Like the bench on the hill in the big park.'

Candy had been scanning her notes when he said this. Straight away, her eyes dropped to the details of his former address. The first letters of the city postcode told her that Wretch had grown up close to where she lived. Some time back that would've struck her as remarkable. Nowadays, it was hard to tell if any kid in her neighbourhood was the genuine article until they'd made it through their teenage years.

'That sounds like a good place,' she said calmly, without wishing to unsettle him by admitting that she knew the spot.

'You can see everything from there,' he went on, with some enthusiasm in his voice all of a sudden. 'All the way to the far horizon.'

The park in question sloped down to the river. It overlooked the cluster of skyscrapers in the financial district. Candy and Greg had taken a picnic there one summer afternoon the previous year. She remembered because Greg had burned the crown of his head and then fretted for the rest of the day about just how much his hair was thinning.

'Well, next time you need to be alone with your thoughts,' she suggested, 'maybe you can imagine yourself being high up on that hill. Just you, the bench and that peaceful view.'

As she spoke, Candy noted how Wretch had pulled focus a little, as if lost in a memory inspired by the same place.

'So, what's made you feel tense today?' she asked, hoping to build on this opening moment. 'Has something happened that you'd like to share?'

It was meant as a gentle line of enquiry, and yet all of a sudden the figure in front of her looked petrified.

'You can tell me anything, you know.'

Wretch began to quiver. Then he looked up and around, before making a buzzing sound.

'There is no fly in the room this time,' said Candy, smiling to herself. 'Let's work on putting what's bothering you into words.'

The buzzing ceased, unlike the quivering. As that intensified, another sound formed on his lips. It was as if he had started cooing to himself in order to remain calm.

'Richard – I mean, Wretch?' Candy gestured around her. The meeting room looked out onto the corridor, but the door was closed. 'Whatever you share in here remains confidential.'

The cooing grew more intense, increasing in pitch and volume. Candy sat back, unsure how to respond, when the troll jumped to his feet without warning.

'I didn't mean to hurt him!' he cried, before seemingly gasping at his admission and dropping back into his seat.

In the silence that followed, it was Candy who blinked first. Not only had his response come as a surprise, the pitch of his voice was also unexpected. Most trolls could be gruff at the

60

best of times. This one seemed to warble, as if his vocal cords were as taut as his nerves.

'Hurt who?' She reached for her pen, and then set it back on the table. Fighting wasn't uncommon between these guys, after all. A visit to the medical bay would always find the chairs occupied by those who had come off worst in a punch up. What's more, Candy had an opportunity here to prove she could be trusted. 'OK, well, I'm sure you had your reasons,' she said, and waved away the issue. 'But maybe it would be good to talk about positive ways to resolve conflict.'

Wretch simply stared at her. For a moment, it looked as if he had ceased breathing. Candy closed the file. All she wanted to do was engage him in a gentle chat that slowly earned his trust. This seemed like an ideal opportunity.

'Will you do something for me?' she persisted. 'When this session is over, I'd like you to go back, find the individual you hurt and apologise.'

'Huh?'

Wretch's eyes tightened at the corners. At least she had provoked a response, Candy thought to herself.

'It's called *leading by example*,' she pressed on. 'Be big about this and say how sorry you are. Hopefully that person will rate the effort you've made and do the same thing. You never know,' she said to finish, sitting back in her chair, 'you might end up the best of friends.'

*

All morning, the rain fell relentlessly. It drummed upon the streets, washing litter into the gutters and blocking many drains.

Those trolls who braved the wet did so at a lope, anxious to get from one source of shelter to another. Only Governor Randall Shores appeared unconcerned by the deluge. With water dripping from the brim of his hat, he made sure he was seen across each quarter of the settlement. Those trolls unlucky enough to cross his path had all been collared and interrogated. Much to his surprise and increasing frustration, however, not one of them had sung to him about the whereabouts of the missing boy.

'What hijack?' asked one, standing amid curls of torn metal on the actual spot where the coach had been set upon the night before. 'This is a peaceful place, sir.'

Either the low lives knew nothing, he had thought to himself, or they lived in fear of whoever was behind it. One way or the other, as Randall told each and every troll that ran into him, he would bring the perpetrators to justice.

Just after midday, a call came through on his radio pack. At the time, the Governor was finishing a bowl of noodles from a street vendor in return for a stick of gum. Despite the urgency of the news, he took his time with his lunch. The discovery of the kid's mobile at the gates outside the compound wasn't going to hurry Randall Shores. He called the shots around here, after all. If the trolls witnessed him hurrying off at a lick, that would only encourage them to think he was reacting to the situation. By taking his time, they would see that he was effortlessly leading things to a conclusion that would leave them wishing they had just let the coach drive on by.

*

'So, this is what they want?' the Governor said, once back at the compound, on viewing the clip of the young hostage. He looked around at the personnel gathered in his office. Trasker,

62

the kiddiewink from the government, was present. He seemed to have grown in confidence over the day, Randall noted warily, which was in direct contrast to the progress of the search. Well, the Governor thought to himself, pacing the floor in front of them, this was just the beginning. 'Of all the schoolkids they could've picked off,' he went on, and hefted the phone in his hand, 'they had to snatch a bedwetter!'

Governor Randall Shores was alone in chuckling to himself at this, but it was true. Watching the footage, as soon as the camera had pulled back, midway through the kid's appeal for the gates to be opened in return for his life, the faint crotch stain was clear to see.

'With respect,' said Trasker, who showed no sign of amusement, 'the boy, Maurice, is clearly in a stressful situation.'

The Governor could feel the tension in his jaw as he glowered in response. As the figurehead tasked with getting the kid back in one piece, was this not a stressful situation as well?

'With respect,' he replied, echoing the suit but with steel in his voice, 'when they come to reckon with me it's the trolls responsible who should be worried about soiling their pants.'

It was the settlement's security chief who spoke up next, stepping forward to address Randall. The man was stocky and shaven-headed, like so many of the former wardens from the prison system who had come to work here.

'Can I make a sensible recommendation?' he asked, adjusting his clip-on tie.

'I doubt that.' The Governor flashed a grin at the room. 'OK, what have you got?'

Despite his lack of confidence in the presence of authority, the security chief's triangular torso and bulging veins invited plentiful whispers about steroid abuse. Whether it was down to muscle-enhancing drugs or a commitment to the gym, the Governor approved of such a look among his frontline staff. Anything that kept the trolls at bay was fine by him, even if the man did look uncomfortable with an audience all of sudden.

'The softly-softly approach isn't working,' he said. 'They're not listening to you, sir.'

The comment led Randall to consider his life at home. When it came to talking to his wife and daughter, it sometimes felt as if he was completely invisible. Only the other evening, as he'd been sharing the highlights of his day with his other half, Bonita swept in to ask her for money and all of a sudden he had found himself outside the conversation. Things were different in the workplace, however. When the Governor drew breath to speak, people listened.

'So, what do you suggest?' he asked. 'That we *negotiate* with a terror group? Because, frankly, that's what we're dealing with here.'

'We should at least enter into a dialogue,' reasoned the man from the government. 'We can't keep the media quiet indefinitely.'

The Governor considered this for a moment. With his eyes on some imaginary point in the room, he turned the missing boy's phone repeatedly in his hand.

'Very well,' he said eventually, before jabbing randomly at the touch screen with one finger. 'I'll talk.'

Once a member of his staff had helped him to activate the video recorder, Randall clutched the device in his outstretched hand and drew breath to address the camera.

'Let's cut to the chase,' he began, in no mood to introduce himself by name. 'Now, everyone makes mistakes in life, but this is a big one. There's only one way out of this for you, and that's by letting the boy go. You have until sundown.' He paused there to be sure that everyone in the room was waiting for him to set out his terms. 'Hand him over, or you can expect hell to come knocking at your doors.' He finished there, deactivated the camera and tossed it nonchalantly to his chief of security. 'Place it on the step where you found it,' he told him. 'The low lives who left it there will be watching.'

'What if they don't listen?' asked the security chief.

Governor Shores pressed his rear molars together, as he often did at times of tension. In front of him, people whom he had never met before were awaiting his response. What had started out as a minor inconvenience was now threatening to become an embarrassment and all because a bunch of damn trolls thought they could outsmart him. It left him with no option.

'If the kid doesn't show up on my terms, then we send in the tanks.'

The Governor spoke with purpose in his voice and posture, and then closed down further questions by striding for the door.

Kyle Trasker swapped a glance with the security guy, which Randall did his level best not to notice.

'Do we have tanks?' he heard Trasker ask, and took some satisfaction from noting his man shrug like it was the first he'd heard.

Well, of course they didn't possess that kind of firepower, the Governor brooded to himself, on crashing out into the corridor. Not literally. But now the low lives had pushed him this far he planned a personal show of strength that would crush those kidnappers and anyone else who stood in his path.

7

With the gang members taking it in turn to watch over him through the day, Maurice fretted about two things.

His safety was uppermost in his mind, of course. Long Skull had made it quite clear that there would be serious consequences for the boy if the group's demands for freedom weren't met. What threatened to push Maurice over the edge, however, was the belief that somehow he would get into trouble for the whole sorry situation.

'It wasn't my fault,' he muttered to himself.

With their backs to the door, the two female trolls watched him closely but looked utterly blank. The one with the gum moved it around her mouth like clothes in a washing machine. Maurice sat on the bed with his knees drawn against his chest. Outside, the rain had stopped pattering against the window. It brought a silence to his surroundings, as if the world was awaiting his next move. Maurice had thought about just trying to overpower the pair. It was only when the one with the pink hair clip narrowed her eyes at him that he worried these creatures could also read minds. Leaping from the window was also out of the question. It was just too high. Instead, he clung to the belief that behind-the-scenes people were going to great lengths to bring him home safely.

Maurice just hoped nobody would be cross with him.

He had been this way since primary school. Wrongly accused of vandalising a swing, the boy had been made to stand up in assembly so the headmaster could make an example of him. Had he told his mother about the incident, no doubt she would've stormed in and practically called for an inquiry to clear his name. Unwilling to make things worse for himself, however, he had simply stewed on it. Even years later, when the lad that everyone knew had been responsible was revealed to be a troll, Maurice felt no sense of justice. By then, he had become hard-wired into worrying over the slightest thing.

'Will you tell them I didn't do anything wrong?' he asked the two trolls next. 'When they find me?'

'But they won't,' said the one with the clip. 'Nobody knows you're here but us.'

Her friend paused to pluck the gum from her mouth and examine it, which caused her eyes to cross momentarily. 'We're clever like that.'

Under any other circumstances, Maurice would've taken her to task over such a claim. Instead he dropped his head and wondered when they might feed him. So far, the gang had offered him nothing but two cans of sports drink and some boiled sweets. They all seemed to have a taste for the stuff. It left Maurice wondering whether it was the hostage situation or the sugar hit that made them so restless. The girls made no effort to sit, despite being on guard for what felt like hours. They just stood sentry at the door and worked that gum in their mouths. Only footfalls on the stairs prompted the pair to stop chewing and stand aside. A moment later, with several members of the gang in tow, Long Skull strode into the bare, gloomy room. He was clutching the boy's phone. One look at the troll's expression told Maurice that he was about to share news the boy didn't want to hear.

'You have a choice,' he thundered, and held the phone as if he was about to crush it. 'Which body part should we leave outside the compound, Maurice? An ear? Your tongue?' He stopped there and surprised him with a grin. 'Whatever it takes to persuade the man in charge that we're serious!'

'Please –' Maurice drew breath to beg the troll to reconsider, but a catch in his throat prevented him from continuing.

Long Skull dropped to his haunches in front of the boy, staring intently at him. He held out the phone so Maurice could read a message. Maurice didn't dare take his eyes off the troll.

'In one hour from now, the sun will sink behind the perimeter fence.' Long Skull addressed him in a quiet growl. 'That's when the Governor has threatened to come for you . . . what's left, at any rate.'

'You don't have to do this,' said Maurice in little more than a whisper.

Before the boy could find the courage to plead further, Long Skull rose to his full height once more and rolled his shoulders to loosen them.

'I need to prepare,' he muttered. 'What I have to do is going to hurt me as much as you.'

'I doubt that,' Maurice replied bitterly, which only brought the troll right back to him.

'The Governor leaves us with no other choice,' said Long Skull, breathing directly into his face. 'Now you just stay here and keep your fingers crossed that he sees sense and opens the gates. Otherwise, when I come back, one of those digits will belong to the TF . . . the T . . . to *us*!'

Without further word, Long Skull turned for the door. The others followed close behind, including the two girls. For a moment, just enough for his hopes to stir, Maurice thought he was about to be left alone. Then the last troll in the room closed the door behind the others, before facing the boy with his hands plunged into the pockets of his hoodie.

'So, that's it.' Maurice focused on the individual in the shadows before him. He had his hood up again, the short, slight urchin who couldn't stay still when the tension got the better of him. 'You're going to stand by and let that brute assault me?'

The little troll said nothing. He just shifted his weight from one foot to the other, grunting to himself. Maurice looked to the ceiling in despair.

'Can you even understand me?' When Maurice looked back, he found the hooded figure was now considering him closely. Then he nodded, ever so slowly. Maurice sprang to the edge of the bed. 'So speak!' he pleaded. 'Come on! What have you got to say?'

The little troll wiped his nose on his sleeve, and then inhaled, as if preparing to hold his breath for some time. A moment later his eyes began to bulge, and then the quivering kicked in.

'*Sorry!*' he yelled without warning, so explosively that the boy recoiled. 'I'm sorry I hit you with the pan, alright?'

Maurice blinked, and then reminded himself to close his mouth. It wasn't just the response that caught him off guard, or the volume. For such a gruff breed, he thought to himself, the troll's voice was surprisingly high-pitched. It also went some way to explain why he'd been so quiet, he decided.

'Well, that's no problem,' Maurice said all the same, thinking this was the chance he'd been seeking all day. If he could just get him to start talking, surely he could earn his freedom? 'It's also very big of you to apologise,' he added in a bid to flatter. 'Consider it accepted.'

The troll grunted to himself, his gaze back on the floor. A moment later, he peered up from the shadow of his hoodie once more.

'Now *you* say sorry,' he mumbled. 'Like Miss Lau told me you would.'

'Miss Lau?' Maurice leaned forward with his hands on his knees. At once, the little troll gasped and clamped both hands to his mouth. 'Who is Miss Lau?' the boy asked. 'Have you spoken about me to someone?'

The troll shook his head rapidly for a second. Then his shoulders drooped and he nodded once.

'My social worker,' he said in a small voice. 'So, are you sorry?'

'Of course I'm sorry!' By now, Maurice had seized upon what felt to him like a lifeline. He held the troll's gaze for a second, before mustering his best smile. 'Listen, maybe we got off to a bad start, but it isn't too late to change that. Now, what else did you tell this Miss Lau?'

The little troll shrugged. Maurice watched his hands burrow deeper into his pouch pocket. If his face was visible, the boy thought to himself, he would be blushing.

'Is she nice?' he asked. 'Your social worker?'

As Maurice held out for an answer, it looked as if the figure in front of him was attempting to hide inside his hoodie. He shrank into the garment, making strange buzzing noises as if a fly was trapped in there with him. Maurice gripped the edge of the bed, determined to talk the troll around.

'You know, unless you help me out here, they'll lock you up and you'll never, *ever*, see her again.'

Maurice detected the sound of a small gasp.

'Think about it,' he pressed on. 'All you have to do is get me out of here, and everything will go back to normal.' He stopped there to consider another approach. 'I'm sure if Miss Lau knew about this, she'd want you to set me free.'

By now, the little troll was following every word he said. Maurice could see his eyes in the gloom. He looked tense and troubled. The boy drew breath in a bid to secure his passage out of here, only to see his captor blink and fold his arms.

'Be quiet,' he grumbled. 'Or I'll hit you again.'

So much for the apology, Maurice thought to himself, and placed his head in his hands. Of all the trolls in the gang, this one looked the most vulnerable. The boy reckoned he stood a good chance of overpowering him if he made a break for the door. It was what he faced in the grid of hostile streets beyond that stopped him. In his mind, as he dwelled on the worst-case scenario, losing a finger seemed like the better option.

For what seemed like an eternity, with the little troll standing in front of the door, Maurice stared at his feet. He would sigh every now then, as did the troll, which told him they were both simply waiting here for Long Skull to return. It left the boy with a sense of mounting dread. On several occasions he had to focus on controlling his breathing to prevent his chest from tightening. There had to be some way out of here, he told himself. If nobody was coming for him then what choice did he have but to take matters into his own hands?

As for the boy's lone captor, he had chosen to pass the time as the daylight diminished by fiddling with objects from his pouch pocket. When Maurice realised he was toying with a lipstick, his interest spiked. Judging by the reverence with which the troll handled it, carefully popping the lid to sniff the tip, the boy felt sure it didn't belong to him. Then Maurice watched him produce a car key from the pocket, and sat up straight. For dangling from it was a laminated fob. Despite the gloom, he could just make out the wording, which read, *Social workers do it with care.*

Straight away, Maurice knew whose bag was likely to be missing the items.

'You know what?' he said, breaking the silence with a nod towards the key. 'Stealing that is nothing compared to the trouble you'll face for kidnapping me.'

The troll, who had evidently been lost in thought, closed his fingers around the key. Slowly, Maurice rose to his feet. Then, with his eyes fixed on his captor, he held out his hand.

'She'll be missing those, you know? Far from home, feeling stranded, all because you took something that doesn't belong to you. If you let me return them, you'd make her so happy and everything would work out just fine.'

Maurice was braced for a negative response. This time, however, the troll just stared into his eyes. The boy could see him thinking things through. If there were cogs inside his mind, he thought to himself, they were undoubtedly turning very slowly. Even so, he sensed that they *were* turning, and doing so in his favour.

'It's the right thing to do,' the boy added quietly, and turned his palm face upwards. Tentatively, the troll offered him the key. Maurice watched him hold it over his hand, only to snatch it away in panic at the sound of footsteps climbing the stairs.

*

Having rummaged through her bag, Candy figured she must've left her lipstick at home.

'At least I didn't forget the things that matter,' she joked with Serena on preparing to leave after a long day. She showed her the half-finished pack of gum. Everyone who worked here carried a pack at all times. That day, Candy had dished out a stick to each troll she had seen in session. Only one declined the offer, having rushed out just as soon as the bell had sounded for the switch over.

'How did your first session go?' Serena peered over her spectacles at Candy, who had just popped in to wish her a good evening.

Candy grinned. Was it obvious that Wretch had been playing on her mind? He was a nervous little thing at the best of times. Today, he behaved as if he'd started his day by inserting a finger into a power socket. Even so, despite Wretch's hurry to leave, she felt as if perhaps they had begun to make some progress.

'Not as hopelessly as you might think,' she told Serena, who pretended to be disappointed. 'It's all about trust,' she continued. 'Once you start to build it up, they stop being monsters.'

Serena returned to her keyboard, smiling to herself.

'Don't drop your guard for a moment,' she warned Candy quietly. 'Given half a chance, a troll would steal every last possession – including your soul.'

Shouldering her bag with a chuckle, Candy turned for the corridor. As she did so, her mobile began to call out to her. Sighing, she reached for her coat pocket. Greg was always fiddling with her ringtone. This time, she hurried to kill the comedy-voice command for her to come home and clean the flat.

'Will you stop messing with my phone?' she asked before he could speak, and headed for the corridor to be out of earshot. 'I could've been in an important meeting.'

'It's supposed to be subliminal.' Greg seemed deaf to her complaint. 'I'm hoping that if you hear it enough times you'll show up with your rubber gloves and duster.'

Candy smiled thinly. Greg was only joking, and yet he carried on like this so much that she was beginning to wonder if there really was a serious message behind it.

'The flat doesn't need tidying,' she told him, and began to make her way along the corridor. 'I cleaned up at the weekend.'

'You did?'

'When you were out wall climbing,' she reminded him, feeling a little affronted that he hadn't actually noticed. 'Someone had to tackle that coffee mug collection on your desk.'

Candy heard Greg draw breath sharply, as if primed to challenge her, only to exhale slowly.

'I did wonder why there was so much space for my elbows today,' he said, which she took to be his way of apologising. 'Listen, I'm standing at the fridge and it's bad news.'

'What?' asked Candy, heading for the door at the end of the corridor.

'Supper tonight is going to consist of milk unless you can pick up something for us to actually eat.'

'Greg, you've been at home all day. You could've popped out at any time.'

The couple shared a flat just off a bustling high street. Candy knew for a fact that it would've taken him less than five minutes.

'If you buy then I'll cook,' he offered. 'A ready meal would be good.'

'That's not cooking.'

'Ah, but there's still the washing up afterwards. A little bit, at any rate.'

'And you'll do that?'

'Sure,' he said, and then hesitated. 'In the morning, maybe.'

Candy told him she would pick up something on the way home, and finished the call feeling flat all of a sudden. Greg's tolerance of dirty dishes was far greater than hers. Inevitably she would be up to her wrists in soapsuds before bed. Through one of the side windows just then, illuminated by the last light of the setting sun, she noticed a squad of security guards in riot gear. They were massing near one of the perimeter gates. It reminded Candy that there had been talk of an incident. Making her way from the corridor into the staff reception area, she just hoped it had already been resolved peacefully.

8

The blade wasn't the first thing Maurice saw when Long Skull stalked into the room. It was his eyes. With his gaze locked on the boy seemingly before the door swung open, the troll's entrance spoke volumes about his intent.

'This will only make things worse for you,' Maurice told him, leaving the bed to take a step away. He held out his hands, as if in surrender, but the troll just kept on advancing. 'Be reasonable.'

'I've *been* reasonable,' growled Long Skull. 'Now it's time to be taken seriously.'

As he spoke, the little troll who had been guarding Maurice melted into the shadows. The boy shot him a look, as if in appeal, but with no time to wait for a response.

'Not my fingers,' he whimpered, as the knife appeared between them. 'Or my toes.'

'It's your choice.' Long Skull had come so close that Maurice struggled to get out of his face. When a hand shot out to grab the boy by the throat, a cry died inside him.

Behind their leader, the two female trolls had gathered to watch. They strained to see over Long Skull's shoulder, only to step back with a start when he turned to glower at them.

'Join the others downstairs,' he told them.

'What about my hair?' croaked Maurice in desperation. 'You could take a lock, maybe?'

Calmly, Long Skull waited until the pair left the room, each one muttering in disappointment, before facing the boy once more.

'I'm not here to cut your hair,' he growled.

Maurice caught sight of the knife tip as Long Skull raised it into his field of vision. The weapon glinted in the dying light from the window, as did the base of the frying pan that promptly swooped out of the gloom and connected with the back of the gang leader's head.

'Watch out!' Maurice cried involuntarily, but it was too late for Long Skull. His eyes turned upwards, rolling into their sockets as his body crumpled. It left Maurice with a clear view of the figure responsible, who had frozen to the spot with his hoodie slipped to his shoulders and the pan handle in his grasp.

'Oops,' said the little troll, seemingly to himself, and then looked up fearfully at Maurice. 'Did I do a bad thing?'

'It could've been worse.' Struggling to take in what had just happened, the boy's attention turned to the door. The other trolls had left it ajar. With the clang caused by steel on skull still ringing in his ears, Maurice figured the rest of the gang would be drawn to investigate within moments. 'I need to get out of here,' he whispered, and grasped the little troll by the shoulders. 'Will you help me?'

For a moment, Maurice found himself looking into a pair of terror-struck eyes. They only blinked and found focus when a voice from the foot of the stairs called up to check on the figure currently out cold on the floor.

'Outta my way,' said the little troll, spreading his hands to grasp the mattress from the bed frame. With surprising strength for someone so short and stocky, he then lifted it upright and marshalled it towards the door. Maurice watched him push the thick, sprung pad into the frame, where it jammed, and only drew breath when the troll produced a lighter from his pocket.

'Is this wise?' Maurice hissed.

Ignoring him, the troll struck the flint and touched the flame to a corner of the bed sheet still clinging to the mattress.

'*Look!*' he declared, as if had just invented fire. He stood back, flapping his hands in delight as the flame forged across the fabric. In a blink, the light in the room intensified. It cast the little troll in silhouette when he turned to face the boy victoriously.

'What now?' asked Maurice.

The troll seemed totally untroubled. Already, a thick black smoke had started to break and roll over the ceiling.

'What do you think, dumb-dumb?' he asked with a wobble of his head. 'All we need to climb down from the window is a knotted bed sheet.'

Maurice watched him push the bedframe against the burning barricade, feeling dread and despair all of a sudden.

'The only sheet is on the mattress,' he said, and cleared his throat. 'You just set it ablaze.'

The little troll looked startled, as did Maurice on feeling a hand grab his ankle. With a gasp, he looked down to see Long Skull attempt to lift his head off the floor, only to pass out with the effort. At the same time, as the fire took hold, voices could be heard on the staircase. The little troll caught Maurice's eye.

'Well, I tried,' he said simply, just as fists began to beat on the other side of the door behind the burning mattress. 'Miss Lau always says making the effort is what counts.'

*

Governor Randall Shores was a man with a great weight on his mind. The missing boy was an issue, but he would be found. Having cancelled all leave, he'd ordered every member of his security team to sweep the streets. They would have the kid in a fresh pair of pants and crying into his mummy's bosom by nightfall. What troubled Randall now, as he led a detail of armed guards through the old shoemaker quarter, was the text he'd just received from his daughter.

Going 4 a sleepover @ Ryans tonite. Don't wait up xxx

The missing apostrophe, funky misspelling and triple X sign off had soured his mood before he'd even processed the message. Within seconds, he had been on the phone to Bonita to express his reservations.

'I don't care if you're sleeping on the floor,' he had told her. 'It's still not appropriate . . . Anyway, why hasn't Ryan offered to give you the bed?'

'Mum said you'd be like this,' was all she'd replied.

'She knows?'

'And she didn't treat me like an infant when I told her!'

Randall had switched the phone from one ear to the other, as if hoping to understand her better. When it came to pushing her luck, Bonnie always turned to her mother for support, and that had left him with no option but to play the role of the bad guy.

'I'm not happy about this,' he'd told her. 'Why can't you work on your science project with Ryan and then come home?'

A moment's silence followed, which the Governor had judged long enough for Bonita to place her hand over the mouthpiece and curse him.

'Well, Benny's dad doesn't have a problem with him staying over.'

'Benny will be there, too?'

His daughter had done little to lighten his mood by going on to mimic what he'd just said.

'Am I talking to my father here,' she had asked, 'or my grandmother?'

'Bonnie, I only have your best interests at heart.'

'If that was true then you'd stop suffocating me!'

'I'm not suffocating you.'

'I can barely *breathe*, Daddy!'

'Let's not exaggerate.'

'Don't make me block you!'

And that's how the call had ended, just as it always did. If any member of Randall's staff dared to speak to him in that way, they'd be facing a disciplinary procedure. All he could hope for was that his little girl would grow to respect him. The Governor, after all, was a man who could authorise every member of his security team to arm themselves with tear gas and rubber bullets. On his word, these guys were ready to take down kidnappers, and yet when it came to Bonita he felt like one big inconvenience.

Stepping aside to let the sanitation tanker through, Governor Shores began to wonder whether Bonita's refusal to compromise was really just a plea to be trusted. He waved at his team to continue once the vehicle had turned at the next block, and steeled himself against the stink. Leading them between imposing red stone buildings, with his daughter uppermost in his mind, Randall questioned whether he had basically overreacted. Perhaps she really did just want to put her heart and soul into a school project, he reflected. He just hoped that Benny and Ryan would recognise that and even share her commitment.

Moments before the sound of glass tinkling on a nearby street drew his attention, followed by cries of a fire, Randall decided that he would have the college authorities quietly swab the boys as a precaution. All they had to do was test the saliva from the rim of a coffee cup or some such, but chances were it would come back negative. The tell-tale hormone took a while to fully kick in, and only then did the change in body chemistry become detectable. It was just one more reason why the low lives could be maddening, Randall thought sourly to himself on picking up the pace towards the column of smoke now thickening over the rooftops.

'Sir, shall I call in backup?'

The security guard nearest to the Governor was all set with his walkie-talkie in hand. Randall glanced at the man and figured he had to be new in the post.

'Fires break out all the time in this settlement,' he told him. 'Half the population have previous for arson, but we're here for a hostage.'

As he spoke, several trolls raced across the junction at the next block. Randall watched a couple of females scatter away with them. They looked spooked, but hardly capable of staging a hijack on a coach and snatching a schoolboy. It was only as the Governor reached the corner, however, and came within sight of flames licking the upper window of a building, that he turned to the guard with the walkie-talkie and bellowed at him for not summoning reinforcements sooner.

'*Freeze!*' he cried, on seeing two youths descending from a window on a charred and smouldering sheet. It was hard to get a clear view on account of the sanitation truck ahead of them. The driver had seen the drama, halted temporarily, and then wisely decided that no miscreant shenanigans were going to mess with his schedule. With the security detail behind him, Randall raced towards the scene. It took a moment for him to realise that the one without the hoodie was shouldering a limp-looking figure. Clearly unconscious, the troll's hair hung from his skull to reveal prominent temples, while his long torso and swaying arms obscured the individual carrying him down.

Randall couldn't be sure if this meant the schoolkid had been located at last. There was no guarantee that he was even looking at the kidnappers here, but standing back and waiting for them to explain themselves was not an option. Amid a stampede of footfalls, his instinct was to have all three hog-tied on the pavement before finding out. 'Freeze, or I will use force!'

Frantically, the imp with his hood up led the way down what was left of the sheet. Judging by the flames now jabbing from the window, there was no way they could've remained holed up there. The blackened section of the bed sheet snapped before the Governor's patience with the escapees. Helplessly, he watched the trio tumble, only for the sanitation truck to obscure his view of their impact on the ground.

'Dammit, just take them out!' he instructed his security detail with a note of desperation in his voice now. 'I want them incapacitated!'

By now, the wail of the emergency siren over the rooftops told him the cavalry were coming. He hoped an ambulance would be among their number, and that if the kid was among the casualties from the fall he could be patched up before his parents were called. Any bruising from the rubber bullets that began to spit forth would require some charm on his part to justify, Randall realised, but if that's what it took to bring the kidnappers to justice then so be it.

'Get out of the way,' he muttered, slowing by a step until the sanitation truck wisely accelerated from his sight line. A moment later, with a clear view of the pavement, Governor Shores pulled up completely. Every member of his security detail reacted in the same way on seeing the sheet in a heap on the ground. Tangled in amongst it was the figure that had been carried down from the building. The troll was sprawled on his back, nursing his head, and then yelped when a quick-thinking guard ensured he was going nowhere with a bullet that bounced from his buttock. As the target cursed the approaching team, the Governor looked around frantically for the two individuals who had tumbled with him. He knew full well that this whole quarter was a rat run of alleyways, with one such passage leading off right besides the burning building.

'What are you waiting for?' he demanded, and rounded on the guard with the walkie-talkie as he reported on the unfolding scene. 'Hunt them down!'

9

In the face of a fire – one that swiftly spread across the walls, floor and ceiling – Maurice's instinct for survival had taken over from his fears. It was the little troll who had wrenched the burning sheet from the mattress, stamping out the flames before twisting what was left into a cord of sorts. The noise from the blaze was intense, like an outpouring of breath that just continued to build. By the time the pair had secured one end of the sheet to the radiator under the window, it was a struggle for them to hear each other.

'What about him?' Maurice had yelled, and gestured at the figure out cold on the floor.

By then the little troll had already clambered out onto the ledge.

'If he survives,' he said, his voice pitched high over the roar, 'he'll kill us both!'

Before Maurice could reply, the troll dropped out of sight. He looked back around, grimacing at the heat. Then, with his eyes smarting, he grabbed Long Skull by the wrists and dragged him towards the window.

Even on his own, there was no way that the boy would've willingly ventured over the edge. With a dead weight over his shoulder, it had seemed utterly suicidal. Then again, as the room was consumed by fire, he'd had no option. The fire-damaged sheet had begun to shred just as soon as he wrapped his ankles around it. With the little troll leading the way down, Maurice had sensed that it wouldn't hold them for long. Sure enough, as the friction from his desperate slide stung his palms, a ripping sound had marked the moment that the ground rushed up to meet them. Maurice had sensed the troll slip from his shoulder as they fell, only to serve as a cushion on hitting the ground.

He had closed his eyes for a second, winded but alive, only to snap them open when gunfire crackled nearby. The little troll loomed over him, his gaze tight with panic, and offered him his hand. Still struggling for breath, and flinching as a bullet bounced off the pavement beside the groaning body that had softened his impact, Maurice accepted his grasp. He had heard voices, one yelling orders, but it was lost to the rumble of a passing truck. That's when the troll promptly hauled him to his feet, dragging him between the vehicle's front and rear wheels. Under the crackle and snap of yet more gunfire, and with bullets bouncing from the ground behind him, Maurice cried out in terror.

'This is no place to hide!' he yelled, and hurried to stop his feet from being crushed.

'Just hold on!' urged the troll, grabbing the chassis with one hand and the scruff of the boy's shirt with the other. 'Hold on and stay out of sight.'

'But I've done nothing wrong!'

In a bid to stop himself from going under, Maurice found a handhold and then hooked his feet over the rear axle. The only noise now came from the engine, as the truck began to build a little speed, while a wretched stink consumed Maurice's nostrils. It was only when drops of liquid began splashing his face that he realised with a grimace that the vehicle was carrying waste from the settlement's cess pits.

'This is disgusting!' he called across. 'I'm getting off.'

In response, a hand reached out to grab him once again.

'Don't leave me,' the little troll pleaded, and caught the boy's eye. '*Please!*'

In that moment, Maurice found himself looking at a frightened child. At least that's how it seemed beneath the sanitation wagon. He glanced at the ground as it passed beneath them. With the rear wheels rumbling and the axle too low for him to safely drop down and clear, he decided in a heartbeat to put up with the stench until a better opportunity arose. It was several blocks before the truck finally came to a halt, however. Despite the fact that the muscles in his arms and legs were screaming for release, Maurice fought to hold on tight. He could hear voices as some security guy spoke to the driver, while another paced around the vehicle. What caused him to freeze was the patrol dog. As the wolf-like canine circled the vehicle, any urge to make his presence known vanished. Before his kidnap, just seeing one through the window of the coach had persuaded Maurice to skip a visit to the restrooms. Big dogs like this didn't only make him nervous; ever since his mother taught him that even a friendly hound had the potential to go for the throat, they positively paralysed him with fear. Just then, as the patrol dog paused to sniff the air, the boy clung on to the chassis and a chest full of air. Side by side with a troll, he expected the beast to go wild at any moment and quite possibly savage them both. Instead, as the conversation between the driver and the guard came to an end, the dog and its handler simply pulled back from the vehicle as it set off once again. Wrapping his ankles tighter around the axle, and with yet more waste fluid from the tanker spilling over him, Maurice realised what had masked their presence.

'The stink just saved you,' he muttered at the little runaway beside him, whose hoodie now trailed on the road.

'I've smelled worse,' he replied, which left Maurice unsure if the troll was talking about an experience or his personal hygiene.

A minute later, with a slow squeal of brakes, the truck stopped once again. This time, with no sign of any further security checks and silence all around, Maurice chose the moment to drop to the tarmac. Scrambling quickly between the front and rear wheels, in case the truck started moving again, he found they had arrived in a sprawling car park, at the junction to a service road with the traffic lights on red. He climbed to his feet, his nerves run ragged, and looked around. Some way behind the truck and the gates they'd passed through, the perimeter wall loomed large in both directions. In the deepening gloom, floodlights swept across the settlement on the other side. Then the troll rose into his field of vision, his ears like little trumpets, and looked around to see what had caught the boy's attention.

'What now?' he asked, facing Maurice with his brow contorted.

'You're asking me?' Maurice hauled the troll down between two parked cars as the lights turned green for the truck. 'Listen,

I appreciate what you did back there, but let's not forget it was you who kidnapped me in the first place!'

'It wasn't my idea!' he piped up, but Maurice was beyond caring.

'I'm going home,' he said, tucking his school shirt into his trousers, both of which were spattered with spillage from the sanitation truck. 'You can do whatever you like,' he added, before gesturing at him to leave. 'Go on. Shoo!'

The little troll blinked but didn't move. Maurice sighed and looked for somewhere to hand himself in. A high mesh fence bound the car park to the perimeter wall. On the far side, the truck had stopped at another checkpoint. Despite the fading light, Maurice watched a guard with a mirror on a telescopic pole check the underside of the vehicle. He figured trolls must like to smuggle stuff in and out of the settlement. A schoolkid, he thought ruefully, was probably a first.

'You got off at the right time,' he told the troll, and removed his glasses to clean the lenses on his shirt. 'But there's no escape for you now.' Popping them back on and blinking to find focus, Maurice felt a hint of pity at how forlorn the figure beside him now appeared. Then he reminded himself what he'd been forced to endure. 'Next time,' he added, 'you should think twice before hijacking school coaches.'

'So, what am I going to do?' The troll scuffed at the grit on the ground before looking back at the boy with a pleading expression. 'Help me out, buddy?'

'We're not buddies,' Maurice told him, before turning to head for the checkpoint on the far side of the car park. 'And this is where we say goodbye!'

As much as Candy Lau enjoyed the challenge of her job, the security measures could be a pain at times. At the exit from the reception area, she queued for several minutes in order to have her bag checked. It was Jeffrey who scanned her identity badge, and waited awkwardly for the system to release the door lock.

'Orders from on high,' was all he said. 'I can't just buzz you through today.'

'Is this about the missing schoolboy?' she asked.

Jeffrey nodded, his eyes on the computer monitor.

'Let's hope they find him safe and sound.'

Candy knew better than to press the security staff for details. Jeffrey was a nice guy, but operational issues were confidential. Besides, she had other concerns – like what to pick up for supper that evening.

'I'm not sure why I'm in such a hurry to go home,' she told him when the computer finally cleared her to head out into the car park. 'A ready meal is hardly the height of romance.'

'You never know,' said Jeffrey with a wink, 'maybe you'll get back to find a candlelit dinner for two.'

Candy chuckled as he returned her identity badge.

'In another life, Jeffrey, you and I would've been made for each other.'

She enjoyed her exchange with the guard. He'd been happily married for four decades, he'd told her recently. It was something she had dwelled on because it seemed like such an achievement. She and Greg had been together for a good couple of years, but lately it felt more like they were sharing a flat rather than a life ahead of them. Candy had never been with anyone as long as this. She had even found herself wondering if things would ever get any better, and put it down to the fact that they were both just busy people.

'Have a safe journey,' said Jeffrey as the the exit door buzzed open. Candy thanked him and collected her bag. As she did so, the walkie-talkie attached to the guard's lapel crackled into life. Jeffrey pinched it between his thumb and forefinger, and acknowledged the communication. 'You're lucky,' he told her, and gestured for her to hurry through. 'The settlement is about to go on lockdown.'

'OK. I'm gone.' Candy knew not to hang around when the security level rose. If she didn't make her way out now, there was a good chance that supper would be a bag of crisps and a can of Coke from the vending machine in the corridor. 'Miss Lau has left the building.'

*

Maurice trudged between the rows of parked vehicles feeling utterly wrung out. He looked a mess and felt about ten times worse. He coughed into his fist several times, having breathed in smoke on his escape from the burning building, and wondered if he would even need to identify himself. Surely everyone was on the lookout for a lone schoolboy with no business being anywhere but home. At the checkpoint at the far end of the car park, the guard with the telescopic mirror had just returned to the booth beside the barrier. Maurice figured the sooner he made his presence known the sooner he would be back home, which is when an anguished cry caused him to spin around with a gasp.

'*Get down, low life! And stay down!*'

If the sight of another guard circling the little troll surprised Maurice, the level of violence he went on to display froze him to the spot. It took a second for the boy to realise the guy had used a baton across the back of the runaway's knees to floor him, and another before he called out to stop.

'Don't do that! You're hurting him!'

Maurice broke into a trot, still appealing to the guard who was now stamping on the helpless figure as if he was a fire in need of extinguishing.

'Will you devils ever learn?' yelled this uniformed gorilla, and swung the baton hard. 'Break the rules, you suffer the punishment!'

By now, Maurice had pulled up behind the pair. Maurice watched the guard snap out a set of handcuffs from his duty belt, and that's when he found himself in possession of the guy's pistol. As soon as he saw it in the holster, the boy just snatched it on instinct. The little troll had earned himself a lot of trouble, but not this.

'You need to stop what you're doing, sir.'

Maurice's voice was shot through with uncertainty, but the cold metal of the gun's muzzle against the nape of the man's neck spoke volumes. As if compelled by a magic spell, the guard dropped the cuffs and raised his hands.

'Easy now,' he said, as the troll scrambled clear from him. 'We can settle this.'

'Don't look at me!' ordered Maurice, panicking suddenly when the guard tried to glance over his shoulder. With the chambers of his heart experiencing what felt like a tidal surge, it took every effort to cling on to the gun and not pass out on the spot. 'I mean it. Keep your eyes to the front!'

The second time he attempted to look, the guard showed less trepidation. Maurice kept the gun levelled at him as he turned, but by now his hands had begun to tremble.

'Son,' said the guard, before facing him directly and then rising to his full height. 'You're in a lot of trouble, too.'

Maurice watched a grin ease across the guard's face and then promptly contract in shock when the little troll coshed him with the baton. The guard went down so quickly it was as if his legs had turned to twigs. In shock, Maurice dropped the gun. Then, for a second time that day, he found himself facing a little figure that looked utterly surprised by the force of his actions.

'Will you *stop* doing that?' he told the troll. 'You can't keep hitting people round the head. It's really dangerous!'

On the ground between them, the guard groaned and rolled onto his side. For a moment, it looked like he might struggle to his feet, but that threat disappeared when the troll clipped him across the temple with the baton one more time.

'I won't do it again,' he said, and tossed it to one side.

It was clear to Maurice, watching him wince as he pulled his hood over his head, that the little troll had taken quite a beating. He was also well aware of the gravity of what had just happened. Not just the severity of the assault by the guard but the manner in which he himself had intervened. Looking over the rows of cars, Maurice considered the settlement's compound buildings and then the exit checkpoint behind them. Nobody appeared to have witnessed the scene, though it did little to ease the sick feeling that now gripped him.

'What now?' asked Maurice.

The troll blinked several times before touching his thumbs to his breastplate.

'Oh, you want my advice all of a sudden?'

Maurice grimaced, aware that they were letting their voices rise here, and glanced around once more.

'All I know is this doesn't look good,' he hissed. 'It seems your master plan to kidnap me didn't extend to a getaway strategy!'

The little troll held the boy's gaze for a moment. At the same time, he began rummaging in his pouch pocket. Then, with a grin, he produced the car key he had been toying with earlier.

'This is our ticket out of here,' he said, swinging it by the fob in front of the boy's face.

'So, I can add car theft to assault on my charge sheet now,' grumbled Maurice. 'I'm supposed to be the victim in all this!'

The little troll snatched the key from sight. He scowled at the boy.

'Then stay here,' he said, and prodded the guard on the floor with his foot. 'Wait for him to come to his senses and explain there's been a misunderstanding.'

Maurice considered his options, and then apologised for being snappy.

'I'm just feeling a little stressed right now.'

'So, let's hit the road!' The troll bounced on the balls of his feet as he said this, as if struggling to contain a sudden surge of energy. 'Things will look better for us both on the other side.'

Well aware that they could be spotted at any moment, Maurice spread his arms in appeal.

'There's no way we can just drive through the checkpoint,' he pointed out. 'Even if we can find the car, it still belongs to someone. Just what will your social worker write in your report if we steal it?'

'Who says we're leaving without her?' Without taking his eyes from the boy, the troll raised the key high and pressed the fob button.

In response, from several rows of cars behind them, a hatchback chirruped and winked both indicator lights.

*

Making her way from the compound's reception area to the car park, Candy Lau dwelled on the security operation to rescue the missing schoolboy. It was certainly an unprecedented event, and no surprise that the powers that be had attempted to maintain a media blackout. In her view, the press found any excuse to demonise the changelings. If a small minority really had held a pupil to ransom then it was best to let the settlement resolve things peacefully. Sensationalist headlines would only stoke up further prejudice and hatred.

Candy wore a scarf, which she folded around her neck before buttoning up her coat. Since the storm front had moved on, it was shaping up to be a clear evening with a growing chill. Every sound from the other side of the wall carried far. Certainly something was going on, she thought, judging by the sirens. Heading for her car, she quickened her pace a little. A lockdown didn't normally go beyond the compound and perimeter walls, but Candy didn't want to discover it had been extended to the exit barrier, too. Dropping her bag from her shoulder, with the car in sight, she rummaged for her keys. By the time she

95

reached her door, she still hadn't found them, and set her bag down so she could use both hands.

'Ah, come on,' she muttered to herself, well aware that her lipstick had gone missing during the day. If someone had stolen the key as well then she'd have to notify Jeffrey and look forward to a whole heap of grief and paperwork. With an air of rising panic, Candy stepped away from her bag with her hands clasped behind her head. Even with her focus on the dashboard inside the car, she failed to register the object of her search for a second. When she focused on the key fob, dangling from the ignition where she must have left it, the young social worker lifted her eyes to the stars in the sky and asked out loud for a restful end to the day.

'OK, car, this is between us, alright?' she asked, on climbing into the driving seat. Candy felt an overwhelming sense of relief. Not least because it meant she didn't have to call Greg and explain why she would be late. The next thing she did was crinkle her nose in disgust, step out of the vehicle and check the soles of her shoes. Seeing no sign that she had stepped in anything, Candy got back behind the wheel and wound down the front windows. It was only as she manoeuvred from the bay and set off towards the security gate that she began to breathe without the urge to gag. Despite the ventilation, however, she drove with a hint of a grimace. Even after she had been waved through by the guard, just moments before the lockdown siren sounded across the settlement, Candy Lau resigned herself to travelling home with a really bad smell for company.

10

Governor Randall Shores watched the CCTV footage with one hand clutching the back of his neck. He recognised the low life straight away. Under the circumstances, he opted not to reveal that he had run into the very same little troll earlier that day, and then sent him on his way. What's more, having shut down every block across the settlement while his team conducted a search, it came as a personal insult to learn how his quarry had given him the slip.

'This boy with him,' said Randall, trying hard to keep his voice calm, 'he doesn't look like much of a victim to me.'

Kyle Trasker stood beside him in the control room. As far as Randall understood things, the young man's job was to sit at the back, take a bunch of notes and report to the big boys at the government department responsible for the settlement. Instead, Trasker faced the screen with a commanding posture, upright with his shoulders squared and chin grasped in contemplation.

'Governor, as the suspects are now at liberty, the police will have to be informed.'

'Now, let's not panic here.'

Kyle Trasker looked across at Randall, who saw no hint of panic whatsoever in the man's face.

'I've already put the call through,' he told the Governor. 'We'll also release a press statement. This is a public safety issue now.'

'I see,' said Randall, and winced a little on clenching his jaw.

Several minutes earlier, a guard had staggered to the compound gate in a state of some distress. As soon as the radio message reached the Governor, the twinge in his back molars returned. Now, having assembled with his team to watch the playback from the car park cameras, Randall wished that he had held on to a stick of gum to stop him from grinding his teeth. Instead, he'd handed them out in vain to every low life he suspected of knowing something about the kidnapping. Whether they had just been too scared to speak, or unwisely adopted some code of silence, he felt sure that the troll with the high hairline and the headache would crack. Despite a blazing row with the doctor at the medical bay, however, the Governor had been forced to agree that any interrogation would not be permitted until the patient's concussion cleared. Still, the footage Randall had just witnessed told him that he didn't need to wait. Watching the so-called schoolboy hostage hold up one of his best men so his little accomplice could cosh him, the Governor came to one clear conclusion.

'We're looking at an outside job,' he declared, as the monitor showed the car pull away from the checkpoint. 'The kid accessed the settlement with every intention of springing that little troll. Whatever his motive, I can assure you all it won't go unpunished!'

Randall had hoped that such a commanding attitude would restore his authority. Instead, Trasker glanced in the Governor's direction as if surprised to see that he was still in the room, and then fished a ringing mobile phone out of his breast pocket. Randall recognised the model as a sleeker, more sophisticated version of his own.

'Go ahead,' Trasker said into the mouthpiece, and focused on a point in the air in front of Randall. As he listened to the caller, it seemed like everyone in the room was holding their breath. 'Frankly, it's been like watching sand through a sieve,' he went on, and then stared hard at the floor. 'All understood. I'll keep you informed.'

Trasker ended the call, pocketed the phone and then faced Randall once more.

'This case is mine from here on out,' he announced.

'But the police –'

'Answer to me,' Trasker finished for him, and patted his breast pocket. 'Orders from the top.'

'Wow, work experience has come a long way since our day!' Governor Randall Shores shot a look of amusement at his head of security, who did his level best to avoid eye contact with his boss. Randall looked back at Trasker, his smile fading, and then recovered his composure. 'I have to say you look very young for that kind of authority. I'll be happy to continue leading the way –'

'I'm just awaiting confirmation of the resources available,' Trasker told Randall, and then looked at him hopefully. 'Actually, can we get a cup of tea around here?'

A moment passed before Randall registered the question.

'You don't want coffee at a time like this?' he asked. 'Something to fire you up?'

'Tea is fine. Really.'

The Governor assessed him for a second.

'We have tea,' he confirmed a little absently. 'I believe there's a machine in the corridor.'

'Excellent.' Kyle Trasker nodded appreciatively before assessing the screen once more. 'I'll take mint or camomile. Either one is fine.'

Mint or camomile, the Governor thought bitterly to himself. This wetback might as well be drinking his mother's breast milk.

'Our machine isn't that sophisticated,' he explained patiently. 'The only fancy drink is a fruit tea. You know, blackcurrant or raspberry.'

Before assembling here, Governor Randall Shores had only just ended a call from his wife. She had wanted to know what he was thinking in giving permission to their daughter for a sleepover with those boys, and now this.

'Any fruit is fine,' said Trasker, with a hint of impatience that Randall hadn't expected from a guy this young-looking.

Governor Randall faced his head of security and jabbed a thumb towards the corridor.

'One fruit and one coffee, strong and black,' he barked at the guy, like a general issuing battlefield tactics. Randall might've had responsibility for the hunt taken away from him, but it would be a cold day in hell before he had to fix the hot drinks.

'So, let's establish the facts.' Kyle Trasker purposely ignored the Governor to address the assembled staff. 'We have not one but two perpetrators at large.'

'What about Miss Lau?' The question came from one of the guards. Everyone had seen her drive away. What wasn't clear was whether she knew she had company stowed away in the back of her car. 'She was supposed to be heading home to see her boyfriend.'

'Settlement staff remain my responsibility.' The Governor nursed his jaw where it had really begun to hurt. 'And when I find her she has some explaining to do,' he added, glaring pointedly at his head of security as he made his way towards the vending machine. 'Along with anyone else who allowed this situation to become a crisis!'

*

Hiding under a blanket behind the rear seat of the hatchback, Maurice had braced himself to be discovered. It wasn't just the terrible smell that threatened to give away their presence. The little troll balled up beside him just would not stay still. He started fidgeting even before they'd passed through the checkpoint, where the guard had gone no further than wishing the young social worker behind the wheel a safe journey home.

'Will you cut it out?' hissed Maurice finally. With the car beetling along the orbital road, he addressed his fellow stowaway under the rush of air coming through the open windows. 'Stop wriggling!'

'It's the fleas,' the little troll whispered back at him, scratching the back of his leg at the same time. 'The settlement is infested.'

From that moment on, Maurice did his level best to create some space for himself. Such was the extent of the troll's constant shuffling, however, the boy soon found himself trapped in a spoon formation. All he could do was tell himself that the odd bite from a mite was a small price to pay for the chance to clear his name. The surest way to do that, he decided as the car pulled in at a petrol station, was by getting back to the protective bosom of his parents.

First, Maurice realised, he needed to part company with the creature currently nestling into him like they were tucked under a duvet.

That moment arrived, he decided, when the woman in the driving seat pulled up beside a pump. Peering through a fold in the blanket, he waited for her to get out and start filling the tank. Then he tapped his fellow stowaway on the shoulder.

'This is your chance.'

'Eh?' The little troll raised his head, glancing back at the boy.

'As soon as she heads inside to pay, you should go for it!'

'What about you?'

'Don't worry about that,' Maurice told him. 'I know things look bad but at least I can explain myself. You're on the run, so if you want to stay that way I suggest you seize this opportunity.' He paused just then, waiting for the clunking sound as the lady finished filling the tank. Then, just as soon as she headed across the forecourt, he appealed to the presence at his side once more. 'Go. Scram! Time to fly!'

At once, the little troll threw off the blanket. 'All the trouble I've caused,' he said, twisting around to face Maurice. 'Maybe one day I'll make it up to you.'

For the first time, under the artificial lights of the garage canopy, the boy looked directly into his eyes. For all the talk of low lives being a breed apart, this one looked as vulnerable as he felt just then.

'Don't apologise again,' said Maurice. 'Just go.'

The troll responded by clambering over the back seat of the car, planting a foot on Maurice's thigh for leverage.

'Sorry,' he said, seemingly without thinking as he popped up on the other side of the back seat.

Despite everything, Maurice couldn't help but grin. His fellow escapee was a liability, but a considerate one at least.

'I don't even know your name,' Maurice said, glancing through the windscreen to see the social worker enter the forecourt store.

The troll's monobrow dropped.

'Why do you want to know?'

'I'm just being . . . you know . . . *polite*. We've been through a lot together.'

'My name doesn't matter,' he replied. 'You can call me Wretch.'

Maurice extended his hand over the back seat.

'Well, Wretch, be lucky. You're going to need as much of it as you can get.'

The little troll examined his hand, as if this was the first time anyone had ever made such a gesture, and then simply nodded in response.

'I'm gone,' he said, and squeezed between the front seats of the car.

For a second, Maurice wondered what Wretch was doing. Instead of cracking open the car door and creeping out to freedom, he appeared to be wrestling with something under the steering column. Careful not to make himself too visible as he strained to watch, Maurice promptly caught his breath at a crackle and shower of sparks.

'I was hoping you'd stage a getaway on foot!' he protested, and promptly tipped back into the boot when the little troll hurriedly finished hotwiring the hatchback, stamped on the accelerator and fishtailed from the forecourt. 'You're not helping either of us!'

*

Three hours later than planned, carrying only a plastic bag, Candy Lau rang the front doorbell to her apartment.

'Where have you *been*?' asked Greg when he answered. 'I called a while back but you didn't pick up.'

Candy's first thought was that he might've shown more concern than a single attempt to reach her on the mobile. Her boyfriend certainly seemed deeply troubled just then, even though he wasn't actually looking at her. Candy followed his gaze, which was fixed on the road, and saw the real reason: the space where they normally parked was vacant.

'There's a problem with the car,' she explained, and waited for Greg to face her finally.

'Flat battery?' he asked. 'A puncture?'

'It's been stolen.'

'*What?*'

'My bag was on the passenger seat,' she went on. 'I had my card to pay at the petrol station till, but my phone's gone, too. And the keys to the flat,' she added, sounding pained. 'Greg, I'm so sorry.'

Just then, Greg appeared to have lost the ability to blink. He was barefoot, wearing an old T-shirt and those chequered drawstring trousers that told her he hadn't left the flat all day.

'How could you be so –' He stopped himself there, ran a

hand to the top of his head as if to hold himself down before starting again. 'When did this happen?'

Candy told him she'd been shopping for supper in the petrol station store. The next thing she knew, a squeal of tyres had drawn all eyes to the forecourt. It had taken her a moment to realise that the car slicing out towards the road belonged to her. As she told the policeman who had shown up twenty minutes later, the thief behind the wheel wore a hoodie that concealed his face, and while there was definitely a youth in the back, it happened so fast she only took in the fact that he looked utterly shocked by what was happening.

'Most probably a prank that got out of hand,' she told Greg. 'That's what the policeman said after he took my statement.'

'Some prank,' he muttered. 'Whoever did this should be locked away for life.'

Finally, Greg stepped aside for Candy. It was a cold night, and though she had kept moving, her bones were beginning to feel the chill.

'I had to walk back,' she told him and took herself into the hallway. 'The policeman offered to give me a lift. Then an emergency call came through on the radio and he had to leave in a hurry.'

'Did you even lock the car?' he asked.

'Of course,' she said hotly, and showed him the key.

'But you still left your bag on the seat?'

'In a secure car, at a busy petrol station, for a matter of minutes.'

Greg blew the air from his cheeks, and then raised his head to the ceiling.

'We'll have to get the locks changed on the flat, and how are we going to manage without wheels?' he asked. When Candy didn't reply, he looked back at her once more. This time, appearing to remind himself of something, Greg grasped her by the shoulders. 'Are *you* OK?'

Candy thought he would never ask.

'I'm fine,' she told him, and broke away to head up to the flat. 'Just cross with myself.'

Greg followed close behind, but said nothing to ease her mind. Inside, having shrugged off her coat, Candy took the carrier bag into the kitchen. She was tired, cold, fed up and hungry. Before the incident, she had resolved to skip the ready meal and rustle up something fresh for them both. As they saw so little of each other through the day, it seemed like a nice gesture, and so she had been in the process of selecting the ingredients for a pasta carbonara. Even after the theft and the police statement, she chose to go back and pay for the contents of her basket that the cashier had thoughtfully put to one side. It had seemed like a fitting way to save what remained of the day.

'Is this really time to cook?' asked Greg, watching her from the door. 'What about the insurance company?'

Candy responded by cracking an egg into a bowl. As she did so, the phone in the hallway began to trill.

'I'm not in,' she said, as Greg turned to answer it. She heard him pick up, sounding clipped like he did when her family rang, and then silence.

A moment later he appeared at the door again. He held the receiver to his ear and was staring at her solemnly.

'She's right here,' he told the caller, and held out the phone. Candy scowled. 'Who is it?' she mouthed.

'He didn't say,' Greg replied, in no mood to cover for her. 'But he's ringing from your mobile.'

11

By his reckoning, Governor Randall Shores could extract Bonita from the planned sleepover before catching up with the pursuit squad. So long as he put his foot down, he could deal with his daughter and ensure that Kyle Trasker didn't grab all the glory when the troll and his accomplice were finally brought to justice.

The guy from the government was out of his depth. No question about it. Randall had been forced to observe Trasker take a call to confirm that police personnel were now at his disposal. Then, quietly seething that his own phone remained untroubled by such a high-level communication, he'd watched the man pick up a message matching the registration of a car stolen from a petrol station to the one used in the breakout. After that, without further word, Kyle Trasker had just taken off. Had Randall been in charge, he would've remained in the control room, guiding operations like a grandmaster at the chess table. Instead, with the young buck on his way to the scene, the Governor had been left with little choice to follow. When the fugitives were finally brought to justice, Randall intended to be there so Trasker didn't take all the credit. First, however, in a bid to stop his wife from harassing him by phone, he would deliver his daughter back to the house.

Nobody left Randall Shores on the sidelines. Apart from his family, perhaps.

'Where is she?' he asked just as soon as the youth opened the door. Randall couldn't recall which one he was dealing with here – Ryan, Bryan, Benny, Lennie, or whatever these suspect trolls called themselves. 'I'm in a hurry here.'

'It's late, bro,' said the lanky, undernourished figure in a vest and boxers, with a tattoo of two guns crossing his breastplate and a fringe that wouldn't get out of his eyes. 'Don't spoil the party.'

Instantly, Randall's rear molars reminded him of the day he'd had.

'I'm her father,' he said, as if the youth had forgotten.

'Respect.' The idiot bowed his head before moving to close the door. 'And good night.'

Randall responded by stopping the door with his foot.

'*Bonnie!*' he yelled through the gap. 'It's time to go home!'

The youth looked stunned at the imposition, as if manners ever featured in his code of conduct. It was then Randall detected a note of alcohol on his breath.

'Have you been drinking?' he asked.

'Only a little,' replied the young man defiantly. 'I don't like to mix too much with the weed.'

Randall chose that moment to invite himself into the house.

'Bonbon, we're leaving right now!'

Ignoring the youth's protest, and reminding himself that even touching the young fool would leave him open to an assault charge, Randall focused on the summit of the stairs.

There, after what sounded like a stumble across the landing, his daughter appeared in her jeans and a bra. She looked both shocked at his presence and volcanically angry.

'Every time, Dad! Every single time! You're even *dressed* like a prison warden! All I ask for is some space!'

'You'll have plenty of that in your room at home.' Randall dug his nails into his palms. 'What's going on here?'

He addressed the question not to Bonnie, but to the other drongo who had shuffled into view behind her.

'Just a game of special poker, Mr Shores,' he said, and showed him the fan of cards in his hand. 'Can you wait until we've finished?'

'I'm guessing you're winning,' said Randall, who had registered the fact that he was fully dressed. 'Bonnie, fetch your stuff before I make a scene.'

His daughter just stood there, making no attempt to cover herself. Randall held her gaze. Finally, with a sigh so hard it looked like she was deflating, Bonnie scowled and cursed her father.

'As soon as I turn eighteen you will *never see me again*!'

Watching her stomp off to gather her belongings, and taking some solace from this small victory, Randall turned to the young man standing beside him. He looked him up and down, nodding to himself at the same time.

'How is college?' he asked. 'Any problems with concentration at all?'

The youth shrugged, plunging his hands into his pockets, and attempted to flick his fringe from his eyes once more.

'I'm good,' he said.

Randall continued to assess him. Physically, it was very difficult to identify a troll. Many possessed the bushy brow and sloping shoulders that invited such suspicion, but it was nothing a little shaping and an effort to stand upright couldn't hide.

'It's Benny, isn't it?'

'Ryan,' said Ryan.

Randall took a step closer, still smiling, but with a hint of menace now.

'I'm watching you, Ryan,' he growled, turning two fingers towards his eyes. 'You and your friend. I'm watching and I'm waiting.'

'For what?' By now, the youth looked both puzzled and amused. 'We haven't done anything.'

'Not yet,' said Randall breezily, just as his daughter stomped down the stairs looking deeply unhappy at being back in all her clothes. 'But you will!'

*

The little troll called Wretch drove as though he had gleaned all his road skills from a video game. At least, that's how it felt to Maurice, who bounced around in the space behind the back seat as they tore through the streets.

'Just let me out!' he pleaded when they weaved around yet another pothole in the road. 'Pull over – please!'

Wretch clung to the wheel from the edge of his seat. He was so slight and short that Maurice was surprised he could even reach the pedals – given the speed with which they barrelled down a side road just then, it was clear that somehow Wretch had his foot planted squarely on the accelerator.

'I won't go back!' declared the troll, shaking his head vigorously. 'I'd rather die!'

'Speak for yourself!' Maurice broke off there as the car swerved to avoid a traffic island. 'And where are we heading?' he demanded to know, anchoring himself to the back seat head rest.

'As far from the settlement as possible!'

'*Wretch!*'

Ignoring his plea, the troll shot across the junction at the end of the road. He let the back end slide as he spun the wheel with all the purpose of a ship's captain in a storm. On finding themselves facing the headlights of a bus, Maurice began openly screaming.

'*Hoooo yeah!*' crowed Wretch, fishtailing clear with a second to spare and then flooring the accelerator. Revelling in the moment, he went on to punch the radio into life. At once, every seat inside the hatchback began to throb with the bass notes of a dance-floor filler.

'This is no time to party,' begged Maurice, wishing the troll would stop beating out a rhythm on the wheel and focus on staying on the sensible side of the road. 'In fact, driving like this is a sure-fire way to get caught. If you value your freedom then you'll stop this car right now! There are safer ways to disappear!'

For the first time, with a clear run ahead, the little troll caught his eye in the rear-view mirror. Maurice just looked back pleadingly. Somewhere in the distance, despite the radio volume, the wail of a siren struck up.

'Are they after us?' asked Wretch.

'Let me see. You've jumped half a dozen red lights since we took off in a stolen car,' said Maurice, before yelling to really make himself heard. '*Of course they're after us!*'

Wretch switched his attention to the wing mirrors. Then, with a sigh, but no deployment of the indicator, he swung sharply into an industrial park. Thankfully, so late in the evening, the grid of access roads was broad and empty. Even if there had been traffic, Maurice doubted that Wretch would've stopped for anything. It was only when he appeared to run out of road, by speeding onto a patch of wasteland bordering a canal, that the little troll finally showed that at least he knew where to find the handbrake. Moments after, the hatchback shuddered to a halt, having spun full circle into the flimsy wire fencing, Maurice dared to breathe out long and hard. At the same time, the little troll lowered the radio volume and twisted round to face the boy solemnly.

'You have arrived at your destination,' he said, adopting a robotic voice before dissolving into giggles.

Maurice took a moment to allow his heart rate to settle, and then quietly asked Wretch if he'd mind stepping out of the car to open the boot.

'Thanks,' he said, after Wretch agreed like it was no big deal. He waited for the little troll to saunter round, and then unfolded himself from the cramped space. A moment later, having brushed himself down, Maurice grabbed Wretch by the neck of his hoodie and thrust him back against the car. 'You brainless *idiot!*' he yelled, unconcerned that he'd knocked his own glasses into a tilt. 'What possessed you to take off like that?' he asked. 'You could've killed us both!'

Wretch responded like he had lost the ability to breathe. His eyes widened and he began to tremble violently. In a blink, feeling bad at such a show of aggression, Maurice released him from his grip.

'Sorry,' mumbled the troll.

'No, I should apologise.' Maurice straightened out the shoulders of Wretch's hoodie, and then patted him down for good measure. 'I've never threatened anyone in my life. Even after everything you've put me through, I don't think I want to start now.'

In that moment, standing in the gloom behind the stolen vehicle, Maurice felt a surprising sense of peace. It was the first, he realised, since his kidnap from the coach. Only the sound of sirens in the distance reminded him of the chaos they had caused in getting here.

'We should leave,' said Wretch, turning his attention towards the source of the wailing. 'Want to come with me?'

Maurice waited for his attention once more and then spread his arms.

'Seriously, why would I want to do that?' he asked.

The little troll looked lost at this. The sirens hadn't grown markedly louder but were certainly becoming more numerous. In the still night air, the howling shifted in depth and tone. It left Maurice feeling strangely vulnerable; hunted and helpless. The radio inside the hatchback was barely audible now. Even so, as the music made way for a news bulletin, he caught his breath on hearing the lead item.

'I'll turn it off,' said Wretch, and headed back for the driver's door.

'Wait!' Maurice gestured for him to be quiet. 'This is about us!'

'. . . *the break-out from the settlement, which took place earlier today, was masterminded by two youths described as highly unpredictable. The public have been advised to report sightings and not approach under any circumstances. In other news, police are linking the discovery of an abandoned squad car this afternoon to the spate of missing officers . . .*'

Having heard enough, Maurice leaned into the car and killed the radio.

'Buddy,' said Wretch as the boy stood back to face him. 'You're in trouble.'

'*Me?*' Maurice touched his chest, which was tightening in panic, and then addressed the radio inside the car as if the announcer could hear him. 'But I've done nothing wrong!'

As he did so, he noticed the bag on the passenger seat. It was unclasped, and evidently belonged to the poor woman they had ditched at the petrol station. In among the receipts, the perfume atomiser, house keys and pens, the mobile phone was hard for Maurice to ignore. Just removing it from the bag felt wrong, but this was an emergency and he had a call to make.

'I'm going to ring my parents,' he told Wretch, and stepped away with the phone in hand. 'They'll sort this out.'

'Isn't it locked?' asked Wretch. 'They're always locked,' he added, with what sounded like nostalgia for an age when phones came with no such security.

Maurice swiped the on screen activation bar. To his surprise, it opened without any request for a code. He beamed at Wretch victoriously.

'Your friend Miss Lau works in a high-security environment,' he said. 'Either she's very naive or totally trusting.'

'She's trusting,' Wretch said defensively. 'You can tell Candy anything and it won't go further.'

'Right.' Maurice didn't like to point out that he'd probably tested any bond they might've shared by stealing her car from under her nose. 'Will you give me a moment?' He stepped away to punch in his home number. 'This is between me and my parents.'

Maurice took himself behind the hatchback once more, facing the road as the sirens grew louder. It would only be a matter of minutes, he thought, before the police tracked them down. By then, he felt sure his folks would know what to do.

The problem, he realised very quickly, as his forefinger hovered over the phone, was in what digits to press. Ever since he'd owned a mobile, the home number had been on preset. Maurice had never actually needed to dial it from scratch. The same went for the mobile numbers for his mum and dad. Here he was in an emergency situation with no idea how to reach the people who could help him.

'For crying out loud,' he muttered to himself in frustration. 'Just call the police.'

It was a thought he aired out loud but then hesitated. The news report hadn't painted him in a favourable light, after all. On reflection, he decided, glancing over his shoulder to see the little troll going through the contents of the lady's bag, it was vital that he got some kind of support or legal representation before surrendering himself.

'I'm just looking for a light,' said Wretch, with a thin roll-up pinched between his lips. 'Candy doesn't smoke but I know she keeps a box of matches for the smelly candle in her office.'

'Aromatherapy?' said Maurice, thinking it was probably something she deployed to keep the trolls calm and tranquil.

'Whatever,' said Wretch, who promptly dropped the bag on finding what he was looking for. He struck a match, leaned over the flaring light, and then glanced up at Maurice. 'Go ahead and make your call. This is my only smoke, and I plan to relish it.'

Maurice looked upon the little troll as if this was the final wish of a condemned man. Unwilling to spoil the moment, he opted not to share his current difficulty in reaching his parents. Instead, thinking ahead, and mindful of the stolen car in their possession, he accessed the stored numbers in the phone and selected the one marked *Home*.

If he couldn't reach his own house, he decided, turning away to focus as the line began to bleat, he would at least do the decent thing and reunite Miss Lau with her car and the bag.

*

The call had lasted no more than a minute. Maybe a minute and a half once the obstructive guy who picked up finally quit with the threats and handed over the phone. In that time, the sirens seemed to howl from every direction as if multiple squad cars were combing the estate. Over the din, without giving away his name and requesting that she just listen, Maurice hurriedly explained where the social worker would find her vehicle. He stressed that no serious damage had been done, apologised profusely for the trouble caused, and then hit the

117

red button. With the phone in hand, and the police just blocks away, he felt good about having rung her. It could only support his claim that he was a nice boy caught up in something beyond his control. Meanwhile, the individual responsible for all the chaos was enjoying a cigarette behind him. Maurice grimaced at the smell as he focused on his next move with the phone. Unwilling to surrender without first giving an explanation, he figured recording an audio of his testimony could only help as evidence to support his innocence. Even if the police responded to him as a suspect in a crime, the truth was on his side.

'You should go,' Maurice called over his shoulder, coughing as the smoke intensified. 'Leave the car to me.'

'Don't worry about the motor,' he heard the troll assure him, just as the sound of crackling caught his attention. He looked up from the phone. Despite the absence of any street lighting close to this path of scrubland, a widening radius around him was beginning to brighten. 'I've already taken care of it.'

It took the boy just a moment to wheel around. But even before he saw it with his own eyes, Maurice knew the little troll had just set the social worker's hatchback on fire.

12

Pulling up before the police tape in the industrial estate, the taxi driver turned in his seat and asked his passenger if she'd like him to wait.

'If that's your car,' he said, gesturing through the windscreen, 'I don't think you'll be driving home tonight.'

Several police vehicles, with light bars flashing, were parked at right angles across the road before the tape. From the back seat of the taxi, Candy Lau just stared at the scene on the wasteland beyond.

'Greg is going to kill me,' she said under her breath. 'What the hell happened here?'

The taxi driver said nothing for a moment, and watched the recovery truck take up the slack on the chains attached to her hatchback. It was half submerged in the canal, lit up by portable spotlights, and snagged in the remains of the fencing. As the truck dragged the vehicle onto dry land, causing the police in attendance to create some space, Candy took one look at the charred and weed-strewn carcass of her car and wrote it off in her mind.

'Looks like someone tried to put out a fire,' observed the taxi driver. 'Want me to keep the meter running?'

'Thanks, but I'm good.' Candy handed him the cash she had withdrawn with her card on the way there. Greg had offered to pay, which was something, given that he hadn't volunteered to come with her, but Candy assured him she could cover it. He had already made her feel guilty about losing the car. She wasn't going to finish the night any deeper in his debt.

'I hope they catch them,' said the driver, leaning out of the window as Candy dipped under the tape. 'The only good troll is a dead one!'

'Charming,' she muttered under her breath. Ahead, the recovery team had finished winching her car from the water. Candy recognised Governor Shores by his broad-brimmed hat. He was gathered with several police officers. A young guy in a suit was crouched before them. He was handsome and well turned out, she noted, and appeared to be inspecting a spent match he had found on the ground. The Governor just looked bored and distracted, until the guy asked for his input. Judging by the younger man's response to his answer – moving on to one of the officers with them – it looked like Shores wasn't making much of a contribution. When he saw the young social worker approach, Randall backed away from the group before facing her with a solemn nod.

'I don't know whether to fire you first or have you arrested,' he told her in greeting, out of earshot from the suit.

'For having my car stolen, torched and sunk?' Candy felt sick at the sight of the wreckage.

'Miss Lau, two dangerous criminals are at large thanks to you.'

It took a moment for Randall to bring Candy up to speed. By the time he was done, she looked utterly shell-shocked.

120

'I can't believe Wretch could be capable of such a thing,' she said, on learning how the little troll had smuggled himself out of the settlement. 'There was a bad smell in the car, but I had no idea.'

'He has human help,' said Randall gravely. 'Why anyone would want to spring a low life is beyond me, but the boy will pay for his actions.'

Candy considered telling him about the call she'd received, but the Governor's threatening tone stopped her. He was evidently in an unforgiving mood and she had no wish to make it worse for the kid who had contacted her. He hadn't been obliged to ring, and he'd sounded perfectly pleasant. Finding her car trashed like this was a kick in the teeth, but Candy liked to think of herself as a woman who believed in second chances.

'Sir, if I'm responsible here then I apologise,' she said instead, conscious of her position. 'Whenever I come and go from the settlement, I will be more vigilant in future.'

For the first time, Governor Randall Shores faced her directly. She saw some thunder under the brim of his hat.

'Your future is under review,' he warned her. 'Consider yourself suspended until the troll and his accomplice are brought to justice!'

Candy drew breath to protest but took it no further. Ever since she had joined the staff at the settlement, the Governor's uncompromising reputation had been evident in his attitude towards the residents. If a troll didn't respect his authority, as Candy was well aware, he was known to challenge them at every opportunity. Many of her colleagues argued that was

121

how he maintained law and order among a population of vandals and thieves. Only the sound of a car horn behind her was sufficient to stop him from staring at her like she was soaking up valuable seconds in the hunt for the runaways. Turning around, Candy figured it was her taxi driver. Then the headlamps flashed on the saloon with the learner plate. This was swiftly followed by another blast from the horn before a girl in the driving seat leaned out.

'What is taking you so long, Daddy? First you ruin my night out and now this? Hurry up!'

Bonnie addressed her father so forcefully that it silenced the hum of chatter around the crime scene. Even the guy in the suit broke off from his conversation with the officers to see how the Governor might respond.

'I have to take my daughter home,' Randall told Candy in a quiet voice. 'Just be aware that this is a very serious breach,' he added, already heading for the car as he jabbed his finger at her. 'There will be consequences!'

*

The little troll could certainly run from trouble. That much was clear to Maurice as he attempted to keep up.

'Slow down!' he cried as Wretch sprinted along the towpath under the stars. 'Wait for me!'

'Can't stop! Won't stop!'

Wretch had taken off just moments after the front end of the hatchback came to rest in the canal. All Maurice had done was appeal to the little troll to put out the fire he had started on the back seat. With mounting disbelief, he had watched Wretch respond by releasing the handbrake and rolling the car towards the water. As the vehicle was already sitting over the fencing that marked the boundary between the wasteland and the canal, it hadn't taken him much effort. In that time, the flames gathered strength with frightening ferocity and then went out with the kind of hiss that Maurice associated with the appearance of a panto villain. For a moment, the pair simply looked on at the semi-submerged wreck in silence. Then Wretch had glanced at the boy and turned tail.

Ten minutes later, after what felt to Maurice like several miles, the damn troll was still going strong. Even though the sound of the sirens had ceased, Wretch tore along the path as if pursued by wild dogs. Driven by a rising sense of anger as much as anything else, Maurice made every effort to close the gap. This impulsive, reckless low life in front of him had shown no consideration for the predicament Maurice now found himself in. Taking off, having torched the car, was the final straw. In fury he threw himself at the troll, bringing them both down in the dirt.

'All you're doing is making things worse for us both!' he yelled, pinning Wretch to the ground by his wrists. 'You owe me some answers!'

Such was his anger that Maurice barely recognised his own voice. The troll on the ground just faced up at him, panting hard. His cheeks glowed, but his eyes looked stricken. For a moment, it looked as if he might burst into tears.

'Don't send me back,' he begged. 'It'll be curtains for me.'

'But it's a safe place for your kind!' said Maurice, who tightened his hold as Wretch wriggled to be free from underneath him. 'You can run riot there and nobody else has to suffer!'

Maurice felt bad just as soon as the words left his lips. More so when he saw how the troll grimaced in his grip.

'Just get off,' Wretch grumbled, his face contorted. 'Get off and leave me alone!'

'Are you injured?' Releasing him, Maurice clambered to his feet. 'Did the guard hurt you?'

'None of your business!' Wretch grimaced as he rolled onto his side, and then gasped when Maurice grabbed the edge of his hoodie, exposing his lower back.

'Good grief,' he whispered after a moment. 'Who did this to you?'

Even in such poor light, there was no mistaking the cross-hatching of scars. Without a doubt, they had been inflicted with great violence.

'I don't belong there!' Wretch repeated, his voice shrill with fear as he pulled free. 'None of us do!'

Still utterly stunned by what he had just glimpsed, Maurice extended his hand uselessly.

'We can sort this,' he said, as Wretch backed away from him. 'You shouldn't be so frightened.'

'Frightened? Have you any idea how frightened feels?'

'After the last twenty-four hours I can hazard a guess,' said Maurice, and then decided to stop there.

'When you live in constant fear,' the troll continued, 'any chance to escape is worth a shot.'

'Like kidnapping?'

Wretch nodded, breaking from Maurice's gaze.

'I always thought it was a bad idea, but what else could I do?'

Maurice was well aware that trolls tended to act in groups. This was down to a combustible combination of low self-esteem and a tendency towards excitability. Even so, he wanted to point out that Wretch was perfectly capable of independent thought. He'd just obliterated a hatchback without instruction, after all.

'Why don't we put that behind us for now?' he offered. All of a sudden, in light of what he'd just seen, Maurice felt as if he was faced with a timid animal in the wild here. Wretch's eyes darted about, searching for a chance to get away, which made Maurice feel even more uncomfortable. 'We've been through a lot together in a short space of time. Let's not go our separate ways like this.' He paused and spread his hands. 'Come on. We hardly know each other!'

Wretch furrowed his brow.

'So, now you want to go on a date with me?' he asked, looking amused all of a sudden. 'No touching my tummy banana.'

'All I want to do is help.' In no mood to make light of their situation, Maurice pushed his glasses back to the bridge of his nose. 'I'm offering to stick around while we work out the right thing to do.'

Wretch's brow see-sawed to one side as he processed the situation. Then, taking a step back, he shook his head vigorously.

'You'll turn me in,' he said. 'I can't trust you.'

'We wouldn't have come this far without some trust in each other,' countered Maurice. 'Think about it.'

The proposition seemed to create some kind of challenge for the little troll. He looked pained for a moment, even with the light from a nearby streetlamp casting half his face in shadow.

'If you're caught with me,' he said finally, 'you'll be in big trouble.'

Maurice sighed to himself, nodding at the same time.

'At least let me try to make things good for us both.'

Still eyeing him, Wretch smiled cautiously.

'The thing with the car back there,' he said. 'I was just taking care of the evidence.'

Maurice shook his head incredulously.

'It wasn't much help,' he told the troll, 'but it's done now. We'll sort it out, I'm sure.'

Wretch looked to his feet.

'Miss Lau is going to be mad at me, isn't she?'

His comment reminded Maurice of the mobile in his jacket pocket. Part of him wanted to call the social worker once again. She hadn't freaked out when he'd identified himself as one of the two stowaways in her car. If anything, she had sounded concerned about them. Then again, he figured there was every chance that by now she'd be wise to the fate of her motor. With this in mind, Maurice opted to power down the phone.

'Everything will be alright,' he assured Wretch, before looking around. They had reached a stretch of the towpath that took them past a small square lined on three sides by terraced houses. For a second, Maurice considered knocking on a door where some lights were still on and just giving up there and then. The police would be called for sure, but that way he'd also be reunited with his parents. Then he looked at Wretch, and wondered who would come for him. 'You know what?' he said after a moment, 'I'm sure things will look better for us once we get some rest.'

126

'There's no way I'm stopping.' Wretch pulled his hood up over his head. 'It's high time I went home.'

'Huh?' Maurice watched him set off along the towpath once more. 'Where's home?' he called after him, well aware that every troll inside the settlement had been disowned by families who once believed they were their own flesh and blood.

'I'll find it,' said Wretch breezily, walking with a swagger now, as if his centre of gravity was located midway between his shoulder blades.

Despite the sudden upswing in Wretch's spirits, Maurice remained troubled by the scars he had glimpsed. It left him feeling oddly protective. An escapee from the settlement was just too likely to cause trouble to last long in the open. Without someone to look out for him, Wretch would quickly wind up behind the perimeter wall again, but the boy couldn't allow that to happen if that's where he had suffered.

With a sigh, Maurice realised there was only one option available to him now, and set off to catch up. He said nothing on drawing alongside the little troll. Just glanced across and caught his eye. In response, Wretch looked ahead once more and purposely scuffed a stone so it skittered into the dark.

PART TWO

PART TWO

13

Towards dawn the next morning, Candy Lau abandoned any further chance of sleep and slipped out from her side of the bed. Her grandmother had once warned against finishing the evening with an argument. Padding through to the kitchen, Candy figured this was the reason why.

'Didn't I tell you that working with trolls spells trouble?' she muttered to herself in a parody of Greg's voice when he was cross. 'Now it's cost us our car!'

Frankly, the way Greg responded on her return from the canal side had spoken volumes about the state of things between them. Candy waited for the kettle to boil, the first bars of sunshine breaking over the skyline, and asked herself out loud what she was doing here. It was her first thought on waking that had prompted such a big question. She had barely registered the man snoring fitfully beside her. If anything, her thoughts had rested with the little troll responsible for trashing their hatchback.

What on earth had possessed Wretch to go to such an extreme? she wondered, on waiting for her tea to cool. Of all the settlement residents she saw in her line of work, he was one of the sweetest in nature. Yes, he could be uncommunicative, twitchy and erratic, but Candy would've never marked him down as one with designs on a breakout like this. Sipping her tea, even though it scalded her lips, she figured the Governor was right about the schoolboy. He had to be in on it somehow.

It was with this in mind that she picked up the home phone and dialled her mobile. The kid had seemed perfectly polite when he'd called, she thought, with the receiver pressed to her ear. When the phone went straight to answer machine, however, Candy killed the call. Just hearing her own voice came as a surprise. For a moment, it felt as if she was out there with the two runaways and not stuck in her kitchen as dawn broke, feeling strung out about her partner's lack of support.

'What am I doing here?' she asked again out loud. Her first thought was to head out for some fresh air. Space was her usual remedy at times of stress, as Candy remembered telling Wretch when he briefly opened up about the subject, and that's when she set down her mug as if it was a dead weight. 'That's it,' she whispered to herself, pushing her chair back as she rose. 'Got you!'

When Wretch had shared where he once liked to get away from it all, the location had been of passing interest to the young social worker. At the time, her aim was simply to encourage the little troll to put his thoughts and feelings into words. Now, the place in question seemed loaded with significance. Leaving the rest of her tea, Candy Lau returned to her bedroom. There, she dressed as hurriedly as she dared without disturbing the man in her bed who'd positioned himself as far from her side as possible.

'Well, this is nice,' said Maurice with a yawn as the early morning sun bathed his face. 'If we weren't wanted criminals I might even be able to relax.'

Sitting beside him, the little troll sniggered wheezily. It wasn't funny, as far as the boy was concerned, but in the brief time they had been together Maurice had learned that Wretch responded in this way to pretty much everything.

'I'm getting my bearings,' Wretch grunted a moment later. 'Let me think, alright?'

This was the third time he had asked for a moment to work out where they should be heading. It had been in the middle of the night, after trudging for miles along the towpath, that Wretch peeled off towards a park on a hill, jumped the fence and then climbed towards a bench under trees near the top. All the way the little troll had jabbered about getting home. He had just failed to respond when the boy pressed him on where that might be.

'It would be good if you worked it out sooner rather than later,' suggested Maurice just then, and looked around nervously. 'We can't stay here for ever.'

*

It was still dark when they had settled on the bench. In the stillness of the night, a mist had thickened over the canal and spilled across the fringes of the park. From their spot at the top, it felt as if they were castaways on an island surrounded by a moon-silvered sea. It came as a comfort to Maurice, in some ways. He was cold, scared, tired and confused, and yet somehow cut off from the world. Worrying about the events that had overtaken his life had proved exhausting, and the chance to just rest his feet felt like bliss.

With his school blazer buttoned, his collar turned up and his arms folded, Maurice had closed his eyes and found just a semblance of peace. Wretch meanwhile had simply retreated inside his hoodie like some kind of streetwise tortoise. Despite the occasional muttering from the troll, the boy had eventually nodded off. When he had next opened his eyes, roused by birdsong, he had been met with a vision of sunlight flaring against the east-facing walls of distant skyscrapers, and an urban sprawl spread far and wide. With the mist evaporating, and the paths around the park dotted with early dog-walkers and joggers, Maurice had felt uneasy all over again. Wretch didn't appear to have slept at all. With his eyes fixed on the view beyond the park, as the rush hour hum began to build, he appeared to be no closer to working out where to head next. It was only when Maurice registered a scratching sound that he turned to his companion on the bench.

'What are you doing?' he asked, having noticed that the troll was absently working on something in the gap between his thighs.

'Nothing.' With the tip of his tongue peeping from his mouth, Wretch looked downwards. 'Well, something, but it has to be done.'

'What has?' Maurice rose from the bench for a better look. The troll made a vague attempt to hide his handiwork, which he'd crafted with the ring pull from a can that lay at his feet, but there was no mistaking what he had just etched into the seat.

Maurice tutted disapprovingly.

'That should be *were here* not *was*,' he said. 'If you're going to leave both our names then it's plural.'

The troll blinked up at him.

'Eh?'

'*Wretch and Maurice was here* makes you sound grammatically challenged,' said Maurice, who gestured for him to hand over the ring pull. When Wretch obliged, the boy promptly marched to the bin beside the bench and flicked it in. 'Just how dumb are you?' he demanded, spinning around full circle to address the startled troll. 'I'm here with you because I'm worried what will happen if you're caught, and what do you do? *Leave an inscription on the bench!*'

The little troll glanced down at the carving once more.

'Are you sure it's *were*?' he asked. 'Shouldn't that be with an *h*?'

Maurice closed his eyes for a moment, and reminded himself that he faced an extraordinary situation. It demanded calm and sensitivity, he realised, and duly sat back down beside the little troll.

'Listen, Wretch, if this is about finding the courage to go home, the fact is you won't be welcome there. Those people you considered your parents have been robbed of their real child at birth. Chances are you represent everything bad about what's happened. If you show up, my guess is they'll slam the door in your face.'

'I know that,' said Wretch, who had been listening closely. 'Those guys threw my stuff out onto the street when the test results came through.'

'You're kidding.' Maurice wondered whether Wretch had ever really enjoyed a decent break in life. 'That must've been tough.'

Wretch shrugged like it was no big deal, only for his gaze to fall. It left Maurice feeling a little awkward. He had no doubt that his parents would be frantic with worry at this moment in time, and hopefully going to great lengths to clear his name. That their son had volunteered to accompany one of his kidnappers following the breakout would take some explaining. Like most people, neither his mum nor dad had time for trolls. Even Maurice had surprised himself with his decision. Just then, looking at the little figure with the weight of the world on his shoulders, it still felt like the right thing to have done.

'Anyway,' sniffed Wretch, and nodded towards the hills on the horizon beyond the city, 'I have another home in mind.'

'So, your family had two places?' asked Maurice, struggling to keep up. Some said that trolls intentionally sought to smuggle their offspring into affluent households. Others argued that a wealthy family didn't guarantee a happy upbringing, though many pointed out the breed lacked the sophistication to be that selective. 'Do you mean like a holiday cottage?'

'I mean my *birth*place.' Wretch turned to face the boy, his eyes shining in the strengthening sunlight. 'The place where I belong.'

*

Facing her father over the breakfast bar, Bonita Shores pulled a face like she'd just found a mummified mouse in her cornflakes.

'Seriously?' she said, dropping her spoon with a splash. 'You're asking me to take the *bus* to college?'

136

'Bonbon, we have a crisis situation at work. I just don't have the time today.'

'You don't have the time? For your own daughter? Do you want me to fail my driving test?'

'Now you're being unreasonable.'

'Oh, *I'm* being unreasonable.' Bonnie shoved her bowl away, kicking back her stool at the same time. 'This is not what we agreed when my provisional license came through, Daddy, but that's fine! Leave me to take public transport. I'll run the risk of being molested or picking up some minging cough. No *problem*!'

'Bon –'

Randall's appeal was cut short by the kitchen door as it slammed shut behind his daughter. He turned to his wife, but she had already crept out into the utility room with the washing basket. With a sigh, Randall finished his toast and then reached for his mobile. It had been pinging at him since his alarm went off that morning. A glimpse at the messages from his office confirmed that the two runaways had yet to be apprehended, which only added further steam to his shower.

Minutes later, having been forced to dry himself with a towel that Bonita had left damp on the floor, the Governor noted he had missed a call from the local radio station. He wasn't sorry. The story might've broken out, much like the damn troll and his accomplice, but in his view it was no more newsworthy than a couple of livestock escaping from their pen. Yes, there might be some damage, but ultimately they'd be caught out by their own stupidity. All he had to do was keep his head down and it would soon be yesterday's news.

More immediately, Randall didn't want to be a disappointment to his daughter. Having been sprung from the sleepover, she had only just started speaking to him civilly again. Was it really worth earning her displeasure, plus a weighted silence from his wife, simply for a delay of no more than half an hour in tracking down two delinquents who would probably turn themselves in once they realised there was nowhere to hide? Finishing his coffee, including the grit at the bottom of his cup, Randall wiped his mouth on the back of his hand and called for Bonita a second time.

'OK, I'll take you to college,' he said, tipping his head back so she could hear him from her bedroom. 'But I'm not picking up any more boys,' he muttered under his breath, brushing the toast crumbs from his lap as he rose from his stool. 'My car. My rules.'

14

At school, everything Maurice was taught about trolls could fit on an essay paper. That was pretty much the objective in modern history at sixth-form level. He'd already covered the sinkhole phenomenon, and the discovery that low lives had long been switching human newborns for their own bawling offspring, while the trip to the settlement was supposed to have formed the basis for the study of the social implications. Maurice hadn't banked on gaining such first-hand experience, though he doubted his account of kidnap, assault on a security guard and car theft would help him in exam conditions. Even so, spending time with Wretch had opened his eyes to one clear fact: the little troll was living in a dream world.

'You can't go back to wherever your kind comes from,' he pointed out, as the sun climbed over the park on the hill. 'Nobody knows how to get down there.'

Wretch stood before him, having climbed off the bench as if lifted up by a sense of optimism. He seemed to deflate a little at the boy's response, but it didn't stop him from glaring defiantly.

'I'll find out,' he declared. 'All I have to do is put my ear to the ground.'

Maurice couldn't be sure if he was talking literally here. The number of trolls on the surface, whether squirrelled away with families still or in secure facilities, was far outnumbered by those said to dwell in the vast, unexplored tunnel system below their feet. There had been talk, in the beginning, that the trolls must have originated from subterranean Scandinavia and just burrowed endlessly as the population grew. Academics and historians put forward a convincing case that some truth might lie behind the myths and legends, but to date no search had proven successful. That Wretch thought he had it all figured out was just a fantasy.

'Can I make a suggestion?' Maurice folded his collar down now some warmth had eased into the morning. 'Why don't we head for the nearest police station and turn ourselves in?'

'No way!'

'I'll go there with you. My parents will be called and together we can work this out.'

'Don't make me hit you again,' warned the troll, jabbing a finger towards the boy. 'I'd rather die than go back to the settlement!'

Maurice hadn't expected to spark this level of agitation, and quickly raised his hands to calm the moment.

'I'll stand by you,' he promised, thinking of the scars he had seen. 'I give you my word that nothing bad will happen again.'

The troll responded with a snort.

'I'm going home,' he insisted.

Just then, some distance behind Wretch, a dog tore after a Frisbee. Maurice watched it hurtle after the plastic disc, followed from behind by its owner. He glanced around. The park was beginning to host the noise and activity of an everyday morning.

All of a sudden, the boy felt like he didn't belong. He looked to his shoes, playing out the consequences of stepping up to the duty sergeant's desk without the little troll, and chuckled ruefully.

'I've done nothing wrong,' said Maurice, 'but only you can clear my name.'

Wretch pushed out his lower lip, considering the point before nodding to himself.

'You make it sound like *you* need *me*.'

Maurice couldn't disagree.

'So, have you worked out what direction we should be heading?' he asked, which drew a small smile from the figure on his feet.

'There's only one way.' Wretch turned to look beyond the city sprawl. 'Over the hills.'

Maurice waited for him to look back once more.

'Over the hills,' Maurice repeated, as if testing out the statement. 'So, should we be on the lookout for a yellow brick road or anything like that?' When Wretch looked at him blankly, Maurice sighed and shook his head. 'We're not in Oz,' he pointed out. 'You can't just head for the horizon and hope for the best.'

The little troll continued to hold his gaze. It was Maurice who blinked first.

'Watch me,' beamed Wretch, and then made his way towards the path that wound down the hill.

Maurice remained where he was for a moment, staring into space. Then, with a curse under his breath, he hurried to catch up.

'We won't get far on empty stomachs, and I'm starving,' he told Wretch. 'What's good to eat around here that's free? That's right. *Nothing!*'

The troll chuckled to himself, walking with a swagger and sway once more.

'You really do need me.' Fishing inside his pouch pocket, he produced a purse with a clasp. Immediately Maurice recognised who it belonged to, and not just because it had been in the bag on the seat of the car when he borrowed the mobile phone.

'You should give that back,' he said quietly, having stopped in his tracks.

'It's too late for that now.' Wretch swung around to address him, waving the purse in the air. 'The burgers are on Miss Lau!'

'That'll be my pleasure,' declared the woman who had just trotted across the grass to block their path. Even before the little troll had spun back to face her, Candy plucked the purse from his grasp. 'But seeing that I'm paying, it'll be a proper breakfast. There's no way I'm taking charge of this situation if you're stoked up on junk food.'

All Maurice could do was nod solemnly, shocked by this intervention but relieved. Not least because everyone was well aware that a troll gone hyper on sugar and artificial food colourings could be a recipe for disaster.

*

Governor Randall Shores took the call from the settlement's chief of security on his car speakerphone. On being informed that the missing pair had been sighted, his daughter responded by pulling up at a set of traffic lights just as they turned to amber.

'We could've got across then,' Randall complained, having listened closely to the additional details before the security guy rang off. A moment later, though it felt like an age, the light turned to red. 'Bonnie, we had time. I can't hang around here!'

Bonita set about examining her polished nails.

'You're supposed to be the responsible adult,' she said. 'Responsible adults don't encourage learner drivers to jump the lights.'

Randall became aware of his back teeth, still tender from the previous day. With his broad-brimmed hat in his lap, he found himself turning it repeatedly through his hands.

'Is this about last night?' he asked. 'That was me being a responsible father.'

'Well, it's done now.' Bonita waited for the green light before carefully checking her mirrors. 'I'll just have to hope that Benny and Ryan understand what you can be like.'

'Just pull over and let me drive,' said Randall.

Bonita eased the car forward, taking her time between gears.

'Aren't you impressed?' she asked. 'No crunching sounds or wheel spin.'

Randall conceded that it made a change, but his role as an instructor was over now. Behind the wheel, it would take him at least forty minutes to reach the location of the sighting, reported by a park warden who had noted two suspicious figures on a bench before the gates had opened. If he put his foot down, or even picked up a police escort, he could make it in half an hour. More importantly, according to his security chief, the guy from the government had yet to check in for the day. Most likely his mum had forgotten to wake him, Randall thought resentfully. Nevertheless, he felt driven by the need to have the case closed before Trasker showed up.

Right now, however, as Bonnie crawled along, Randall feared the park gates would be in danger of closing for the day by the time he showed up.

'Did you hear me?' he asked, turning to glare at his daughter. 'Stop the car before I –'

'Before you what, Daddy?' She glanced across. 'Before you beat me black and blue?'

'Of course not.' Randall took a breath and faced the road once more. 'I'd never do anything to hurt you, honey.'

Bonita said nothing, while signalling in good time for the college road. Even so, Randall knew what was on her mind. Not once had he lost his temper with her. Not physically, at any rate. Yes, there had been a moment when he'd been so angry with her relentless defiance that he'd reached for the belt strap he kept in his briefcase. Thankfully, he'd reminded himself that he wasn't at work before it was too late. The episode had occurred after a deeply testing day with the trolls. Not that he could use that as an excuse, and his daughter knew it.

'So, what will happen to the two runaways?' Bonita asked next, having left him to stew for a minute.

Randall knew what she was thinking, and quickly stressed that they would face the due process of the law.

'They have nothing to fear,' he added pointedly.

Bonita shot him a glance like she didn't believe it for one moment. Then she looked back at the road, only to tut and curse to herself.

'I've left my mobile at home,' she said, braking so abruptly that the driver leading the queue of cars behind them was prompted to sound his horn. Bonita showed him the finger before embarking on a multiple-point turn. 'I can't go to college without it.'

'You're in lectures,' complained Randall. 'You don't need your phone in lectures and I really don't have time for this!'

With the traffic held up in both directions, Bonita took a moment to unwind the window and hurl abuse at the motorcyclist who had lifted his visor to ask what she was playing at. As she did so, a message flashed up on Randall's phone, forewarning him that the pair had been seen leaving the park with an adult female.

With a sarcastic cheer from the motorcyclist, Bonita pointed the car in the opposite direction and noisily found first gear.

'We're going home for my phone,' she insisted.

In that same moment, what Randall wished for more than anything else was a car with dual controls. That's what flashed through his mind as he reached for the handbrake and yanked it upwards.

'What are you doing?' screamed Bonnie as the car felt like it had driven into a pool of glue. She pulled to the side of the road and threw her hands in the air. 'Do you want to kill us both?'

'Swap places right now, young lady!' Governor Randall Shores glared at her with such rare fury and purpose that his daughter instinctively reached for the door handle. 'From here on out, I'm driving!'

*

The trio chose a table at the back of the café, close to the fire exit. Wretch sat across from Candy. She had regained possession of her purse and phone, and was studying the laminated menu closely. Maurice sat beside her, mortified.

'Wretch,' he hissed, and kicked him under the table. 'Stop staring.'

Ever since they took to their seats, the little troll had set eyes on Candy's cleavage. He appeared to have lost the ability to look anywhere else.

'Just because I'm buying you guys breakfast,' she said without glancing up, 'doesn't mean I've forgiven you for anything.'

On the way out of the park, Candy spent some time pointing out that their actions had cost her everything from her car to her job. Maurice had apologised at every opportunity, while Wretch simply trailed after the young social worker without once uttering a word.

'I'm really sorry,' Maurice said again, which drew Candy's attention from the menu.

'By rights I should be on the phone to the police.'

'Miss Lau, I know it looks bad but I really haven't done anything wrong.'

Candy flattened the menu on the table.

'Are you trying to heap all the blame on Wretch?' she asked. 'In my book, that makes things worse.'

'I didn't mean it like that!' Maurice reached for his glasses, not that they needed adjusting.

'So, how long did you have this planned?' she asked. 'I don't know whether to be appalled or impressed.'

'You have to believe that I'd never willingly do anything bad!' Maurice struggled to keep his voice above a whisper. He glanced around nervously before continuing. 'I just happened to be in the wrong place at the wrong time . . . on quite a few occasions,' he added on reflection. 'But all that's come to an end now you've found us.'

'I'm no lawyer,' she told him. 'But I'm here to help.'

Candy Lau studied the boy for a moment before breaking off to order from the waitress. Keeping his head down, Maurice opted for the same breakfast as Candy, and then suggested they make that three when Wretch failed to respond.

'Look at me, Wretch,' he hissed as Candy thanked the waitress. Briefly, the little troll dragged his eyes across to him. 'If you can't stop staring then at least close your mouth!'

Wretch complied with the latter request, returning his attention to Candy's chest at the same time. Maurice pressed his lips together, and then apologised once more just to break the awkward silence.

'I work with individuals like Wretch every day,' Candy pointed out. 'At least I did until you two decided to go sightseeing. But I can handle myself, OK?' She stopped there, faced Wretch directly and snapped her fingers. 'One, two, three, eyes on me,' she said firmly, raising her voice as if addressing a coma patient. With a blink, the little troll emerged from the shadow of his hoodie. As his hair sprung outwards, he met her gaze directly. Candy smiled in greeting, though Maurice could see it was a little forced. 'Do you remember our talk?' she asked Wretch, who responded by wiping his nose with the heel of his hand. 'When I said that at times of stress you should go to your special place, I meant in your imagination. Not, you know, *literally*!'

'We had no choice,' said Maurice in his defence. 'I can explain everything.'

The way Candy switched her attention onto him, Maurice could tell that she was at the limit of her patience. He couldn't blame her, but figured it had to be worth bringing her up to speed. Starting from the moment he was snatched from the coach, and not dodging the fact that he'd coshed a guard to save the little troll, he only paused for a moment when the waitress delivered their food to the table.

'So,' said Candy once he'd finished, and turned her attention to Wretch. 'What do you have to say about all this?'

While Maurice had been explaining that the whole sinking of the car in the canal thing was essentially a misguided attempt at firefighting, the troll had dived into his breakfast as if his plate might be seized at any moment. He only paused when Candy repeated her question, midway through licking his knife clean.

'Maurice needs me.' He jabbed the utensil across the table. 'We're a team.'

'Partners in crime, eh?'

Candy sat back with her arms folded.

'Absolutely not!' Maurice drew breath to protest further. This wasn't helping his situation, and yet he felt oddly flattered. The little troll might have been part of the gang behind his kidnapping, but the boy no longer felt threatened by him. In fact, it was almost refreshing not to be subject to the usual mockery and belittling that he put up with from his classmates. OK, so nobody at school had ever whacked him with a saucepan, but Maurice figured he might've done the same in such a desperate situation. Collecting his knife and fork, he cut into the bacon on his plate.

'Wretch has his reasons for escaping,' he said quietly, and glanced across at Candy. 'I just want to make sure that he's safe.'

Candy held his gaze for a moment, as if attempting to read his mind, before addressing the little troll.

'Would you mind fetching a napkin or two?' she asked. 'I'd be very grateful.'

Without a word, Wretch slid from his seat and left the table.

'Wow,' said Maurice. 'I had no idea he could be that obedient.'

Candy lifted her mug of tea with both hands.

'Changelings expect nothing but criticism and abuse,' she told him. 'A little positive encouragement goes a long way. I'm also familiar with handling partial disclosures,' she added, her tone changing as she faced Maurice once more. 'Without a doubt, Wretch is in a lot of trouble here. There will be consequences when he's caught, but at no time will he be in any danger. Now, you strike me as a sensible, sensitive young man. Do you want to tell me what's behind your concern for his welfare?'

Candy had the seat by the wall, but just then it was Maurice who felt cornered. He glanced over his shoulder at Wretch. The little troll was hunched over the cutlery and condiments trays beside the serving hatch.

'Terrible things have happened to him at the settlement.' The boy faced her once more. 'All this could just make it worse for him.'

Candy listened to what Maurice went on to say without blinking. He told her of the scars he had glimpsed across Wretch's back, clear signs of violence, and the troll's reluctance to talk about it. Maurice looked for some sign that she believed him, but saw only shock in her eyes.

'Do you think another resident is responsible?' she asked eventually.

Maurice dwelled on her question a moment. Then he shook his head.

'Whoever did it made sure his injuries weren't easily visible,' he said. 'I've seen some brutal behaviour in that place with my own eyes, but this is different. It's clever, calculated . . . evil.'

Candy ran her thumb around the handle of her coffee cup, considering what Maurice had said. Then, like many other customers in the café, her attention was drawn to the sound of a voice raised in anger.

'A couple of napkins you are welcome to.' The man in the apron had just stepped out from behind the counter. He crossed the floor to grab the stack from Wretch's hands. 'Helping yourself to the whole lot is just theft!'

The little troll reacted by backing away by a step, only to screw up his face, snatch the stack back and glare defiantly. The cook attempted to seize them once again, but this time Wretch clung on. Before Maurice could rise from his chair, the ensuing tussle saw the pair crash into a table. Several diners rushed to get out of the way, one tumbling backwards over a chair.

'What shall I do?' asked Maurice, grimacing as the cook dragged the flailing troll around in a headlock.

'Get him out of here,' Candy told the boy, while hurrying to open her purse. 'I was planning on leaving a tip but now this is really going to cost me dearly.'

150

15

Think like a troll. That's what Governor Randall Shores told himself as he travelled at pace towards the scene of the reported sighting in the park. How would such a creature hope to slip away given his offensive attitude and disruptive instincts? Even if a schoolboy had masterminded the operation, Randall concluded, there was no way that a low life could get far without causing upset or falling foul of the law.

'What would you do, Bonnie?' he asked. 'In their shoes?'

His daughter sat in the passenger seat with her arms folded tightly.

'Get as far away from you as possible,' she muttered under her breath.

Randall gripped the wheel a little tighter. He recognised that she might be somewhat put out, given that he'd kept her from college in his haste to hit the trail. Even so, having stopped off in a hurry at their house so she could at least pick up her phone, Bonita's sulk was really beginning to needle him.

'I'll drop you into lessons just as soon as I've checked this out,' he told her, following their race to the park. 'Besides, you could've caught the bus.'

'I will *not* put my health at risk,' she told him with a note of finality. 'Or my reputation.'

'OK, but now you're here I'd really appreciate your advice,' he pressed on. 'You're about the same age as the troll and his accomplice. Where would you go?'

Bonita issued a little groan, as if his request caused her actual physical pain.

'You're supposed to be in charge,' she said. 'Why ask me?'

'It's a polite request.' Randall glanced across at his daughter. 'Help me out here?'

Bonita stared at the road ahead. Finally, she dropped her hands into her lap and sighed. Randall enjoyed a small sense of achievement. Parenting was tough but persistence could only strengthen the bonds.

'Honestly?' she asked him.

'Your insight could be key.'

'Well, if I'd been locked up for so long I'd definitely want to get off my nut. Maybe score a little weed and party.'

Immediately, Governor Randall Shores felt tension in his jaw muscles.

'They're with an adult female,' he pressed on, choosing not to raise the temperature.

'Most probably a hooker,' Bonnie suggested confidently.

'Well, it isn't the boy's mother.' Randall wound down his window by a fraction just to get some air. 'Both parents have been called in as possible accessories to the breakout. Nobody just breezes out of a high-security facility without a sophisticated back-up plan. This troll has people protecting him, and I won't stop until everyone involved is brought to justice.'

As he spoke, swinging onto the park road, a squad car swooped by in the opposite direction. Randall watched the vehicle tear away in the rear-view mirror, the siren engaging as it shifted up a gear. This close to his destination it had to be related, which only left him all the more determined to be leading this hunt. Bonnie seemed to read his mind as he embarked upon a frantic turn in the road. Juicing the air between her teeth, she pulled out her phone and began to thumb deftly at her keypad.

'Benny and Ryan will be wondering what's happened to me,' she said. 'I'll have to let them know I'm on the worst Bring your Child to Work Day *ever*.'

*

It had been Candy's idea to catch the bus, simply to get away from the café before anyone reported the incident. Together with Maurice, having barrelled into the street and spotted the vehicle at the stop, she had ushered Wretch on board first. In hindsight, thought the young social worker as she climbed on to diffuse the stand-off with the driver, it would've been better had she led the way.

'It's an adult fare or he walks.' The guy behind the wheel was glaring at Wretch. 'There's no way he's nine.'

The little troll glanced up at her like he'd given it his best shot.

'Cheaper fare,' he said.

Without word, Candy Lau paid for three adults before shepherding Wretch down the aisle. Maurice followed close behind, taking the seat beside her midway down the coach.

'The last time I was on one of these,' he said anxiously, 'I left through the roof.'

Candy craned her neck to see Wretch heading for the rear seats.

'What's he up to now?'

As the bus pulled off, Maurice twisted around to see for himself. 'I can only think he feels most comfortable there,' he suggested.

Candy eyed the small group of youths slouching at the back and hoped this wouldn't spell more trouble. Wretch dropped into the seat in front of them, keeping one leg stretched out into the aisle. The youths were talking noisily amongst themselves. Candy didn't like to just assume she was looking at changelings. She came across that kind of judgmental attitude whenever people learned about her job and it wasn't helpful. OK, so they looked a little slack in the shoulders, and made a rapid, guttural din when they laughed, but unless their behaviour let them down then she saw no reason to suspect they were living with families under false pretences. It was only when Wretch began a hushed conversation with one of them that Candy wondered if they might share some common interest.

'I have a bad feeling,' she muttered.

'About those guys?' asked Maurice, turning back round to face her, 'or this whole mess?'

Candy understood exactly what was going through the boy's mind. The sun had not long cleared the skyline but already she'd amassed enough trouble for herself in one day to last her a lifetime.

'We need to get help,' she said. 'Running away only makes a problem worse.'

'I just don't feel we can hand him over,' replied Maurice. 'Not without some assurances.'

'I could always contact the Governor,' suggested Candy, as the bus progressed along the high street. 'I'm not exactly in his good books right now, but I'm sure he'd guarantee that Wretch would be treated with respect.'

'Are you sure about that? The way the trolls spoke about the man in charge when they held me hostage, I suspect he might be at the heart of the problem.'

'Don't be ridiculous.' Candy laughed briefly, only to compose herself when Maurice remained quite sombre. 'Really?'

'Well, someone gave the order to open fire on us with rubber bullets,' he said simply. 'This whole nightmare has left me questioning who I can trust here.'

Candy nodded as he spoke.

'You can trust me,' she said. 'As can Wretch.'

The bus slowed for the next stop. Several shoppers climbed on board, took one look at the youths gathered at the back and opted for seats near the driver. Both Candy and Maurice glanced towards the rear. The way Wretch was nodding while listening intently to a few members of the group, he seemed to be taking instruction.

'The two of us are in a big enough mess as it is,' said Maurice, returning his attention to the young social worker just as her phone signalled an incoming message. 'You don't need to get involved.'

Candy looked at the screen, her resolve hardening as she read Greg's demand to know where the hell she had gone, before stowing her phone away.

'In the last twenty-four hours, I've lost my job, my car, and possibly also my boyfriend,' she told Maurice. 'Brooding about it in my flat is the last thing I want to be doing.'

As the bus continued on its way, Wretch appeared in the aisle beside them. He flopped down in the seat opposite and grinned in a way that displayed a set of small, slightly overlapping teeth.

'What have you done?' asked Maurice. 'Please don't say anything illegal.'

'You wanted to know where we should be heading.' Wretch offered a nod of thanks towards the group at the back. 'I just put the word out.'

Having refused to draw conclusions about the youths, Candy now felt certain that Wretch had been conversing with his own kind. While many trolls who were still at large had no idea of their true identity, there were always some who had worked it out for themselves. She had never seen them pick up on each other's presence as Wretch just had. Then again, as recent events demonstrated, it struck her that there was still a great deal to learn in the field.

'Is it far?' she asked, trying hard to sound calm in the face of it all. 'Do we head for the north like some people say?'

'Only idiots say that,' replied Wretch breezily. 'But this is the right direction.'

Maurice exchanged a glance with Candy.

'Maybe we should just give ourselves up and hope for the best,' he said on reflection. 'We're going nowhere with him in charge.'

'You can say that again,' she replied as the bus began to slow. Ahead, a police car had blocked the bus lane. Standing in front of it, an officer gestured for the driver to stop. 'It looks like this is the end of the road.'

16

Watching the bus brake as he stood behind the police vehicle, Governor Randall Shores adjusted the brim of his hat.

'Stay well back and observe,' he told his daughter as the cop signalled the bus driver to kill his engine. 'You're about to learn a lot more in the next few minutes than you would from a week at that college of yours.'

'Whatever you say,' replied Bonnie, in a way that was so loaded her father couldn't help but feel insulted. She was hanging back from him by a few paces, toying with her phone. 'Can I film this?'

Randall ignored her request, choosing instead to follow the officer as he boarded the bus. He had tailed the police car on instinct, called in for an update on the situation as it evolved, and now here he was, set to personally bring the runaway troll into his custody. The officer had been a little difficult with him at first, which was understandable when Randall struggled to provide adequate identification to back up his reason for tailing him. With his official lanyard on his desk in the office, it had taken a couple of phone calls to the settlement before the guy got off his high horse and began addressing him as *sir*. The Governor's sense of satisfaction had risen by another notch when Kyle Trasker tried to ring him back – a call he'd killed just as soon as the man's name flashed up on his phone. No doubt the kid had sauntered into the control room, the mark from his breakfast bib still visible on his neck, to learn that it took experience and dedication to successfully hunt down a loose low life. So, if Bonnie wanted to record this moment, Randall decided, no doubt for sharing on social media, then at least he would be in the frame ensuring that justice was done.

'Police,' he told the bus driver, and flashed his pass for the settlement canteen.

The man looked up questioningly, but by then Randall was up alongside the cop in search of the three reported suspects. 'Stay calm, ladies and gentlemen,' he announced, and began to work his way down the aisle. 'There is a troll on board, but everything is under control.'

Several gasps rose up from the passengers, which came as no surprise to the Governor. The low lives had earned themselves such a bad reputation over time that just suggesting to people that they were breathing the same air caused some to cover their mouths. Switching his attention from one individual to the next, he continued to scan each row in turn. It was only on hearing a presence close behind him that he wheeled around and found the lens of Bonnie's mobile in his face. 'Can you just give me some space?' he hissed, and then quickly composed himself in case she was live streaming the event.

'So, where are the suspects?' she asked, peering out from behind her phone. 'This is hardly internet gold, Daddy.'

It was a disturbance from the rear of the bus that stopped Randall from balling out his daughter for placing herself in danger like this. With a start, he turned to see the emergency exit flapping open in the sunshine, and promptly bundled over the police officer on registering the sudden flight of passengers from the back seat.

'Why didn't we have this covered?' he yelled, fighting to get back on his feet as the cop called for reinforcements and the last of the youths scrambled into the open. Rising to his full height, Randall became aware that every passenger was now looking at him in stunned silence. 'They won't get far,' he assured them, and followed the officer as he crashed down the aisle in pursuit.

'There's only one hashtag to go with this,' said Bonnie, who stopped filming, flipped the phone in her hands and began to type. 'A big fat *fail*.'

*

Wretch had immediately withdrawn inside his hoodie on seeing the Governor climb on board. Across the aisle, Maurice had simply stared at his feet, as did Candy beside him. The boy's heart had thumped so loudly he feared that everyone could hear it. His first thought on seeing the road block was that another sinkhole had opened up. It wasn't uncommon, after all. Then the cop had made a beeline for the door to the bus, followed by the man in charge of the settlement, and that's when panic set in. As the Governor announced the purpose of his search, addressing the passengers while standing level with Maurice's seat, the boy felt like all the trouble he had earned himself was bearing down upon him. That he'd been seized from a school trip seemed like no excuse any more, given how far he'd come. Then the group at the back, evidently trolls, had

159

taken flight. In the time it had taken for Maurice to exhale, the threat of capture seemed to pass right by him.

'Are we in the clear?'

It was Candy who dared to whisper this just after the Governor flew through the emergency exit along with the policeman, trailed by the girl who had been filming it all on her phone. Together with Wretch, Maurice strained to see through the rear window.

'He's gone,' he said to confirm, before rising to his feet. 'And so are we.'

All of a sudden, Maurice felt a desperate need for some fresh air. At school, he'd only have to spot some troublemaker in the corridor to feel his chest tighten. This had been enough to charge his system with so much adrenalin that he couldn't help but hurry to the front.

'Slow down!' Candy urged him under her breath as he hurried towards the front of the bus. 'Just act like nothing's happened.'

Maurice cleared the steps to the pavement in one bound and then wheeled around to face her.

'That's not so easy,' he snapped, fighting for breath as Wretch jumped out behind her. 'My life is ruined thanks to him!'

'What have *I* done?' Wretch looked insulted for a moment, and then a little guilty, as if he'd just remembered the answer.

Candy grasped Maurice by the shoulder.

'Can we discuss this elsewhere?' she hissed. 'There are people here.'

'There are people *everywhere*!' Maurice shook free from her, gesturing at those who had stopped on the street to witness the drama. Despite the fact that the boy was behind all the noise, it was the hoodie in their number who attracted suspicious looks. 'That's the problem,' he continued, well aware that Candy had also picked up on the attention. 'There's nowhere we can go without getting into deeper trouble!'

Without word, Candy grabbed his upper arm and led him away from the bus. Wretch scampered close behind, quietly cursing those who watched them go. Maurice even suffered a little shove from the troll as Candy hauled him down a passage between two shop fronts.

'Keep your mouth shut!' he told the boy, before spilling into giggles. 'Do as the lady says.'

'Just let me go!' yelled Maurice, his head spinning now, only to express surprise when Candy did just as he had asked.

'You're having a panic attack,' she told him firmly, her gaze sufficient to pin him to the wall. 'Breathe slowly and it will pass.'

Just hearing this stopped Maurice from snapping back. It wasn't the first time he had felt this way under pressure. He also knew she was right about how to bring it under control. The last occasion had been during a mock exam, which he had cut short because it felt like he was suffocating. Back then, his form tutor had been clear that in order to get on in life he needed to learn to embrace his anxiety and find ways to deal with it. Confidence, so he had been told, was the key to his future. Well, in terms of immersing himself in a whole world of worry, Maurice thought with no sense of satisfaction, he'd done a fine job there. He stood with his shoulders heaving for a moment, and then rested his hands on his knees. Slowly, as his composure returned, his temples throbbed and his skin prickled inside his school shirt. He also felt a little foolish when he finally straightened up and apologised.

'It's not you guys,' he told them. 'It's me.'

'We're all out of our comfort zones,' Candy assured him. 'The only way to get through this is by working as a team.'

'We should stick together,' echoed Wretch, who was standing so close to Candy it looked like he hoped to do just that. 'Stop worrying and follow me.'

Maurice was feeling calmer by the second, but no less puzzled by the little troll's plan of action.

'Wretch, you can't just set out for some place without knowing where it is.'

'Brother, I'm not an idiot.' He jabbed a thumb towards the street at the mouth of the passage. 'According to my sources, I just have to follow my nose.'

Maurice straightened his glasses and stared at him.

'That sounds about as effective as tapping your red shoes together three times and making a wish.' He paused there to address Candy directly. 'Do we really want him calling all the shots here?'

'Wretch and his kind evolved in darkness,' she said as if to remind him, 'Their sense of smell is second to none.'

'What kind of stink pit were you born in?' he asked the little troll irritably. 'Does your home really honk that bad?'

'I think what Wretch means is that he has a homing instinct,' she suggested, cutting in first. 'Something shared by his own kind.'

'That's it!' declared Wretch. 'I'm like a bird.'

162

'A pigeon,' said Maurice to clarify. 'The skanky type, no doubt.'

'As the crow flies,' the figure in the hoodie pressed on, 'we could be there in twenty-five hours.'

'Twenty-four,' said Maurice. 'Twenty-four hours is the accepted expression.'

'Whatever it takes, I know we can make it.' Wretch spread his hands wide. 'Who's in Team Troll?'

Noting the air of confidence in his voice and manner, Maurice reflected on how certain Wretch had been about heading over the hills. At the time it had seemed like an expression of wishful thinking. Having seen him go on to seek guidance from a bunch of abrasive-looking strangers on the bus, he wondered whether there could be something behind it. Still feeling deeply unsure about the situation, however, Maurice slumped back against the wall with his eyes on Candy.

'Even if Wretch can take us to his people,' he said, 'what are we going to find?'

'Some back-up.' The little troll pretended to draw two pistols from hip holsters, squeezing off several capping sounds before putting them away again at Candy's request.

'Who knows what's out there?' she told Maurice, and then turned away from Wretch before lowering her voice. 'But if he feels it's his only place of safety, and the scars you've seen are from his time in the settlement, I'm not going to pretend that I can guarantee it anywhere else.'

From some way down the high street, the sound of a police siren reminded Maurice of their immediate options.

'This is going to take some faith,' he said reluctantly. 'Part of me wants to give up on you guys, turn myself in and hope I

163

get my life back. After everything that's happened, the other part has no intention of abandoning you guys.'

Candy smiled.

'Then why don't we give Wretch the one thing he needs to see it through?'

'What's that?'

Candy stood back from Maurice, addressing them both now.

'A chance,' she said, which seemed to surprise the troll, as if it had never been offered to him before.

Maurice waited for Wretch to settle. Slowly, he began to nod.

'Very well. But I'm not travelling any further by bus.'

'Leave the wheels to me.'

Before anyone could respond, Wretch broke away from the pair. A cobbled mews was visible at the far end of the passage. Dotted with potted plants and hanging baskets, it looked like a private urban oasis. Maurice took one look at the little troll heading towards the gleaming vehicles parked in the bays and faced Candy. She didn't look as stricken as he did. Instead, she slipped two fingertips between her lips and whistled with such force that Wretch spun around on the spot.

'Stealing a car is not the answer.' Opening her purse, Candy plucked out her debit card and driving licence. 'I'll hire one.'

'*What?*'

Wretch took a step back at the same time as he spoke. His gaze tightened on her in sheer disbelief.

'We won't be breaking any laws,' said Candy. 'At least let's learn *something* from this adventure.'

17

Towards late afternoon, back at the settlement's compound, Governor Shores considered seeking emergency dental treatment. His rear molars throbbed as if each socket contained a pocket of tiny bees, but with a runaway troll and his two partners in crime still at large it would have to wait. In a bid to cope with the discomfort, Randall washed down several painkillers with his coffee and wished his daughter would learn to give him some space.

'I can't even pick up the internet in this dump,' complained Bonnie, interrupting her father as he discussed the situation with his security chief. 'You might as well deprive the place of oxygen.'

Randall closed his eyes for a second, his train of thought derailed.

'The perimeter fence ensures the settlement is a wireless black spot,' he said patiently, despite the strain in his voice. 'The trolls survive without phone and web access. I dare say your status update can wait.'

Bonnie turned to the security guy, clutching her mobile in one fist.

'It works for you,' she said, which stopped him from thumbing his phone pad.

'I have the Wi-Fi code,' he said apologetically, and glanced at his boss for guidance.

'The Wi-Fi is for operational purposes only,' Randall told his daughter, and then glared at his head of security so fiercely that the man immediately pocketed his phone. 'So, what's been happening while I was away?'

They were gathered in the compound's control room, following Randall's return from a fruitless trawl of the area surrounding the city bus he had boarded. The Governor remained convinced that he had missed the troll by moments, along with the schoolboy associate and mystery woman.

'The kid's parents are still assisting police with the investigation,' his security guy told him. 'Both still claim to know nothing about it.'

'Big surprise,' muttered Randall. 'If the interrogation was in my hands, they'd be squealing within minutes.'

The Governor paused there. Not because he realised that thinking out loud in this way might've made him sound like he operated on the fringes of the law. It was the sight of his daughter in the background, clambering onto a chair with her phone raised high over her head.

'If the boys don't hear from me soon they'll just find another party girl,' she muttered, and then examined her screen once again. 'Not even a single bar,' she grumbled. 'How do you even survive in here?'

Randall glanced back at his chief of security.

'Kids, eh?' he chuckled.

'I only see mine every other weekend.'

'I should be so lucky,' muttered Randall under his breath,

and broke off to bellow at his daughter to stop hunting around the room with her phone like some digital diviner. 'The quicker you let me deal with this situation,' he told her, 'the sooner you'll be home!'

It was the chief of security who drew his attention to the wall clock, pawing at the back of his shaved head as he reminded Randall of the schedule.

'The press briefing is due to start downstairs,' he said. 'Mr Trasker has authorised you to handle it.'

Since returning to the settlement, Governor Randall Shores had done his level best to avoid the man in charge from the government. No doubt Kyle Trasker would want to know why he hadn't been involved in the swoop on the public bus, and Randall would have to stand there taking a dressing down from a kid whose exam certificates had yet to yellow with age.

'There are two things I don't want to deal with right now,' he told the security chief. 'Anyone who drinks herbal tea for pleasure and questions from the media.'

'Media?' Bonita Shores climbed down from the table and combed her fingers through her tresses. 'Are there cameras here?'

Ignoring her, the Governor reminded himself that Trasker was unlikely to discuss operational failures in public. If he had to face him, now was the time. In front of a small pack of journalists who had taken it upon themselves to blow this episode out of all proportion.

'I'll be five minutes,' he told Bonnie, and turned to leave the room. 'After that, I'll take you home.'

'*Wait!*'

The temptation to just ignore his daughter steered him onwards towards the door. On hearing her hurry to catch up, and with no time for a scene, Randall made the snap decision to let her follow.

'Just promise me you'll keep your mouth shut,' he told her quietly, heading into the corridor.

'I'll stay quiet if you take off that cowboy hat.' Bonita walked alongside her father as if she was the one that the press in the room downstairs were expecting. 'Don't make me a laughing stock, Daddy.'

*

Candy Lau had been driving for several hours when Wretch suggested that they could steal a better vehicle.

'No way,' she said, with just a glance at the troll in the rear-view mirror. 'This car might be slow, but at least I have the paperwork.'

'It's perfectly adequate,' agreed Maurice who sat up front beside her. 'I must say I'm really impressed by how economical it is.'

'Yeah, but can it outrun the cops?' asked a voice from behind her. Candy found the little troll in the mirror once more. He sat with one foot pressed against the back of the passenger seat, much to Maurice's annoyance. 'I'm not even sure it would beat a pizza delivery bike.'

'At least we're on the move,' Maurice reminded him. 'More importantly, are we nearly there yet?'

They had stopped for directions twice on their drive out of the city. On both occasions, Wretch had spotted figures loitering in the street and urged Candy to pull over so he could speak to them. Maurice hadn't like it one bit, and yet each time Wretch had returned with a renewed sense of purpose and fresh directions. As a result, since setting off from the city, the route had taken them briefly south, and now west.

'We're getting warmer,' the little troll told him just then. 'I can feel it in my bowels.'

From the corner of her vision, Candy noted Maurice pull a face.

'Nobody has ever successfully located a troll in their underground environment,' he reminded her quietly. 'What makes you so sure Wretch isn't just taking us for one big, long ride?'

'Nothing,' she said, 'but you've seen how trust can bring out the best in them. They're so used to being frowned upon and told what to do. If you just give them an opportunity to prove themselves, they rise to the occasion.'

It was clear to Candy that Maurice didn't share her outlook quite so confidently. To begin, on crawling through the city streets in the hire car she'd rented, all three had maintained a tense silence. Despite the changes in direction, both Candy and Wretch had begun to relax on joining the motorway flow. Only Maurice remained on high alert, shrinking into his seat whenever another vehicle drew level with them. In his eyes, every car was potentially an unmarked police vehicle.

'Have you always been this way?' she asked as Maurice quietly shielded his face from the traffic in the slow lane. 'It must be tough.'

'It would be weird if I wasn't worried right now,' he said, before falling silent for a moment. 'What's going to happen to us?'

169

Candy indicated to rejoin the inside lane. All the way she had been careful not to break the speed limit or drive in any manner that would attract attention.

'I've always tried to help people less fortunate than me,' she answered eventually. 'In my job, I did that by the letter of the law. Now I no longer have one, and under the circumstances,' she added with a nod over her shoulder, 'I'm prepared to do the wrong thing for the right reasons.'

'I've never done anything wrong in my life,' said Maurice. 'It feels weird.'

Candy smiled to herself. The sun was beginning to set, triggering the first of the lamps that flanked the motorway. She flicked on the car's sidelights and glanced in her rear-view mirror.

'Are we going to be there by the time it gets dark?'

In her mirror, the little troll shook his head and yawned. He didn't cover his mouth, stretching instead with his hands tightened into child-like fists.

'Home is over the hills,' he said again.

'And far away?' asked Maurice bluntly.

Candy noted the air of surprise in the way Wretch reacted.

'So, you do know where we're going?' he said.

Maurice closed his eyes.

'We're chasing a fairy tale,' he told Candy. 'Are you sure you want to keep driving?'

'We could always stop for the night,' suggested Wretch. 'I could use the full thirteen hours to function normally.'

'Eight,' said Maurice with some impatience this time. 'Eight hours is what's required.'

'Not if you're a troll,' said Wretch.

Candy stifled a laugh and focused hard on her driving. Staying in bed until midday had fast become one of the primary indicators that a teenager might soon require a cheek swab test. It had also been responsible for many false alarms.

'Anyway, how can you be thinking of sleep?' asked Maurice. 'I'm too scared to blink.'

'Don't fight it.' Wretch slotted his hands behind his head, and leaned back in the rear seat. 'Trust me, curling up in bed makes a bad day go away.'

'Wretch, you and I are on the run. We can't just check in some place cosy.'

'But nobody is looking for Miss Lau.'

Maurice twisted round in his seat.

'So, what are you and I going to do? Kip in the car?'

'You just have to trust me,' he said next, smiling as he swapped his attention to the rear-view mirror. 'Isn't that right, Miss Lau?'

Had this been a session at the settlement compound, thought Candy to herself, Wretch would've scored highly for demonstrating a willingness to engage. It was her mobile phone that prevented her from sharing this with the little troll, however. As soon as it rang out, all eyes turned to the ashtray where she'd slotted it.

'Who's Greg?' asked Wretch, leaning between the front seats in order to read the caller display. 'Your dad?'

'My boyfriend,' said Candy with a sigh. 'We had a big fight earlier but he's bound to be worried. I'll let it go to answerphone and call him back later.'

'A fight?' Without warning, Wretch lunged forward and grabbed the phone. 'Anyone who picks a fight with you, Miss Lau, has to answer to me!'

'That's a private call!' cried Maurice, but Wretch was too quick for him.

'Yo, whassup?' he asked in greeting, and manoeuvred himself out of reach from Maurice. 'She's driving,' he continued. 'Miss Lau can't talk to you now . . . not ever, in fact.'

'Wretch!'

The troll heard her clearly, but kept the phone pinned to his ear. Judging by his pained expression, it didn't look as if Greg had reacted positively.

'Finish the call,' hissed Maurice. 'You're putting us all at risk!'

'It's over,' Wretch said next. 'Yes, she asked me to tell you exactly that.' He stopped for a second and held the phone away. Maurice could hear a man shouting down the line.

'I'm fine!' Candy yelled, which prompted the little troll to cover the mouthpiece. 'Greg, we can talk about this when I get home!'

Wretch cradled the phone for a second. Maurice continued to glare at him, but Wretch was simply waiting for the caller to calm down.

'Greg, you have some anger issues. I suggest you work on that, along with your kissing skills.'

'What?' The car veered a little as Candy snapped around. 'Will you cut it out?'

'I heard you snog with your eyes open,' Wretch went on gleefully, resting his head back on the seat as if to compose his next utterance. 'Greg, are you a serial killer? Do you keep human skin-suits hanging in the wardrobe or anything like that? Because that kind of kissing is for weirdoes. No wonder she's running away . . .'

'That's enough!' hissed Maurice, but the little troll was on a roll.

'Who am I?' he asked, repeating the demand from down the line. 'Buddy, I'm your worst nightmare,' he said, staring right back at the boy, and then tightening his gaze. 'I am Wretch. Lighter of fires. Destroyer of hatchbacks.'

'Will you just think before you speak!' Maurice asked out loud, though the troll was focused on the phone. At that moment, it appeared to be spitting a range of threats and expletives into his ear.

'Now don't start again, Greg,' Wretch grunted. 'I'm going to give you a chance to apologise, in fact. Can you do that for me? Go on. Give it your best shot! I'm listening . . .'

The little troll gave the caller a moment to draw breath, presumably to continue shouting, and then hit the red button. In the rear-view mirror, Candy saw him grinning victoriously. If there was one thing Greg hated more than anything, she thought to herself, it was a lack of respect. Mortified by what had just happened, she focused on the road ahead. Even so, when Maurice weighed in to reprimand Wretch, she felt no desire to back him up.

'That's such typical troll behaviour!' snapped the boy, and this time succeeded in grabbing the phone. 'You just steam in, causing upset and distress with no thought for the consequences!'

'It's OK,' said Candy in a bid to cool things. 'Things weren't great between us anyway.'

Having finished the call in such high spirits, a weight suddenly appeared to settle on the little troll's shoulders. Warily, Wretch looked at Candy and then back at Maurice once more.

'Why?' the boy asked. 'What possessed you?'

'I did the wrong thing,' Wretch admitted, before his mouth twitched into a smile, 'for the right reasons.'

Exasperated, Maurice turned to the front. Candy could've told him that asking a troll to justify himself was just an invitation to make things worse. For a minute, they drove without a word, marked by the drone of passing traffic, and then Candy chuckled. It was only brief, a momentary loss of self-control, but that was laid to waste when Wretch sniggered to himself and she promptly exploded into laughter. Maurice looked across. Candy did her level best to compose herself, but just glancing at him made it worse. Finally, Maurice succumbed to the same response.

'Greg does like to kiss with his eyes open,' she confessed finally, squeezing out the words before cracking up again.

'I'm not exactly a world expert,' said Maurice, who peeled off his glasses to wipe his cheeks, 'but even I know that kissing is an eyes-closed activity.'

'What did I tell you?' crowed Wretch as Candy recovered sufficiently to move out into the fast lane. 'I've saved you from being carved up in your sleep!'

18

Governor Randall Shores swept into the meeting room commandeered for the press briefing. He took his place in front of the whiteboard, purposely ignoring the gloomy budget cut calculations that the finance director had forgotten to wipe clean, and surveyed his audience. It came as a small relief, after his bad start to the day, to find many of the plastic chairs were empty.

'What else does a troll on the loose have to do to stay in the headlines?' he asked, grinning broadly at this bid to break the silence.

The audience, some half dozen hacks, stared back at him impassively. The only photographer in the room, standing at the side, took a picture and then cursed when his flash failed to go off. Randall glanced at the wings, where Kyle Trasker had elected to hover. No doubt with a successful capture the room would've been full and the man centre stage to soak up the glory. Instead, presumably as punishment for going rogue earlier, the government guy had invited Randall to take the questions. Standing there with his back to the exit door and both hands in his pockets, Trasker nodded as if to prompt Randall into accounting for that morning's missed opportunity on the city streets. Unwilling to accept responsibility alone, the Governor prepared to invite his so-called superior to join him. He extended his hand, beaming broadly, only for Trasker to slip away into the corridor. His exit left Randall with an empty smile as he switched his gaze back to his audience. The journalists seemed a little restless all of a sudden. Clearing his throat, he resigned himself to rustling up a spin on the lack of developments.

'OK, the headline news is that the troll was spotted but got away,' piped up a voice from behind him.

'Bonita!'

Randall wheeled around, glaring at his daughter who waited expectantly for the photographer to take her picture.

'But it's obvious,' she said, and gestured at the journalists. 'Dad, these guys aren't stupid. Just let them know you've blown it and we can all go home.'

Facing the front once more, with a smile that now hurt to maintain, Randall assured the room that the situation was fluid and on-going.

'My gut tells me they're heading north,' he announced, and took a moment to make it clear that he had read all the academic papers on troll origin theory, or at least the summaries. 'We will of course inform you of developments just as soon as they happen,' he told them.

'Don't hold your breath.'

Pretending not to hear his daughter this time, the Governor read out a description of the low life and the schoolboy. That their ages prevented either of them from being identified by name was ridiculous, in Randall's opinion. What was it with this obsession to protect the young when they used it as a licence to create mayhem? All he wanted to do was give out their names and get away. Instead, having painted a picture of some saucer-eared slugbrow and the junior mastermind behind the breakout, he looked up and invited any questions.

'No? Well, I think that concludes the briefing,' he said quickly before anyone had raised their hand, and began to usher his daughter out of the room. As he did so, the security chief appeared breathlessly at the door.

'You need to take this,' he said, and held out a mobile.

'Oh, so now you guys get a phone signal as well?'

Bonnie turned to round on her father, and then promptly backed away. It took Randall a moment to realise it was most likely down to the murderous look on his own face. In a blink, he did his level best to soften his composure.

'Who is it?' he asked, and took the phone even after the security chief had shrugged.

'His name is Greg,' was all he could offer. 'Says he has news of the missing troll.'

Clasping the phone to his ear, all Randall could think was that at least Trasker wasn't there to claim authority over the call. 'Hello?'

On hearing nothing, and with the journalists in the room still watching, Randall examined the device in his hand. He jabbed at a couple of buttons in a bid to summon the caller, which he unwittingly achieved by engaging the loudspeaker.

'*Governor Shores? I know where you can find the scum you're seeking.*'

To the sound of notebooks flipping open, Randall attempted in vain to deploy the mute function.

'Everything is under control,' he insisted, while rather wishing that Kyle Trasker would come back and take over. At the very least, being the owner of a more sophisticated version of the phone in his hand, the government guy would know how to disable the loudspeaker.

'*I've tracked a mobile in the car with them, and they're travelling –*'

'North?'

Governor Randall Shores faced his audience once more, awaiting confirmation.

'*Pretty much every direction but that,*' the caller continued, and relayed the current coordinates.

'Who owns the mobile in their possession?' asked Randall, thinking that at least a name might distract the press from his guess at their location.

'*One of your employees.*'

In silence, the Governor responded as if a sour taste has just crept into his mouth.

'Is this a crank call?' he asked in desperation.

'*Her name is Candy Lau.*'

*

It was Maurice who insisted that they park the hire car far back from the motel entrance. For his sake, Candy pulled in one row away from the section reserved for trucks, wide loads and RVs. As soon as she switched off the engine, however, Maurice noticed one of the lorry drivers scoping them from his cab.

'Maybe we should move,' he told her, glancing at the guy in the vest with the tanned right arm.

'You shouldn't be so quick to judge.' The little troll prodded the back of Maurice's seat with his foot. The boy turned to face him.

'Let's be frank here. All truckers have killed at least a couple of times, no? It's like a job requirement or something.'

'Maurice.' Candy closed her eyes, which was welcome after all the hours she had spent behind the wheel. 'Not now.'

'But it's the long, lonely journeys,' he pressed on. 'They pick up a friendly hitchhiker, and bad thoughts get the better of them.'

'I wouldn't let him hear you say that,' warned Wretch. 'I reckon he'd struggle to see the funny side.'

Candy opened her eyes, looked at Maurice and then waited until she had his full attention.

'Shut up and let me check in,' she said finally. 'No doubt Wretch will look out for you while I book us a room. Just do as he says, OK?'

They had been through the plan on the motorway. Candy had listened to Wretch put forward the idea, and then surprised Maurice by agreeing that it was worth a shot.

'I don't like it,' the boy said again, as he had when they first hatched this move. 'We could get caught.'

Using the rear-view mirror, Candy exchanged a glance with Wretch.

'We could get caught at any time,' she reminded Maurice, before reaching for the door handle. 'This is one way of minimising that risk.'

Leaving the pair behind in the hire car, Candy Lau approached the motel entrance. Despite her level best to look confident, she understood Maurice's caution. Was this wise? she asked

179

herself. Before Wretch had taken off in her hatchback, and cost her a job in the process, the young social worker had judged herself to be more or less on the right side of the law. OK, so Greg liked to smoke the odd joint in the flat, and the university library was still short of a textbook she had forgotten all about until recently. What she faced here, on pushing through the revolving door, was in a different league. The motel was nothing special. It was just a part of the motorway service stop. It felt nicely anonymous, though Candy didn't expect to find herself to be the only guest in the lobby. As the receptionist made eye contact from behind the desk, giving her no way to simply follow the revolving door right out again, Candy reminded herself why she was doing this.

'I'd like to book a twin room for the night,' she said, and then took a breath. 'On the ground floor.'

The receptionist didn't blink, but looked like she needed to.

'I'll check,' she said, consulting her computer screen.

Candy pressed her hands flat on the reception counter. It helped to stop them from trembling.

'I'm scared of heights,' she added, smiling sweetly when the receptionist glanced up at her. 'And I like my space.'

Across the floor, the lift doors slid open to disgorge several guests. Candy looked pained. She told herself that could only help in her bid to appear convincing.

'You're in luck,' said the receptionist, before attacking her keyboard for several seconds.

'That's good to hear,' replied Candy, and meant it sincerely. *Let's just hope it lasts*, she thought as the receptionist took her card and turned to the machine to swipe it.

Governor Randall Shores was a man in some pain. The dentist could take care of the physical grief, if only he had time to make an emergency visit. Just then, as he waited impatiently outside the ladies' staff lavatory at the settlement facility, it was his responsibility towards his only daughter that caused him most discomfort.

'Will you hurry up in there?' he asked, and kicked the door with his boot heel. 'We really need to hit the road.'

A moment later, following the sound of the bolt snapping back, the door opened and Bonnie appeared looking freshly made up but with no hiding her sheer irritation.

'You wouldn't hassle Mum like that,' she grumbled.

'Your mother doesn't take twenty minutes,' he snapped, and led the way through the corridor. 'Bonita, are you aware of the gravity of this situation? Everyone in that press briefing set off at the first opportunity. Even Trasker has gone ahead with my security guy,' he added bitterly, well aware that a police operation was in danger of starting without him. 'Bonbon, I should be *leading* this pursuit!'

'But I look hot, right?'

Randall glanced around to see that Bonnie had stopped to await his answer. It was then he noticed that she had gathered the front of her school shirt and knotted it to expose her midriff.

'I'm taking you home,' he declared, having made a snap decision.

'Daddy! I've trailed after you all day. Now there's a chance I might get on the TV and all of a sudden you can't wait to get rid of me!'

'This isn't an opportunity to be famous,' he told her. 'There's a dangerous troll on the loose out there!'

'But you've no idea where,' she pointed out, and placed her hands on her hips.

'We have a last known location,' he told her. 'And a vehicle registration.'

Immediately after the tip-off from Candy Lau's partner, the security chief had taken over the call and sought to establish more details. Once Greg stopped ranting about how he felt like he'd been living with a stranger, it was quickly confirmed that Candy's phone had been subsequently switched off. Randall knew that it was highly unlikely that the trio would just be waiting for him on the hard shoulder of the motorway. He still found it hard to believe that a member of the facility staff, someone he had employed, who seemed so devastated about the loss of her hatchback, would betray him for a troll. Still, now they had a name, and established that Miss Lau was in possession of a hire car, it could only be a matter of time before he faced her once again. He just hoped it would be at the point of arrest, and not later at some debrief in which Trasker muscled in on his moment.

'If I was a troll I know what I'd want right now,' said Bonita, checking her reflection in the corridor window at the same time.

'What's that?' Randall was already wondering if he needed to phone his wife to forewarn her of their daughter's return home.

'Sleep,' she said, while playing with the way her hair fell. 'You're always saying that low lives only get out of bed to cause trouble. It doesn't take a team of crack detectives to realise this one's earned himself some down time.'

By now, Randall had stopped in his tracks to listen intently to her reasoning. Focusing on the door ahead, a smile crept across his face. In his experience, low lives did indeed like to crawl between the sheets at the first sign of stress. It was unusual to see any of them up before mid-morning, when spot checks often found them with the sheets pulled tight over their heads. If Wretch had been living by his wits since escaping, he decided, there was a very good chance he'd be desperate for some shut eye.

'Bonbon,' he said, beaming at her now. 'You've just shown an insight into this young upstart's motives that outshines everyone else on this case.'

'I have?' Bonita looked taken aback, but only for a second. 'Then shouldn't I be getting paid?'

Randall stepped forward to place his arm around her shoulder. In the space of a minute, she had provided an informed opinion he could pass off as his own to the police. Once the troll and his accomplices had been apprehended, he had no doubt it would restore his reputation at the top of the command chain.

'What would I do without you?' he asked, and squeezed her affectionately. 'Now let's get you back where you belong. Once all this is over we can look at raising your allowance a little.'

As he moved towards the door, Randall found that the soles of Bonita's shoes appeared to have stuck fast to the linoleum floor.

'We really need to talk about my allowance *now*,' she told him, folding her arms. 'My expertise doesn't come cheaply.'

'Bon –'

'I'm tracking down this troll with you,' she said, and promptly walked past him to the door. 'You need me at your side, Daddy. Even if it is going to cost you dearly.'

19

Twenty-five minutes after Candy Lau left the hire car to check in, Maurice began to wonder whether they had been abandoned.

'We could be here all night,' he grumbled. 'Is your door locked?'

'Stop being a such a lightweight.' Wretch had taken over the driving seat. Even though Candy had the keys, the little troll fiddled endlessly with every switch and button. 'We're totally safe.'

'But someone might try to get in,' Maurice told him. 'That trucker is still checking us out,' he added. 'Don't look now but he's properly staring. If he makes a move, Wretch, after everything I've done for you, promise you'll offer yourself first.'

The little troll grasped the wheel and peered over the dashboard.

'The guy is a gorilla alright,' he observed, and then turned his attention to the cover that housed the ignition slot. 'Maybe we should just leave.'

'No way.' Maurice raised his forefinger. 'We're not going to hot-wire the hire car.'

'So, where is she?' Wretch turned to squint at the motel entrance.

Mindful of a troll's tendency for poor eyesight, Maurice reported that she was nowhere to be seen. 'We've come too far,' he added reassuringly. 'Candy wouldn't just walk away from us.'

Wretch sat back. Resting his heels on the edge of the seat, he began to chew his nails.

'It wouldn't be the first time I've been abandoned.'

Maurice looked across at Wretch.

'Did it come as a shock when your family found out?' he asked.

'It did to them,' said Wretch with a chuckle, though it sounded bittersweet. 'I'd figured it out some time before, and hoped nobody would notice.'

Maurice faced the front once more. The trucker watching them from his cab had opened a packet of crisps. Without even blinking, he popped several into his mouth at the same time and mashed them without care for the bits that dropped in his lap. His lorry was the largest in the lot, the boy observed. He could only guess what was in the long, featureless container, but didn't like to dwell on it.

'When my parents find out why I chose to stick with you,' he said, 'I'd like to think they'll understand.'

'Your folks sound cool,' said Wretch.

Maurice smiled quietly.

'They won't understand,' he said to clarify. 'It's wishful thinking on my part. Their idea of high excitement is the karaoke evening at the campsite we go to on holiday *every* year.'

He glanced at Wretch, having offered him an easy target for mockery, but the little troll just continued to gaze into the middle distance.

'We used to do stuff like that as a family,' he said next.

For a moment, the pair retreated into silence. It was only when Maurice noticed the trucker ball up the empty crisp packet that he sat forward in his seat.

'Look at that,' he said as the guy tossed the packet from his cab window. 'He knows we're watching, too. How can he be so blatant?'

'Just leave it, brother.' Wretch moved to stop the boy from unstrapping his seat belt, but by then Maurice had opened the door. 'Trust me, it's not worth it!'

It was only when he stepped out of the car that the night air cooled his impulse to do the right thing. Briefly, he reminded himself of the consequences of trying to save his teacher from the shocking breakdown of law and order that had befallen his class in the coach. Even so, having drawn the attention of the trucker, it was too late to pretend he had just left the car to stretch his limbs. All he could do was approach the cab, collect the crisp packet, and politely appeal to the guy's civic nature.

'Excuse me, sir,' he said, and held up the packet to the window. 'You dropped this.'

The trucker looked down at the boy. His elbow partially obscured his face, but Maurice was close enough to see two well-travelled eyes tighten on him from underneath a duck-billed cap.

'Have I just done something without thinking things through?' he growled, and then picked at his teeth.

Maurice wondered whether the man was asking him to reflect on his own actions here, but chose not to clarify things.

'It's just you missed the bin by about twenty metres.' He gestured at the litter basket. By now, the trucker had leaned out sufficiently from the window of his big rig to reveal a grizzled face beneath the duck-bill cap and a moustache that dropped down each side of his mouth. All of a sudden, Maurice felt two foot tall. 'I thought maybe you'd like to try again,' he added quietly. 'That's if you want.'

The trucker responded by swinging open the cab door. Maurice took a step back to avoid being hit in the face by the handle. Then he retreated by a further step on seeing far too much butt crack as the guy clambered down the ladder. With his feet on the ground, the trucker rose to his full height and faced the boy. Maurice wondered why he had bothered using the ladder at all.

'So, how should we settle this?' he asked in a deep, slow-sounding voice.

The menace in the man's voice was at odds with the fact that he wore his long hair in a pair of plaits better suited to a milk maid. Not that Maurice even dared to dwell on that in case it registered on his face.

'Sorry,' was all he could think to say, his voice shrinking. 'I'll take it to the bin for you.'

With a feral growl, the trucker snatched the packet from Maurice and stuffed it into the lapel pocket of his school jacket.

'There,' he said, and patted the boy on the cheek. 'So you don't drop it on the way.'

'Thank you, sir.' Maurice spun around, focusing on reaching the litter basket as quickly as possible, only to find himself jerked backwards.

'You know what? Maybe I *should* make more of an effort.' Having grabbed him by the collar, the trucker hoisted Maurice onto his tiptoes. 'Follow me, my friend!'

In shock as the brute began to march across the car park with him, Maurice could do nothing but scuff his feet over the tarmac.

'You've made your point!' he protested with a gasp on being effortlessly manhandled into an upside-down position. 'It doesn't have to come to this!'

The trucker said nothing, just kicked the dome-shaped lid of the bin into the dark and prepared to drop the boy inside.

'*Wait!*' The voice came from behind the pair, high-pitched but urgent. The trucker turned, clipping Maurice's head against the inside of the bin. Despite the blow, he caught sight of Wretch approaching with his hands stretched wide under the glow of the car park lighting. 'He's one of us.'

As if in response, Maurice experienced the world flip the right way round. Dropped back onto his feet by the trucker, but with the blood rushing from his brain, he grasped the bin to stop himself from toppling sideways.

'Thank you,' he said, exhaling so sharply that for a second he thought he might faint.

Removing his cap, the trucker studied him intently.

'You're lying,' he told Wretch after a moment, before grabbing Maurice by his jaw. 'If he was one of us he'd have cussed my mum by now at the very least. Look at him! There's

188

no fight in this drip. No urge to get the better of me or even have the last word. Nothing!'

Maurice attempted to protest at being manhandled in this way, but the meaty paw clamped across his mouth prevented it.

'Can we speak in private?' Wretch faced up to this animal in the chequered flannel shirt and held his gaze. 'Like, *now*?'

The trucker glowered at Maurice, who feared his jaw was about to collapse in his grip, and then shoved him free. This time, having gathered his glasses from the ground, Maurice scuttled well clear. Nursing the side of his face, he watched as Wretch took the man to one side and found his ear. He strained to hear their conversation, but it sounded monosyllabic, and peppered with grunts and curses. Still reeling from such a disproportionate response to what had been a polite request, Maurice listened to this mumbled exchange for a moment longer and then came to his senses with a start.

'You're a *troll*,' he said under his breath, gazing at the trucker. 'And a big one at that!'

Out of earshot, but close enough to Maurice to remain a deeply intimidating presence, the figure in question broke off from the conversation and faced him with an air of astonishment. He planted his cap over the crown of his skull and opened his arms as if inviting the boy into a bear hug.

'So, *you're* the good Samaritan we've been hearing all about!' he declared, crossing over to slap Maurice so hard on the back that it knocked the air from his lungs. 'The word is out about you guys!'

189

'I can think of better ways to make headlines,' grumbled Maurice.

'Not on the news!' said the trucker, as if the boy needed to engage his brain a bit more. 'On the *streets*! Everyone is talking about the schoolkid who staged the breakout for our brother here!'

'I didn't start this,' said Maurice, but the trucker was too busy swapping a high five with Wretch.

'The name's Byron,' he said. 'My folks had high hopes that I'd make my mark in the arts. A poet, perhaps, a painter or a pianist,' he added, and then offered up his hands as if for inspection. Maurice took one glimpse at what looked like a bunch of sausages poking from two ham hocks, and figured a sonata would be a struggle.

'I guess everyone is good at different things,' was all Maurice could think to say. 'Driving a heavy goods vehicle is an art,' he added, and then rather wished he hadn't.

The trucker rested his hands on his waist.

'Nowadays, friends call me The Bulge.'

The trucker was wide set and paunchy. Judging by his stance, however, Maurice had a horrible feeling he wasn't referring to his stomach.

'Pleased to meet you . . .' he said, and nervously accepted the offer of a handshake, '. . .Byron.'

'Fella,' he said next, squeezing just enough to draw a gasp from the boy, 'if you're going to see this little guy back to his home turf you need to keep your head down. Taking strangers to task is a risky business in this day and age.'

'I think I've just learned that for myself,' grumbled Maurice, who finally freed himself from the trucker's grasp to tuck his shirt back inside his school trousers. 'Even so, it doesn't take much to use a bin.'

On hearing an irritable growl from the trucker, Maurice chose to abandon his complaint altogether. He looked for support from Wretch, only to find his attention had been drawn towards the motel.

'Never mind the litter,' said the little troll. 'Our room is ready.'

Maurice turned to see a figure at a window on the corner of the lower floor. Candy waved cautiously and then gestured towards a ground-lit path that led around the side of the building.

'There she is,' said the trucker, as if the final piece of the jigsaw had just fallen into place. 'The beauty and the brains behind the getaway.'

Maurice drew breath to claim some recognition for getting Wretch this far, took another look at the trucker, and thought better of it.

'It's time we turned in,' said Wretch. 'It's been a long day.'

'With another one ahead,' said The Bulge.

Maurice looked across at him with interest.

'Do you know where to go?' he asked. 'All we've had so far is vague directions.'

'I'm a king of the road.' The trucker gestured at the hedge that hid the motorway, but barely muffled the constant swish of traffic. When Maurice faced back, he found him yawning with his great arms stretched wide. 'If you need directions in the morning,' he said, and jabbed a thumb at the bunk window behind his cab, 'you'll find me in my office.'

20

Without a doubt, she was sexting.

Since setting out in the car from the settlement, to the sound of bleep after bleep, Governor Randall Shores had been aware of the frantic exchange of messages going on at his side. Every time he took his eyes off the road, Bonita was either reading her phone screen with a mischievous grin on her face or jabbing away as if each word she typed out pushed a boundary of some sort.

'Everything OK?' he asked eventually, no longer able to just ignore the fact that his daughter was so blatantly engaging in the practice. 'Who are you talking to?'

'Nobody,' she said, just as her phone heralded the arrival of yet another unpleasant missive. Bonita glanced at the screen and stifled a giggle. 'Just a friend.'

On joining the motorway, Randall had stuck to the fast lane in a bid to make up lost time. He flashed at a vehicle in front, which was dawdling at around eighty miles an hour, and reminded himself to stay positive. Despite the urgent nature of the journey, this was still the first day that he and Bonnie had spent together for some time. It was an opportunity to bond, he maintained, if only she'd get off the damn mobile.

'This schoolboy with the troll,' he said just then, anxious to focus on the matter at hand. Having agreed to pay his daughter for her time, and being a similar age, Randall figured she could at least provide some insight into his motivation. 'Paint me a picture, Bonbon.'

Another incoming message came between his request and Bonita's answer. Randall pretended not to hear her little gasp of delight and surprise.

'He's a thrill seeker,' she said with some confidence. 'Someone who gets off on fear and adrenalin.'

Randall nodded, squeezing the accelerator now the vehicle in front had finally retreated to the middle lane.

'What else?' he asked. 'The more I know about this boy, the better.'

When Bonita didn't answer, he glanced across to see her furtively thumbing open the top button of her blouse. Randall snapped his attention back to the road, if only to correct the car's sudden veer towards the central barrier.

'Sorry. What did you say?'

'His motivation,' said Randall, grasping the wheel so tightly that his knuckles turned white. 'Focus, Bonnie.'

Bonita sighed like the instruction required some effort.

'Well, he's got some balls,' she said after a moment. 'Anyone prepared to go to this extreme must have big stones.'

'Bonbon!'

'You asked for my advice!' she snapped, raising her voice to make it quite clear she was in no mood to back down. '*Unbelievable.*'

It was Randall's phone that punctured the sudden silence.

Plugged into the car dashboard, he took the call on speakerphone.

'What have we got?' he asked, when the security chief identified himself.

It was with some relief, to his poor teeth as much as his mood, that Randall learned the hire car had been located.

'I'll be there within the hour,' he said. 'We move in on my word.'

The security chief was midway through pointing out that technically only Mr Trasker could issue such an order when Randall cut him off. The Governor just didn't want to hear any more. Not when his mind was filled with how he planned to deal with the troll who had caused such grief. With his eyes locked on the road, he pictured himself as an incoming force for justice, leaving no escape for his quarry, and then realised Bonita had just quietly taken a picture of her cleavage.

'What?' she asked when he barked at her to button up. 'Shouldn't you be concentrating on the road?'

'Which one is it?' he demanded to know. 'Benny or Ryan?'

'Both,' she said barely audibly, and made no attempt to hide her phone as she dispatched the shot. 'Anyway, it self-deletes once they've viewed it, so there's no need for you to come over all *hardline* on me!' Bonita dropped the phone in her lap and folded her arms. 'No wonder the troll ran away.'

'Now, that's enough!' warned Randall, who knew quite well what she was referring to here. At the same time, he knew that further protest would risk her putting it into words. It was then Bonita's phone screen lit up on her lap. 'You've got a reply,' he said in a quieter voice. 'Just let me drive.'

It was rare that a low life pushed the Governor so far that he lost it completely. Even so, he supposed that over the course of his career those moments might have mounted in number. Had he known that his daughter was outside his office one time, listening to every lash of his belt strap and anguished yelp, he would've shown more self-control. He couldn't recall why the troll had been sent to him. Randall saw so many on a daily basis for a range of infringements. Figuratively speaking they were free to kill each other on the settlement streets. Inside the facilities, however, from the assembly points and medical bay to the workshops and everything in between, every last one of them was expected to follow rules and regulations.

All he remembered about that incident, apart from the awful realisation that Bonita had arrived early for her driving lesson, was the fact that the troll had brought the beating on himself. Randall had started out being firm but reasonable, as he always maintained, but when every question was met by silence it simply summoned the red mist. He had given plenty of opportunity, spelled out what would happen if he didn't find his voice, and how did the low life respond? By making a failed bid to break from his office.

Looking back on the way he'd handled the situation, and so many others like it when his temper took over, Randall often wondered if the trolls had been sent to test him. As a younger man, before the sinkholes, he'd never once tightened a fist in anger. Now it had become a habit. A default position in the workplace. It was only on that occasion, however, on finally hurling the battered troll from his office to find his daughter waiting for him, that the Governor was forced to account for his actions. It had taken some time to talk her into seeing things from his point of view, though awkward moments like this one continued to arise when she reminded him of what she knew.

In Randall's opinion, Bonita had also gone on to use it as a licence to push her luck at every opportunity.

As for the troll, it had come as a sharp surprise to discover that he hadn't learned his lesson. Attempting to bolt from a beating was one thing. Busting out of the settlement was quite another. On this attempt, Wretch might've made it way beyond the perimeter wall, but he'd be hunted down in due course. So long as the Governor was on hand to take him in, and issue some quiet advice before he was interviewed about what prompted him to take flight, then all would be well.

If everything went to plan, the Governor decided, following the fast lane as it snaked under the night sky, he might even apologise for not having realised that this particular low life had a tendency to stutter under stress.

*

Candy Lau stepped back inside her hotel room as the two figures clambered through the window opening.

'What took you so long?' Maurice asked her. 'I was beginning to worry something had happened to you.'

'*Beginning* to worry?' Wretch dropped onto the carpet, and paused to look around appreciatively. The room was small, simple and clean, with twin beds divided by a bedside table. 'Brother, you were born to fret.'

Maurice drew breath to protest, but Candy caught his eye. This was no time for bickering.

'I needed a moment.' She closed the window behind them, sweeping the curtains closed. 'But we're safe for now.'

*

Minutes earlier, the sight of her reflection in a mirror had been what stopped the young social worker from summoning the pair. She had let herself into the hotel room feeling only relief at making it past reception, and then reacted as if someone was lying in wait for her.

'Candy,' she had declared, addressing the hunted-looking figure in the glass with one hand pressed to her sternum, 'what are you doing here?'

In the space of a day she had travelled a world away from her former life. Assessing herself in the glass, it had felt as if there was no going back to everything she had left behind. Greg was uppermost in her mind, and that hurt. Yes, she had taken off in the wake of a row, but it wasn't really about the fallout from the loss of their car, or his apparent lack of understanding that it had also cost her a job. Things had changed between them. At university, they were a couple bonded by a shared experience. Since graduating, their paths had begun to fork. By turns, and she figured it was the same for Greg, that bond had begun to feel more like a burden. It was as if they had chosen to yoke themselves together, only to tire of pulling in different directions.

Now Candy had encountered two figures in need of the very same thing she sought so badly for herself: a simple hug and the assurance that everything would work out just fine. The schoolboy, Maurice, had shown impressive courage in coming all this way for a changeling who had played a part in his kidnapping. She liked him. He was plainly terrified, and she doubted he would get a wink of sleep, but his loyalty was admirable.

'Why couldn't you be like that?' she had asked her reflection, as if Greg was skulking in the background at that moment in time.

As for Wretch, Candy felt no desire to press him on the reason behind his escape. Inside the settlement, several sessions in his company had led her to grow fond of him. Initially, it was his reluctance to speak that had singled him out. She had read about the stutter in his notes, and felt sure that he'd find his voice as he gained some trust in her. Candy could never have anticipated that his escape from the settlement would bring him out of his shell. Now, on the run with this little live wire, she wondered if he'd ever shut up.

Seeing her expression brighten in the mirror had brought Candy's focus back to the hotel room. That smile was at odds with how drawn she appeared. There was no mistaking the shadows that cradled her eyes, but despite the smoking wreckage of her car, relationship and career, she was at least still standing. The hatchback was insured. While the break-up was a shame, it had been a long time coming. As for the job, if she was part of a system that allowed individuals like Wretch to suffer, Candy wanted no further part of it. If anything, she still had a duty of care towards him and every intention of exposing any wrongdoing. Quickly, she had retied the band in her hair and then squared her shoulders as she took a step back. This time, standing just behind the downlight from the ceiling, Candy Lau had seen only a determined spark in her eyes.

'Doing the wrong thing never felt so right,' she had told herself, and that's when she crossed the room to crack open the window.

Now, watching Wretch as he found the mini bar, Candy wondered how many wrongs they might accumulate on their path to justice.

'Don't you think we've broken enough laws already?' asked Maurice, as the little troll scooped out two cans of lager and several miniature bottles of spirits. 'Underage drinking is the last thing we need right now.'

Wretch looked across at Candy, his brow hoisted in hope.

'We're here to rest,' she reminded him. 'Not to party.'

Wretch examined the little bottle in his hand. With a sigh, he tossed it to one side and then looked around the room. Candy watched his attention settle on the little kettle on the tray with the individually wrapped tea bags and complimentary biscuits.

'Help yourselves,' she told them both. 'We can't risk ordering room service so that's basically supper.'

'To be shared out equally,' warned Maurice, as Wretch began to pick through the items on the tray. 'Unless there's a ginger nut in which case I call dibs.'

Candy chuckled and picked her way around the pair.

'I'll leave you two to divide them fairly,' she said. 'All I really need right now is a hot soak in the tub.'

Just listening to the pair squabble again reminded Candy that the day had left her exhausted. Turning her back on their bickering, she headed for the en-suite and locked the door behind her. There, she spun the hot tap, poured in the little container of body wash to create some bubbles and finally slipped into her bath. Even with her ears below the surface of the water, she could hear Maurice and the little troll communicating in strained whispers. Just then, Candy thought to herself, it would take an awful lot more than a petty squabble to force her to open her eyes.

A moment later, someone hammered on the hotel room door.

21

Maurice responded to the knocking by staring helplessly at Wretch. In turn, the little troll looked at the boy in sheer panic.

'*Miss Lau?*' a voice called out. '*May I have a word?*'

Wretch's eyeballs swivelled towards the door.

'Say she's not here,' he hissed, which was met with a pained look from Maurice.

The man behind the door repeated his request. He sounded insistent.

'Stay quiet,' Maurice whispered. 'He'll go away.'

'*Miss Lau, I have a master key.*'

The little troll cursed under his breath, looked around the room, and promptly dashed for the open wardrobe.

'Not that!' hissed Maurice, aghast as Wretch grabbed the iron from a shelf and then planted himself with his back to the wall beside the door.

The troll glanced at the boy, silently pleading with him to come up with a better idea before drawing breath to address the figure in the corridor.

'I'll just be a moment,' trilled Wretch, his voice pitched into the realms of a panto dame.

Maurice clamped the crown of his head with both hands. In the space of a few seconds, the situation had slipped way out of their control.

'Don't do it,' he urged as the little troll reached for the door handle, with the iron in his other hand, ready to strike.

It came as a shock to Maurice to find himself brushed to one side. He looked around to see Candy wrapped up in a white dressing gown. Silently but surely, she directed Wretch to back away before taking a breath and opening up.

'How can I help?' she asked sweetly, as Maurice seized the opportunity to sidestep smartly behind the opening door. 'Come in.'

'Ma'am, I'm sorry to disturb you. Our receptionist reported seeing several youths acting suspiciously outside your window. I wanted to be sure that everything was OK.'

Without breathing, Maurice peered through the space between the hinges, just as the visitor stepped across the threshold. It had to be the manager, he thought, judging by the ring of keys and two-way radio he clasped in one hand. What caused the boy's eyes to widen was the sight of the little troll on the other side of the door frame. With the man just inside the room, Wretch was just out of his sight. Even so, he dominated Maurice's field of vision given the way he still brandished the iron.

'*Don't do it,*' the boy mouthed in desperation as Candy assured the manager that she had heard nothing.

'I'm fine,' she said, sounding tense. 'Thanks all the same.'

'If I could just check the window is secure,' said the manager. 'The safety of our guests is as paramount as their comfort.'

Maurice watched in horror as Wretch looked set to belt the guy around the back of the head. Given the little troll's form, the boy had no doubt that he'd see it through.

'Wait!' said Candy, clearly stalling now. 'Maybe I did hear something earlier.'

Maurice spied the man shift his weight from one foot to the other.

'Miss Lau, do you have unauthorised guests in this room?'

The boy couldn't see Candy, but her silence told him she had frozen. Unlike Wretch, who braced himself with the iron once more, only for the manager's radio to crackle and spit. When a voice summoned his attention, Maurice watched the little troll shrink back into the far corner of the room.

'What is it?' he asked gruffly, holding the two-way by his cheek. 'OK. Understood. I'll be right out.'

Maurice leaned back to glimpse Candy. She was facing the manager with one hand on the door.

'You're welcome to inspect the window,' she said, which drew a squeak of surprise from the boy.

'There's no need,' he said with a sigh. 'One of the truck drivers just saw the two youths head off towards the motorway embankment. Most probably low lives,' he added, before stepping back into the corridor. 'Let's hope they've gone to play with the traffic, eh?'

Candy mirrored his laugh but with a nervous edge. As the manager bid her good night, all Maurice could think was that a brute who had earlier dangled him in a bin turned out to be a troll prepared to cover for them. It was only when Candy closed the door that he slumped against the wall in relief.

'Now I wish I'd hit him,' grumbled Wretch. 'Troll haters deserve a headache.'

Candy took a long breath, her eyes closed as she exhaled, and then faced them both.

'There's only one way to keep you two out of trouble until morning,' she said, and then jabbed a thumb over her shoulder. 'Bed. *Now!*'

Maurice cleared a catch in his throat.

'But there are two singles,' he said. 'And three of us.'

Candy folded her arms. Meeting her gaze, Maurice realised he should've worked out the plan for himself.

'Well, I'm taking one,' she told him, just in case it wasn't completely clear. 'You two can share the other.'

*

Inside his cab, the trucker in the duck-billed cap watched the receptionist head back inside the lobby and reached for the handset of his CB radio.

'Breaker one-five to Pearly Gates Pete. Got your ears on, good buddy? I have an eyeball on the runaway hen.'

Depressing the transmission button with his thumb, which was marked by a static click, the trucker tightened his gaze on the motel and awaited a response.

'*I'm listening, my son.*' The voice through the speaker meshing addressed him quietly and calmly, like a priest in a confessional booth. '*Although you have disturbed me during the football, whoever you are.*'

'You're jawboning with The Bulge.'

'*Byron . . .*' The transmission cut out for a moment, accompanied by a horse-like sigh from the trucker that made

204

his lips vibrate. *'Stop being a plum and speak English.'*

The Bulge removed his cap for a moment to scratch his head with the same hand. It was a crying shame, in his opinion, that the rise of sat-nav and the mobile phone had killed this form of communication once so beloved by the haulage community. As a younger man, behind the wheel of a lorry half the size of his current beast, the airways were jammed with voices conversing in a language they had made their own. Now technology had all but made the system redundant.

'Copy that, Pete,' he said anyway.

'Then quit talking in code, dammit!'

The Bulge felt downhearted by his response. Over the years, so many drivers had opted to switch off their CB radios. It left behind just a hardcore of users, and Byron felt deeply protective towards their common bond.

'Ten-four,' he said. 'I mean, OK, Pete. Seeing that it's you.'

Such a solitary job that involved being constantly on the move suited trolls like this one – changeling children who had slipped under the radar as they grew up and then sought to earn a living without attracting attention. With the airwaves all but abandoned, it left those trolls who had turned to trucking free to speak to one another without fear of being overheard. Still, Byron was cautious, and preferred to talk in the terminology of the road. There was just one exception, as he reminded himself now, and that's when it came to reaching out to the individual who once again caused his speaker to crackle.

'What do you have for me, Byron? It had better be urgent. I've got the sound turned down on the match. If I'm talking to you and someone scores, you will regret it.'

The Bulge reached for the coffee flask he kept in the holder behind the gear stick.

'Isn't commentary just pointing out the obvious?' he asked. 'If you see the ball go into the back of the net, it's a goal.'

'Why don't I turn the volume back up on the TV and just imagine what you want to tell me? Would that work for you?'

It had been several years since he'd contacted Pearly Gates Pete, the only voice to respond to him over the airwaves who didn't cruise the motorways and main roads in a big rig. Unlike Byron and his fellow kings of the road, Pete liked to remain in one place for longer periods. From his caravan, with the mini TV and the dogs barking in the background, he could be difficult and abrupt whenever anyone tried to reach him. Byron took a swig from his flask, and reminded himself why that made Pete perfect for the role he served. Despite the fact that the coffee had been on the go for several days now, he nursed the flask while sharing details of his recent encounter with the little troll and the two civilians in his company.

'Don't you listen to the news?' asked Byron, exasperated when his account was met with a grunt of indifference. 'That one has come over the wall from a settlement.'

'Why?' The speaker buzzed. *'That would be like escaping from a holiday camp, no?'*

The Bulge understood Pete's reaction. When a troll went into the system, as everyone understood it, his welfare was assured. The settlements were rough around the edges, but everyone got food and shelter. They weren't there to be mistreated, after all, despite the claims the little one had shared with him.

'Whatever his reasons,' Byron said into the handset, 'I wanted to give you a head's up that he's determined to get home.'

'*He'll be wasting his time.*'

The loudspeaker mesh rattled over the response, which left Byron with the handset in his lap and his mouth flattened in defeat.

'Preesheeaydit, good buddy,' he said finally. 'That's a big ten-ten from me.'

'*Does that mean you're done talking like a tool?*'

'Er, it does.'

'*Goodnight, Byron.*'

This time, the speaker produced a popping sound as Pearly Gates Pete closed communications. Setting down his empty flask, with his focus on the motel once more, The Bulge smoothed his moustache with his thumb and forefinger, and then did the same with his two long hair plaits. In his brief encounter with the runaway, it was quite clear that something bad had caused him to seek shelter with his true flesh and blood. He just hoped Pete would be in a more forgiving mood if Wretch and his friends ever knocked on the door of his caravan. They'd be close to reaching their goal, after all. Based on the conversation that Pete had just ended, however, it seemed to Byron that much depended on what was on the TV at the time.

'I never did like football,' he grumbled to himself, before drawing the little curtains that fringed each window of his cab. 'Real trolls play rugby.'

22

In the hotel room, Maurice lay awake with his breath baited. He'd barely moved in the hour since they switched off the bedside light. Even now, when Wretch started snoring beside him, drowning out the gentle but steady breathing from the bed opposite, the boy simply stared at the ceiling and wondered if he'd ever sleep again.

Earlier, the prospect of sharing a bed with the troll had done nothing to put Maurice at ease. If anyone from school knew he would be wrestling for the duvet with a low life, he figured they'd never speak to him again.

'Wretch needs to shower,' he had insisted, when Candy first set out their sleeping arrangements. 'And I mean a proper wash with soap.'

'I'm clean,' protested Wretch. 'I washed only last week.'

Unable to forget the flea issue, Maurice had crossed to the en-suite and held the door open for him.

'It won't kill you,' he said.

'Do you have a flannel I can borrow?'

'Even if I did there are boundaries.'

Reluctantly, the troll had shuffled inside and then faced the boy.

'Don't you dare try it on with Miss Lau,' he warned. 'Else you'll be crossing the boundary from best friend to big time enemy.'

'Wretch, she's old enough to be my –' Maurice had stopped himself there, well aware that even hushed tones could carry. 'OK, not my mother, but still. We're in big trouble here, and even if this was some fun away day, I'm hardly what you call a player.'

'She's out of your league.' The little troll had looked him up and down dismissively. 'Do you even qualify for a league?'

'Make sure you close the shower curtain before you spin the taps.' Before Wretch could respond, Maurice had shut the door on him. 'And use the soap!' he called out afterwards. 'As much as you like.'

'Don't be too hard on him.' Still in the bathrobe, facing away from him on the other side of the room, Candy had just finished brushing her hair in the mirror. 'Changelings can be deeply testing at times, but you can't deny they're spirited individuals. I might not have a job to return to, but I still believe that spirit can be positively channelled.'

'I'd feel better if we could positively channel him into a third bed,' Maurice said. 'Sadly, there are only two.'

'If it's that much of an issue, I'll take your place.'

Maurice smiled as she found his gaze in the mirror.

'Spirited or not, I've learned a lot about trolls recently,' he told her. 'Trust me when I say it's best you sleep in your own bed.'

'Wretch is harmless,' she said, and rose to her feet in front of the mirror.

Instinctively, Maurice had faced the wall.

'I've seen the way he looks at you,' he said, and caught his breath on hearing her gown fall to the carpet.

'He's easy to read.'

'That's what worries me.'

From the en-suite, over the muffled hiss of the shower, Wretch had begun to sing tunelessly to himself. At the very least, it kept the awkward silence at bay as Candy padded to her bed.

'Someone's happy,' she said.

'I'll feel like that once we reach wherever we're going.' It was then that Maurice had dared to glance over his shoulder. With relief, he saw Candy settling under her duvet in a T-shirt, and turned to address her once more. 'Something tells me we're not on our way to the Royal Palace of Oz.'

Candy had grinned and adjusted her pillow.

'Wretch is confident that he'll find help.'

'What about us?' Maurice asked. 'Even if he really does know how to reach his underground family, we still face a whole heap of grief. I mean, we could do time for all this. Frankly, prison scares me.'

Lying on her side, Candy had tucked the duvet tight around her.

'Get ready for bed,' she told him, sounding close to making it an order. 'Whatever tomorrow brings, we can face it feeling recharged.'

Maurice had mulled this over for a moment, and then reluctantly shook off his school jacket. That was when a more immediate predicament crossed his mind. One that Candy seemed to read without asking.

'I'm closing my eyes, Maurice. You're free to get undressed.'

Quietly, as if somehow any noise might disturb her, the boy had removed his shoes, then his socks, his shirt and finally his trousers. Stripped down to his pants, and covering his nipples with one forearm, he reached down to peel back his duvet, and that's when Wretch crashed out of the en-suite. He had towel-dried his hair, and even used his fingers to comb in a side parting. What caught Maurice by surprise was the fact that he had got dressed again. The little troll looked him up and down, which left him feeling all the more self-conscious.

'Can I trust you not to interfere with me?' Wretch asked. 'You look like you're in the mood for love.'

'There's no need to sleep in your hoodie,' said Candy, which caused Wretch's amusement to taper. 'You'll be too hot in a top.'

Maurice had watched a hint of panic push into his eyes. He knew just why.

'I'll be fine,' grunted Wretch. 'Just fine.'

'This is your side,' Well aware of the scars across Wretch's back, Maurice had invited him to climb in with his clothes on. 'Whatever helps you to sleep soundly, that's alright by me.'

The next few minutes had shuttled between wriggling, complaints about space, duvet hogging, and finally a little laughter. It was ridiculous, Maurice had observed when he finally settled, but if they couldn't see the funny side, what chance did they have of sticking together through this testing time? Then Candy responded with a question that signalled a moment of quiet and reflection.

'So, tell me,' she asked. 'What was the most exciting thing to happen in your life before it got turned upside down?'

'Me?' Maurice was propped up on his pillow, his glasses folded on the bedside table and the duvet pinned to his chest with his elbows. He had dwelled on the question for a moment, and then shrugged. 'I can't think of anything worth sharing,' he said. 'I'm an only child with a mother who still worries if I show signs of a cold. We go on a camping holiday every year on the first weekend after the summer term where my dad's idea of risk-taking involves peeing in the hedge at night rather than walking to the toilet block.'

'Your dad sounds like an animal.' Beside him, Wretch was lying with his hands behind his head. Maurice had glanced across, saw the grin on his face and elected to ignore him.

'How about you, Wretch?' Candy asked. 'What was life like before . . . well, you know.'

At first, it looked like the little troll hadn't registered the question. Then he exhaled, as if it were his last breath.

'I used to make things with my brothers,' he said. 'Until the truth came out about me.'

'What kind of things?' asked Maurice.

'The usual.' Wretch had continued to stare hard at the ceiling. 'When I was little, we had these action figures. We used to make them parachutes from tissue paper. Throwing them from the top window was fun, especially when we set light to the paper.'

'Was that bit your idea?' Maurice had glanced at the little troll beside him, who smiled privately. 'So, how did they find out?' he asked. 'What did you do?'

This time, Wretch turned to look at him.

'I set light to some bigger things.'

Maurice had chosen not to push for details. He just hoped that the hatchback marked Wretch's retirement from his career as an arsonist.

'At your age, all I wanted to do was leave home,' said Candy from the other bed. Maurice had turned his head to face her. She was lying on her side with both hands nested under her cheek. 'I didn't get on with my dad back then, and boys were to blame. As soon as I started dating, he just reacted like I was deserting the family.'

'Dating,' said Maurice wistfully. 'What's that, then?'

Candy had smiled at this.

'My first boyfriend was sweet, but terrified of calling round at our house in case Dad was in. Then I got involved with a guy who was two years older than me. He drove a renovated Ford Capri. A sports car back in the day. Dad hated him, so I made sure he had good reason by staying over at his place.'

'You mean you did it with the guy?' This was Wretch. A voice out of nowhere and also out of turn, it had seemed to Maurice.

'That's private,' said Candy after a moment.

'In the car? Back or front seats?'

This time, Wretch's persistence was met by a groan of disapproval from his bedmate.

'I think it's time for lights out.' Maurice had reached for the lamp switch. 'Sometimes, Wretch, you need to know when to stop.'

He had hoped for darkness. Instead, they were left with a sodium glow through the curtains from the car-park lighting. Still, the gloom was enough for Maurice to feel some sense of solitude.

'Stopping doesn't get you anywhere,' a voice piped up beside him. 'Sometimes you got to keep pushing if you want to go places.'

'That's the trouble with trolls,' Maurice replied quietly. 'Everything you do in life, you guys are relentless. You just keep on tunnelling until the roof collapses –'

'– and opens up a whole new level in life.'

'OK, time out!' Candy had called across to them. 'If you ask me there's room for everyone. Both sides need to recognise that if we're ever going to get along.'

Just then, Maurice had found himself exchanging a glance across the pillow with Wretch.

'Is she talking about the bed?' asked the little troll. 'Or something bigger?'

'Good night, boys.'

This time, Candy had addressed the pair so assertively that silence quickly settled over the room. While Wretch sighed and snuggled down, Maurice remained in the same position with two pillows behind him. Unable to relax, he had simply stared through the gloom at the cheap print of a village fete that hung on the far wall. Finishing the conversation on such an awkward note left him tense, though he reminded himself that he was hardly at the tail end of a relaxing day. Listening to Candy's breathing settle, he had closed his eyes and hoped it might draw him deeper. Then, out of nowhere it seemed, but clearly coming from right beside him, he had detected a gentle rocking motion. Slowly it gathered momentum, and was joined by the sound of an unmistakably rhythmic beating.

'Wretch,' he whispered, praying that Candy had already dropped off. 'For crying out loud, stop doing that right away.'

Immediately, the rocking had ceased.

'Stop what?' he muttered.

'You *know* what! I can't believe you even started.'

'I thought you were asleep,' Wretch offered. 'And I couldn't stop thinking about what she said about doing it in the car –'

'I don't want an explanation!' hissed Maurice. 'It's about showing respect,' he added, and edged towards the side of the bed. 'If we're ever going to get along in this world it's something your kind really needs to recognise.'

'Gotta keep pushing, brother.'

'Look, maybe you have a point about some things in life,' snapped Maurice. 'But this is not one of them, alright? Stop being disgusting and settle down, low life. You're very lucky I don't make you sleep on the floor!'

Even as he turned to face away from Wretch, Maurice regretted his words. It might've been the sort of thing that tripped off his tongue before the school trip, but things had changed. Yes, trolls could be challenging and maddening creatures, but having spent time with Wretch, even under strained circumstances, Maurice recognised how much they had come to depend on each other. 'I'm sorry,' he said after a moment. 'But promise me you won't start pleasuring yourself again. I mean, we all do it, and no doubt after tonight Candy will feature highly in my fantasies. Even so, there's a time and a place –'

'Maurice.' A voice piped up from the other bed, and marked the moment the boy lost any chance of sleep. 'Stop talking.'

*

As advised by his security director, who had called in with an update, Governor Randall Shores pulled in on the blind side of the service station car wash. There, out of view from the motel beyond the petrol pumps, the police and several members of the press had gathered. It was gone midnight, and way out to the west, with a low mist rolling down the grass bank behind them, Randall switched off his engine and cranked the handbrake.

'You're supposed to switch off your headlights straight away.' Bonnie unclipped her seat belt. 'Keep a low profile, like you were instructed.'

Randall was just reaching for the lamp stick when she said this. Pointedly, he unbuckled his seat belt first.

'I should be running this whole operation,' he muttered. 'On my watch, there'd be no pussyfooting around. If our troll and his associates are holed up for the night, we should be straight in with a battering ram and a snatch team.'

Randall extended his focus beyond the forecourt, towards the motel car park. Lamps dropped pools of light over the vehicles that had stopped for the night. The hire car was in among them all. They had confirmed that much by the registration. But it wasn't the rental as much as the building beyond that contained the reason the Governor had travelled this far. There was nothing of note about the motel: a three-storey block with identical windows and a lobby that lacked any sense of a soul. It was the perfect choice for three fugitives.

'Can I get something to eat?' Bonita gestured at the petrol station, which was still open for business despite the late hour.

216

'What do you want, Daddy? Chocolate? Crisps? Anything but cheese and onion. That's the smell of public transport in a bag.'

'Food is out right now.' Randall curled his palm around the car keys until he'd made a fist. 'We didn't come all this way for snacks.'

'*What?*' Bonnie regarded her father like he'd just announced his intent to join a nudist colony. 'I'm a teenage girl. This is a sensitive time for me! You can't go messing with my relationship with food. Do you want me to catch anorexia?'

'You can't catch an eating disorder.' Randall spotted his security chief. He was with a group of officers in tactical uniform. Gathered around the bonnet of a squad car, they appeared to be in a briefing. Recognising the individual issuing instructions, it suddenly felt as if the air inside the vehicle had begun to thin. 'They need me out there,' he said with his eyes on Trasker. 'For your own safety, just promise me you'll stay in the car.'

'Are you worried I might inhale petrol fumes or something?' A note of sarcasm had edged into Bonnie's voice. Randall didn't like the sound of it one bit.

'What we're dealing with here could lead to a siege or even a shoot out,' he warned her, having twisted around in his seat with the crook of his elbow resting on the wheel. 'Your insight into what makes a loose troll tick has been invaluable, Bonbon, but right now I need to know you're out of harm's way.'

'Whatever you say,' she grumbled, and fired up her phone in a way that left her father in no doubt that she was about to portray herself to Benny and Ryan as neglected and misunderstood.

Climbing out of the car, Randall reminded himself not to slam the door. He inhaled through his nostrils a few times, allowing the night air to freshen his mood despite the taint of diesel. With the right direction, he thought to himself, on planting his hat on his head and making his way towards the police briefing, they could all be on their way home within the hour. Then he caught sight of Kyle Trasker once more, still addressing the group, and duly added an extra thirty minutes to his estimate. A guy this far out of his comfort zone, he decided, was liable to make some poor decisions.

'What have we got, guys?' The Governor positioned himself between the shoulders of several officers, resting his hands on their backs, and strained at the same time to see between them. 'Will someone fill me in?'

Randall's security chief was listening in from the other side of the vehicle. Randall attempted to get his attention with a little wave, only to be shushed and then shrugged off by one of the officers in front of him.

'Give us some space,' the guy muttered, 'we're trying to work here.'

For a second, the Governor was lost for words. In contrast, with a blueprint spread across the bonnet of the vehicle, Kyle Trasker continued to instruct the group about the hotel layout. He made eye contact with Randall, but didn't even pause to acknowledge his presence as he assigned officers to the building's main exit points. Randall pretended to listen, thinking at the same time that his smart casual suit was in no way appropriate for this moment. He smiled to himself, wondering whether this poor sap would've felt more comfortable with the help of a PowerPoint presentation, only to compose himself when Trasker brought his hands together smartly.

'Is everyone clear of their roles?' he asked, and began to gather the blueprint from the bonnet. 'Any questions, now is the time.'

'I have one.' Randall raised his hand, and was pleased to see attention turn towards him. 'Will you guys be armed when you follow me in? As the settlement boss, this has got to be my call from here on out. I have first-hand experience of handling this troll, and let me tell you we're looking at one desperate low life. In my opinion his accomplice is no schoolkid either. It's more likely to be some kind of cover for a professional. Even the adult female, Candy Lau, has nothing to lose.'

The Governor's contribution was met by an uncomfortable silence. Kyle Trasker finished rolling the blueprint and then calmly told Randall he should stay with his vehicle until the operation was complete.

'It's in our hands now,' he told him, with a glance towards the settlement's security guy, who promptly looked to his feet. 'With respect, we can't afford to have this trio on the loose any longer.' As if anticipating that Randall would protest, Trasker raised his palm and fixed him with a stare that asserted just who was in charge here. 'What matters now is that we move in both quickly and quietly.'

Governor Randall Shores had plenty to say in response. In a heartbeat, a surge of fury swamped his system. Trasker simply hardened his gaze, only for his attention to be drawn by the squeal of a security alarm. The sound cut through the night, rising up over the service station and causing everyone to look towards the source. When Randall spotted his daughter hurrying from the petrol station kiosk with a selection of snacks in her grasp, he sensed his back molars might not be able to take any more pain. Then the till guy bundled after her, yelling for someone to call the police. Watching Bonita scurry for the car, dropping a tube of sweets from her haul onto the forecourt, he knew he had no choice but to put his poor teeth to the test.

23

When Candy snapped bolt upright at the sound of the alarm, she found that Maurice and Wretch had already done the same thing in the bed beside her.

'That's been triggered by a security tag,' said Wretch confidently. 'I know my alarm systems, and that one has nothing to do with us.'

'Well, it almost gave me a heart attack!' Maurice pressed a hand to his chest, blinking in the dim light. He turned to Wretch, who swung his great feet to the floor.

'It was good timing,' declared the little troll, padding to the bathroom. 'I nearly wet the bed there.'

Resting on her elbows, Candy listened to Maurice respond in disgust and figured he hadn't got a wink of sleep.

'He does appreciate what you're doing for him,' she said quietly. 'If it helps I really don't mind swapping places.'

Maurice glanced across as if to check he had just heard her correctly.

'Please make that the last time you offer,' he told her. From the bathroom, despite the loud, cheerful whistling, there was no mistaking the sound of the little troll urinating prodigiously. Maurice caught Candy's eye once more. 'It might be better for us both if we just locked him in there for the night.'

Outside, the alarm fell silent.

'Just close your eyes and think of a special place,' said Candy. 'It's what I always told the changelings when they were feeling wound up.'

Maurice scratched his scalp.

'Does home count?' he asked. 'It isn't special, and I could do without having to explain myself to my parents, but right now I'd really like to be back in my own bed.'

'Home counts.' Candy settled back on her pillow. 'Though when all this is over I think I'll need to find a new one.'

Wretch reappeared from the en-suite just then, leaving the light on behind him.

'You forgot the switch,' said Maurice, and drew his side of the duvet around him protectively 'The switch and the flush.'

'You sound like someone's mother.' Wretch climbed back into bed. 'Next you'll be telling me I should've washed my hands.'

'OK, that's me out of here!' Maurice was clear of the bed before Candy could draw breath to calm things. Wearing only his boxers, and evidently beyond caring, he paced the room like a trapped tiger. 'Just a nap is all I want! Is that too much to ask?'

'Maurice,' said Wretch calmly, and showed him his hands. 'I was joking. They're clean!'

The boy stopped in his tracks. He peered through the gloom at the little troll, who wiggled his fingers as if to dry the last of the tap water. Candy nodded her appreciation.

'If Wretch can learn to be considerate then you can find it in yourself to get some sleep,' she told him. 'Get back into bed, Maurice. It really is about seeking out your special place. Isn't that right, Wretch?'

The changeling grinned and patted the free side of the bed. It was clear to Candy that he relished Maurice's discomfort. Even so, there was something about the way Wretch engaged with the boy that told her deep down he cared.

'My special place is no longer a bench on a hill overlooking a park,' said Wretch next. 'I've got my sights set on somewhere new.'

Maurice smiled, despite himself, and then faced the curtain as it lit up from outside. When the grumble of a truck's engine began to build in volume, and the light intensified into beams that swayed across the room, the schoolboy looked across at Candy. With a violent gasp of air brakes, the vehicle pulled up right alongside the window. On hearing the truck door swing open, and then a pair of boots on the ground, he clutched fretfully at his bed sheet.

'I think perhaps I should get dressed,' he said in a whisper. 'Facing a drama naked is the stuff of nightmares.'

It was Wretch who obliged him, flinging his jacket, shirt, socks and trousers in turn.

'Follow me into the lobby,' Candy told them, having scrambled to dress at the same time. 'Just be prepared to run.'

'I think it might be too late.' Balancing on one leg, Maurice hauled on his trousers while staring aghast at the window. Someone was out there for sure.

Tentatively, Candy peeled back the curtain and then jumped with a start at the face looking in at them. Candy had only just recognised the figure when Wretch hurried forward and released the catch. He pushed the window outwards, and a familiar figure dipped up from underneath, grasped the ledge with oily hands and jabbed his thumb over his shoulder.

'Climb into my office and let's hit the road,' said The Bulge, with a glance across the car park towards the service station. 'Right now you're about as easy to find as a mullet haircut at a hauliers' convention.'

*

Having taken the precaution of locking his daughter inside the car, Governor Randall Shores hurried towards the motel entrance.

In the gloom, several groups of police could be seen fanning towards different points around the building. To the rear of the car park, an officer was inspecting the rental car that had given away the location of the troll and his accomplices. The Governor had every intention of joining the lead group when they knocked at the hotel room. As they had already swept inside the building, he was well aware of the catching up ahead of him.

Randall figured he probably had some more apologising to do as well. Bonita could have found herself in real trouble back then. Had he not made every effort to smooth things over with the petrol station manager, paying for the stolen goods and standing by her claim that it was one big misunderstanding, his daughter would be tearfully facing the duty sergeant with her fingertips stained from the inkpad and her chances of a place at university in tatters. Instead, Randall had left her hammering on the inside of the passenger window and then looked around in shock when he realised the operation had commenced without him.

'What's going on?' he asked, catching up with his security chief midway across the car park.

'We're not allowed to proceed into the building, sir. They say it's for our own safety.'

Governor Shores switched his attention to the motel. Two small teams of uniformed figures were now scurrying alongside the hedge that fronted the building, staying low as they moved. Outside the lobby, several officers had just taken position with their backs to the revolving door. In front of them, three journalists could be seen prowling under the awning with mobile phones pressed to their ears. Randall turned back to his security chief, dwarfed by his formidable frame, and laughed like a man who believed he had just missed a joke.

'Are you scared to see some action?' he asked, raising his voice to be heard as a truck engine revved and bit into gear. 'Because if you're scared then you're sacked.'

'I'm not scared.' The security chief sounded surprised, as if nobody had ever dared question a man of such muscle. 'I just don't want to be arrested.'

Randall eyeballed the guy, wondering how he had ever been capable of running a prison wing. He could feel a rage awaken. From experience, it wasn't something he could guarantee to control. Then he glanced in distraction at an articulated lorry as it headed noisily from the car park.

'Typical truck drivers,' he muttered, before recognising that even if people were trying to sleep at this hour they were about to be awoken by the discovery that a troll on the loose had been hiding out under the same roof as them. 'So, are you coming with me?' he asked, returning his attention to the security chief, 'or do you want to go home and change your soiled panties?'

The guy's face turned the same shade of red as the veins in his neck and forearms, which finally reminded Randall that he was addressing a possible steroid abuser. Fearing that a man with a system pumped with such a drug might be prone to outbursts of emotion and violence, he quickly broke into a grin in a bid to diffuse the moment.

'But I'm not wearing panties,' the security chief said after a moment, sounding confused and a little hurt.

Unwilling to be drawn into a conversation about underwear and figures of speech, Randall turned his attention to the motel entrance.

'Let's do this,' he said, and was relieved to hear the guy fall in behind him as he marched towards the building. The Governor fully expected the two officers to block their path. He was already fishing in his pocket for some identification when they stopped him.

'Wait,' said one abruptly, and held up a hand just as Randall produced the laminated card that allowed him one hot meal a day from the facility canteen. In response, the officer turned away from him. Someone had started buzzing in the guy's earpiece, judging by the way he pressed it with two fingertips.

'What is it?' asked Randall, just as the press hawks picked up that something was developing here.

The officer acknowledged the message, faced his colleague and then shook his head.

'We're too late,' he said quietly, addressing everyone now.

Randall had overheard enough. If this operation had been under his authority, there was no way that the troll and his accomplices would've given him the slip. As the journalists closed in on the officer for more information, Randall seized the opportunity to leave his security guy behind and join a segment of the revolving door. Inside the lobby, he only had to follow the sound of activity from one of the corridors to find the lead team. Alongside them, Randall spotted the individual who had earlier scoffed in disbelief on seeing Bonita fleeing from the till guy.

'This is a potential crime scene.' Kyle Trasker took a step forward on seeing Randall thunder towards him. 'We can't have just anyone breezing in here.'

Randall had every intention of ducking around the guy, incandescent at the suggestion that he was a civilian and not a major player in this hunt, only for Trasker to step right in front of him. Slowly, the Governor looked down at the palm pressed to his breastbone, and then raised his face so there was nothing else for Trasker to look at but a man at the very limit of his patience.

'Don't make me angry,' Randall said, addressing him from the pit of his throat. 'It's something we could both regret.'

A twitch in the young man's expression told Randall that he might just possess some wisdom beyond his years.

'Are you threatening me?' asked Trasker hesitantly.

Governor Randall Shores nodded, mindful not to put it into words. By now the young guy from the government looked desperate to swallow. Randall was well aware that he could cross a line here. He had the guy on the back foot at last. Already his hands had formed into fists at his side. Even with several cops just metres away, picking their way around the empty room, his gaze remained locked on Trasker. Just then, he felt as if he was facing the tongue-tied troll all over again, and not an individual who had been promoted over him to lead this operation.

A moment later, with a blink as if an eyelash had just come loose, Kyle Trasker wisely removed his hand from Randall's chest. Then, closing the incident with a quietly confident smile, Trasker turned to face the room his team were now examining.

'How do we know the low life has even been here?' asked Randall, who felt as if he had just snapped out of a trance. Outside, under the car park lights, the police detail despatched to cover the window could be seen wandering about like they had lost a dog. Focusing on the interior, where Trasker's team were treading carefully, the Governor took one look around and found the answer to his question. 'Oh.'

There was nothing about the main space to confirm a troll had been present. The state of the twin beds suggested that at least two occupants had departed in a hurry. What told Randall that the fugitive low life had been among them was the en-suite. The towels in the tub didn't confirm this, or the unspooled toilet roll. It was the obscene graffiti, carefully squeezed out across the mirror in toothpaste, as if intended just for him.

'Let's just say that's not a rocket ship,' said Trasker.

It was the officer inspecting the open wardrobe who turned and tipped his head.

'A rocket ship firing a laser,' he observed.

Governor Shores closed his eyes for a moment, waiting for the pain in the hinges of his jaw to subside.

'I know what it is,' he assured them, mindful of the fact that practically every surface in the settlement was adorned with such a crude phallic symbol. 'And I don't need forensics to know who was behind it!'

24

When sleep finally claimed Maurice, he went down deep. Wedged between Wretch and The Bulge as the truck rattled through the night, he dreamed that his head was coming adrift from his neck. The boy stirred on several occasions. Each time, with a start, he discovered he had nestled into the accommodating slope of a shoulder on one side or the other. He'd straighten up, only to drop off again, and eventually just gave up any sense of resistance. Somewhere deep in the recess of his mind, it came as a comfort to be supported in this way.

When he finally surfaced, on account of a swerve undertaken by the truck to avoid an old sinkhole, Maurice found himself looking out along a road that cut between mist-enshrouded flatlands. The dim orb low on the horizon ahead told him morning had broken. Sitting up in his seat, he wondered just how long they had been travelling. Over the rumble of the engine, a radio phone-in show was in full swing. Maurice listened for a while as he sought to get his bearings. Whatever the subject, the presenter seemed to be fending off a string of angry callers with poorly constructed arguments and insensitive opinions.

All of a sudden, it seemed to Maurice that trolls had taken over the world.

'Where are we?' he asked with a croak in his voice.

'You know how Wretch took us south and west?'

Candy sounded wide awake. She sat beside the passenger door with her hands in her lap and the window wound down slightly.

'I'm not sure I'll ever forget,' said Maurice.

'Well, now we've gone east.'

Judging by the way Candy had tilted her head as she spoke, the fresh air coming in through the gap was important to her. 'Three times now I've asked if we're nearly there yet. Three times I've had the same answer.'

Wretch jabbed the boy with his elbow. Maurice turned to find him grinning.

'The more you ask, the longer it'll take.'

Maurice frowned, unsure if he was deliberately trying to sound like the responsible adult. Beside the little troll, The Bulge chuckled to himself. Maurice noted how the trucker's belly enfolded the lower section of the steering wheel, which he grasped with two tight fists.

'Aren't we going out of your way?' asked the boy. 'Like, a *long* way out?'

'The delivery can wait,' said Byron with a shrug. 'Let me worry about that.'

'Really? What are you carrying?'

'That's confidential.' The trucker glanced across at the boy, who saw himself, Wretch and Candy reflected in his shades. Above all, Maurice could see that he was uncomfortable with the question. 'Contamination control.'

Maurice took a moment to consider this.

'Are we at risk?' he asked. 'It sounds dangerous.'

The Bulge returned his attention to the road, bouncing in his seat a little as the truck clattered onwards.

'You know, I liked you better when you were sleeping,' he told the boy. 'Right now, there's a troll in need and I won't turn my back on flesh and blood.' Briefly, the trucker lifted one paw from the wheel, reached behind Maurice and clasped Wretch reassuringly by the back of his neck. The little troll squealed happily. 'If bad things are going on inside those settlement walls,' he said, 'it's time the word went underground.'

'You make it sound easy,' said Candy.

Maurice knew just what she was driving at. Ever since the sinkholes had begun opening up and the changelings exposed, every effort to track down the creatures responsible had met with failure. Those trolls who remained underground, along with the newborns they had spirited away were as elusive as ghosts. Now, Maurice found himself riding alongside a brute with a bandit moustache and bizarre plaits. One who casually claimed to share the same bloodline as the little troll along with knowledge of access to a domain that had so far eluded the world.

'We're family,' said The Bulge after a moment, as if somehow he had been tuned into Maurice's thoughts, 'and family look out for each other.'

It was a brief response, but the boy found himself nodding all the same. It also left him thinking about what was in store when he finally went home. After a lifetime seeking to protect their son, his parents would no doubt see this adventure as confirming their worst fears. He wondered whether they would ever let him leave the house again.

For a few minutes, they travelled in silence. The radio show continued to give airtime to vocal callers with vacuous and sometimes dangerous opinions. The subject, Maurice gathered, was the country's obesity epidemic. He doubted that a tax on cake for the overweight would prove effective, while the little troll sniggered throughout a rant from a man who felt that muffin tops and beer bellies should join dive bombing and heavy petting on the forbidden list at public swimming pools.

Throughout, Candy rested her head against the window with her eyes closed. Maurice was relieved to see that The Bulge showed no sign of wanting to do the same thing. Even so, he reminded himself, a responsible driver would be aware that a brief stop could only help concentration and potentially save lives.

'How about a break?' he asked. 'Just to stretch our legs, you know?'

'You're talking to a trucker, son. Truckers don't stretch their legs. They learn to tune out and just focus on the way ahead.' The Bulge fished around in the door bucket to produce a plastic water bottle. It was three-quarters filled with a straw-coloured liquid. 'Same with stopping to take a leak', he added, before offering it to the boy.

'I'm good, thanks.' Maurice quickly pressed himself into his seat when The Bulge reached across to offer it to Wretch. The bottle had no cap. As the truck bumped along, the fluid inside was sloshing horribly close to the rim.

'If you're lucky,' said The Bulge, waggling the bottle, 'there's enough space left for one more go.'

'We'll all pass for now,' said Candy, before the little troll could accept, which only prompted The Bulge to swish the bottle back over Maurice's lap.

'It's probably best you keep that in a safe place,' the boy suggested, and didn't relax until The Bulge returned the bottle to the door. 'Actually, would you mind if we swapped places?' he asked Wretch. 'I could use some air.'

Since waking, it had taken Maurice a while to register the sour funk in the cab. Without doubt, it was wafting from the trucker, whose vest offered unrestricted access to his armpits.

'Suit yourself.' Wretch hoisted himself from the seat so the boy could wriggle underneath.

Manoeuvring himself into the seat beside Candy, Maurice buckled himself in and then found her leaning in towards his ear.

'It's safe to say that washing isn't for truckers either,' she whispered, which prompted him to smile.

Up ahead, the road continued to materialise through the mist. It was flanked on both sides by livestock fencing. Maurice looked around, but saw no sign of sheep or cattle. Only the odd tree was visible as the truck rumbled along. They passed one that was just an arrangement of blackened branches. It led Maurice to think anything that drew attention to itself on this terrain risked being struck down. Switching his attention to the wing mirror, the boy watched the route behind them fade away.

'At least we're not being followed,' he observed.

'There's no reason to come out here.' The Bulge nodded at an approaching tractor. He waved cheerily at the man astride the vehicle, who stared at them hard as he passed by. 'It's for people who don't like being bothered.'

'They call it the countryside,' said Wretch helpfully.

Maurice pondered his comment. The little troll made it sound like something he'd heard about from others. The boy couldn't be sure how far they'd come, but the city and even the hills seemed like a world away. Settling back in his new seat in the cab, he realised that for once he didn't feel strung out by his situation. Maybe the sleep had helped. Above all, however, he knew that it was down to time spent in the company of someone with an unshakeable belief that everything would work out fine. Briefly, he turned to Wretch, sitting with the heels of his trainers on the edge of the seat and his eyes pinned to the road.

'So, having travelled every which way but north to get here,' he said, 'we're finally on the right track, aren't we?'

'Just sit tight, brother.'

Two things served to stop Maurice from celebrating this moment. The Bulge was responsible for the first. It was the way he glanced in his mirror, cursed to himself, and then squeezed the truck's accelerator. The second was the dull, repetitive beating sound that began to cut through the air behind them.

'What is it?' asked Candy, straining to see.

Stuck in the middle seats beside Wretch, and with the volume mounting rapidly, Maurice looked up through the windshield. At first he saw nothing, only to blink in surprise. Then, with the noise threatening to punch through his eardrums, a helicopter swooped so low over the truck that its skids almost scraped the roof.

Locked inside her father's car, Bonita Shores had witnessed the wanted troll and his friends make their getaway just seconds before the police entered the hotel. She had hammered on the inside of the windscreen in a bid to raise the alarm, only for the truck to rumble into the night.

'You couldn't catch a cold,' was the first thing she said when her father returned and disarmed the lock. Climbing out of the vehicle, her face reddened from all the shouting, Bonita had glared at him with utter contempt.

Knowing how his daughter possessed a flair for turning a minor inconvenience into a major crisis, Governor Randall Shores fully expected her to be upset. He had wanted to remind her that being confined to the car was better than being under arrest for theft, but figured that would only fan the flames. With Trasker gathering the officers around the bonnet of the squad car once again, including his security chief, Randall simply wanted to be in on the debrief, not dealing with his daughter's drive for a drama.

'If you treated people with *respect* this would never have happened!' she added, loud enough to turn a few heads.

It had taken several minutes before Bonita calmed sufficiently to relay what she had witnessed. As police radios squawked intermittently around them, she described seeing the wanted trio slip through the shadows from the hotel window to the lorry cab before leaving everyone looking like lemons.

'Are you sure?' Randall turned his attention back across the car park. He remembered the lorry huffing noisily as it moved off. Even that late at night, however, it was hardly a suspicious sight at a motorway stopover. With doubt creeping into his expression, he had switched back to Bonita. In response, as if pained on the inside all of a sudden, her eyes tightened and creases rippled across her brow. Before she had even drawn breath, Randall knew that he was about to face an overreaction.

'Are you calling me . . . a *liar?*'

'No –'

'I can't believe you'd accuse me of such a thing!'

'But I didn't –'

'*Leave me alone!*' Glowering, with her nostrils flared, Bonita snatched the car keys from his hand. 'Someone's got to catch this low life!'

As Bonita threw herself back inside at the driver's seat, Randall tried in vain to stop the car door slamming behind her.

'Calm down,' he yelled, hammering his palms on the glass. 'Be reasonable, Bonbon!'

In response, Bonita fired up the engine. She shouted something unspeakable back at him, her voice lost under the crunch of gears. Immediately, Randall sensed his patience stretching like a perished band. It was his instinct for survival that stopped it from snapping when Bonita swept the car into a ninety-degree reverse sweep that forced him to leap out of the way. Well aware that heads were turning, including those of several journalists, he forced a smile, as if this was just a case of a father fooling around with his daughter.

'There had better be a reward for bringing him in,' she told him, having found the window button. 'A big one.'

Governor Shores appealed to her one more time, reminding his daughter as discreetly as he could under the circumstances that she had yet to pass her driving test. Bonita responded with a squeal of tyres. Helplessly, Randall watched his motor fishtailing away from the petrol station. Across the forecourt, drawn by the vehicle's dramatic departure, he noticed Kyle Trasker had broken away from the debrief to watch. By now, Bonita was well on her way towards the motorway slip road. Like Randall, he flinched and grimaced when the distant car tipped forward abruptly, the ground giving way beneath the front wheels, and came to a crunching halt.

'Sinkhole,' he called across to Randall, who needed no such explanation. 'Always opening up when you least expect it.'

Beyond caring about the pain in his jaw now, in the face of this unfolding grief Randall watched his only child clamber out of the car. It wasn't uncommon to see a vehicle like this, teetering over a pit with the rear wheels off the ground, but it pained him greatly to know this one would see his insurance premium rocket. It hadn't helped that Bonita then set about expressing her unhappiness by repeatedly kicking the side of the car and swinging at it with her bag.

'She's having a bad day,' Randall said, as if that might satisfy the group of law enforcers and media hacks now watching her in baffled silence. 'Aren't we all?'

'Is she even qualified to drive?' Kyle Trasker crossed the forecourt to join Randall, his attention still drawn by the ranting teenager. The Governor saw him coming, well aware of the learner plate on the rear of his stricken car, and prepared to share a lead that he prayed would serve as a distraction. By the time he had finished relaying Bonita's claim that a truck spirited away the troll and his accomplices, she had stomped back from the stranded vehicle.

'Those trolls are a menace to society,' she complained angrily, and rounded on the man with the side-swept hair and suit. 'What are you going to do about them?'

By way of response, Trasker hit the speed dial on his phone. With his free hand turned outwards, as if preparing to cast a calming spell over the young lady in front of him, he then requested permission to summon the closest eye in the sky. Bonita faced him with her jaw dropped, which fell by another degree when the government representative confirmed that a chopper was indeed on its way.

'I'll need you on board to help identify the truck,' he told her on shutting down the call. 'After that we just observe from a distance and bide our time. These guys are on the run. Pursuit vehicles could just spook them, so we'll come from above, and strike when there's nowhere they can hide.'

'Can you do that?' asked Randall, who had been taken aback by the reach of the young man's authority. 'A *helicopter?*'

Pocketing his phone, Kyle Trasker shrugged like it was no big deal.

'I've had one pulled from the cop kidnap investigation,' he said. 'In my view, that search is futile. Every time an officer goes missing, there's never a demand or ransom. It's a serial killer case. No question.'

'I see.' Randall blinked before clearing his throat. 'And my loose troll takes priority?'

'It's time we came down hard on these fugitives,' Trasker told him, and then dropped his voice to stay out of earshot from the loitering journalists. 'I have to say I'm surprised you didn't call one up as soon as he went over the wall.'

'All my choppers were booked,' Randall blustered. 'For an air show,' he added just in case Trasker needed more detail, and then pulled a face like something had just disagreed with him.

Bonita responded to her father with a look that effectively dismissed him from the conversation.

'You should call the recovery services to sort the car,' she told him, before sidling up to the man from the government and clasping him by the elbow. 'Kyle and I have work to do.'

25

It was the end of the road. That's how Candy Lau saw things from the cab of the speeding truck. As soon as the helicopter deftly dropped down and rotated to face them, she could see no escape.

'Everyone on the floor!' cried Maurice, tugging on her sleeve as he and Wretch scrambled to fold themselves between the bench and the dashboard.

'Does that include me?' asked The Bulge, who seemed to relish the sudden appearance of a police chopper now travelling backwards right in front of them. 'Room for a little one?'

'This is serious!' snapped Maurice. 'If they're here for us, then this whole thing is over. They can see right into the cab. We're hardly invisible!'

The Bulge made a buzzing sound, as if the boy had just offered the wrong answer.

'So, what do you suggest?' asked Candy from the foot well. Wretch contributed with a nervous laugh, which just reminded her that their lives were currently in the hands of a troll behind the wheel of a lorry travelling at maximum speed, and trolls thrived on thrills without caring for the consequences.

'Now would be a good time for you guys to climb into my

boudoir.' The Bulge jabbed a thumb over his shoulder. 'You'll find a space under the bunk. Nobody will find you there.'

Candy glanced back. The rear of the cab was hidden behind a sun-bleached, drawstring curtain.

'Do we really want to go there?' hissed Maurice under the noise. With the chopper still low over the road ahead, and with no time to address his concerns, Candy crawled from her hiding place and clambered over the bench. Maurice followed close behind, then turned to yank Wretch through by the scruff of his hoodie.

With the curtain blocking the natural light, it took Candy a moment for her eyes to adjust. Looking around, she found herself in a narrow space with a foam mattress spanning the rear ledge. A lumberjack shirt hung off one corner, and looked like it might crumble to dust if touched.

'I don't like it,' whispered Maurice.

'It's hardly the bridal suite.' Candy peered up and around. 'But what choice do we have?'

Wretch inspected the bunk, running his fingers along the seam between the ledge and the floor. When he found a point in the panelling that clicked, Candy watched him turn and waggle his brow.

'After you guys,' he said, pulling open a hatch. It fell forward on floor hinges, and was clearly designed to conceal the area underneath.

'I'm not going in there!' Maurice sounded panic-stricken. 'I'd rather take my chances with the police!'

Over the roar of the truck's engine, an amplified hiss of static preceded a command from the sky.

'*Pull over!*' boomed the voice over the megaphone. '*Don't make this hard for yourself.*'

In response, The Bulge howled like a wolf and pushed the lorry even faster.

'Just buying some time,' he called back through the curtain. 'Hurry up and make yourselves comfortable.'

'Crawl in!' urged Candy, as Maurice continued to show some reluctance. 'I think we've come far enough to trust him, don't you?'

She placed a hand on his shoulder, resisting the urge to grab him by the ear and guide him in. Instead, a gentle smile was enough to persuade the boy to take a breath and go for it. Wretch needed no such encouragement. She watched him wriggle into the confined space with ease, as if burrowing underground. It reminded her what she was doing here, far away from home but feeling strikingly liberated. Easing through feet first, in order to close the hatch behind her, she wondered what Greg would make of it all. She pictured him with that expression he could pull of contempt and sheer disbelief. Having squeezed through the gap, and bunched in with the other two, Candy lifted the panel back into place with a sense of defiance. This was her time now. It was reckless, for sure, but at least Greg wasn't here to say just that.

*

'Have you got the shakes or something? It's never too early for a whisky hit, you know.' Seated beside the helicopter pilot, Bonita Shores addressed the man with a little too much bite in her voice for her father's liking. 'Keep this bird steady, for crying out loud. I'm trying to shoot a clip here!'

'Bonbon,' he reminded her from his seat behind them both, 'you're here to help the police with their inquiries. In these conditions it's really important that you let the man concentrate. Besides, you really can't go uploading this kind of thing to the internet. It could prejudice any possible trial.'

As everyone on board wore a pair of headphones with a mouthpiece, Randall was keen to show his authority. Even if it was just in the role of a parent keeping his daughter in check, it was better than just sitting quietly.

'She's done you proud.' Kyle Trasker sat beside him, preparing to use the megaphone in his lap.

Ignoring him, Bonnie continued to film the truck below them. She had whooped with excitement when the pilot first executed the move that placed the chopper in front of the vehicle, and then continued travelling backwards rapidly. In direct contrast, Governor Randall Shores squeezed his eyes shut and hoped the sandwich he'd purchased legitimately from the motorway garage, insisting the till guy kept the change, was not about to decorate the back of the pilot's seat.

The Governor had been reluctant to climb on board the helicopter when it finally arrived in the field behind the service station. It was only when Bonnie insisted on taking up Kyle's invitation that he figured he had no other choice. As a responsible parent, and with his car half beached in a sinkhole, Randall had ducked under the whirling chopper blades and hoped he didn't look as ashen-faced as he felt.

On the upside, he had reminded himself, when they ascended over the group assembled beside the petrol station, it meant he no longer had to face difficult questions from the media pack. Even his head of security had seemed frustrated by the failure to capture the troll, and Randall didn't want to push a guy with no neck and a head like a knuckle into questioning his leadership here. As a precaution, he'd ordered him to return to the settlement and ensure the lockdown remained in place. The last thing he needed was for the low lives to get restless because one of their number had gone over the wall.

As for Wretch, Randall had reminded himself throughout the flight, he and his accomplices would pay for all the trouble with their liberty and more. Now, having pretty much crossed the country with a visual on the vehicle that carried them, he figured it could only be a matter of time before the little low life was face down on the tarmac and hog-tied like his friends. First, however, they had to stop the truck.

'This could get ugly,' said Trasker just then, after having broadcast an appeal for the vehicle to pull over. As soon as the trucker responded by picking up the pace, he set down the megaphone and instructed the pilot to get in his face.

'Really?' Randall didn't intend to sound startled, but they were already flying horribly close to the vehicle's windscreen. What the young guy had in mind sounded like suicide. 'Can't we just wait for them to run out of fuel or something?'

Bonita twisted around in her seat. The last time she looked at her father in this way they had just come to a halt at the end of a rollercoaster ride. Once again, it left him wishing he'd kept his feet on the ground.

'If you haven't got anything constructive to offer,' she told him, 'don't say anything at all.'

Trasker leaned forward and tapped the pilot on the shoulder.

'Whatever it takes,' he said. 'This thing ends now.'

Randall swallowed hard, pressing his legs together as the chopper's sudden manoeuvring left him feeling funny in the groin.

'Oh, God,' he muttered to himself, and pressed his brow against the seat rest in front of him, 'make this quick.'

'Sir, that's my intention.' Kyle Trasker sounded as if his confidence had returned and redoubled since their face off in the hotel corridor. Randall glanced across at him, feeling dizzy and sick, and detected just a hint of amusement play across the man's smug face. 'I have some mints, if that would help?'

*

If the sleeping quarters at the rear of the cab were gloomy, Maurice expected to find the hidden space under the bunk to be engulfed in darkness. Instead, on making room for Wretch and then Candy, he found himself in a cramped, coffin-like recess crisscrossed by small beams of natural light. Small holes had been drilled into the lorry's sides, he realised, and reached out to touch one with the pad of his thumb.

'At least we're not going to suffocate.' Candy drew alongside him on her elbows. The roar of the engine was deafening this low down in the truck, and was accompanied by the rumble of huge wheels. 'What does he keep in here, do you think?'

Wretch appeared behind her, crawling into several beams of light. He showed them a coil of rope he'd just found, along with a clutch of plastic ties.

'Must be storage,' said Maurice, just as a squeal of brakes brought the vehicle slowly to a halt. Instinctively, he peered through one of the holes. It afforded a view of the side of the road and a seemingly endless expanse of fenland. He heard doors slamming and activity on the road just out of eyeshot, but it was only when he pulled back from the spyhole that he caught his breath. The voice commanding the driver to climb out of the truck with his hands on his head wasn't responsible, though. It was a glimpse of a word, scratched into the metalwork around the hole he'd just been peering through. It looked like it had been etched by a spike of some sort – or a fingernail, he realised, on considering the jagged, desperate-looking lettering.

HELP US!

With his senses reeling, and well aware that a drama was unfolding just metres away on the roadside, Maurice turned to face the others. As he did so, the little troll beside him removed an object from under his chest that was causing some discomfort. In the beams of light, the hat with the chequered black and white strip above the peak was unmistakable.

'Are we in a dressing up box?' whispered Wretch, who then held up a pair of cuffs. 'What's with all the police gear?'

Movement from outside seized Maurice's attention just then. He glanced through the spyhole, saw The Bulge step towards the side of the road with his palms pressed to the crown of his head. Someone bellowed at him to stop and turn around. They sounded tense but in charge, as if perhaps they had a weapon drawn to back up their instructions. The Bulge complied, looking strangely untroubled. In fact, there was a confidence about his manner that Maurice didn't like one bit.

Then he spotted the tyre iron, tucked behind the trucker's belt, and feared that very bad things were about to happen.

'There's something else in here,' Candy said quietly. Maurice looked around to see her examining a rag of some sort. Even before she sniffed it, a disarmingly sweet and intoxicating smell invaded the boy's nostrils.

'Chloroform,' he hissed, and immediately felt moved by Candy's expression to add that chemistry was a favourite subject in school. Then he considered just why she was looking at him in horror. It was with a gasp that Maurice realised it had nothing to do with his impressive nose for the knockout drug. Taking a moment to regain a grip on his composure, he faced the pair through the shaft of light from the spyhole. 'Well, let's just hope a serial cop killer likes to be consistent,' he suggested, 'and not spoil things with a few civilians.'

26

Moments before the chopper settled on the road, having successfully stopped the truck, Kyle Trasker produced the pistol. Governor Randall Shores watched him slip it coolly from the shoulder holster hidden by his jacket, and struggled to contain his shock.

'You've been packing all this time?' he asked, summoning a phrase often used in the crime drama he was halfway through on box set.

The man from the government had eyed him wearily.

'I'm licensed to carry a firearm,' he confirmed. 'And I'm here to do whatever it takes to close down this event before the public start to question if the troll situation is slipping out of control.'

Randall waited for the pilot to power down the blades before unstrapping his seat belt.

'Stay here,' he instructed Bonnie, who was still filming Trasker as he approached the truck.

'Daddy, nobody is listening to you any more,' she replied calmly, without even taking her eyes from the scene. 'I'll do as I please.'

Randall was painfully aware that this was no time to lose his temper. With his blood coming to the boil, he jabbed at the pilot's shoulder and instructed him not to let Bonita out of his sight.

'If she steps onto the tarmac,' he warned, and reached for his broad-brimmed hat, 'you'll never fly again.'

Hurrying from the cockpit, and hunching low to avoid the slowing blades, the Governor had made his way towards the driver's side of the truck. Cautiously, he stepped around the corner of the vehicle and immediately shot up his hands. On the verge, Trasker faced him with the pistol in hand. A moment later, Randall realised he was in fact aiming at the figure just to one side of him.

'I sincerely hope you're able to remain calm here,' said Trasker, addressing Randall with his gaze turned back on his target. 'I need your assistance after all.'

'Just say the word.' Randall pretended to scratch the small of his back before dropping his arms to one side. The guy at his side, with the gun trained on him, had made just a vague effort to hold up his hands. He was quite a brute, this trucker with the bandit moustache, weirdo hair plaits and a frame that didn't look suited to being squashed behind the wheel.

'Can I say something?' the trucker growled. 'I'll be polite.'

'Go ahead,' replied Trasker, who reasserted his grip on the pistol.

'I just want to apologise to you gents for what's about to happen.'

Randall crossed the dirt to join Trasker, who stood with one foot behind the other as if braced for the recoil when he opened fire.

'Where are they?' he asked the trucker.

'Where are who?'

'The troll, the social worker and the schoolboy,' Trasker responded. 'Don't take me for a fool.'

'Search me,' said the trucker with a shrug.

Trasker glanced at Randall.

'You heard the man,' he said. 'Search him.'

'What, *now*?'

In response, the Governor found himself being assessed by Kyle Trasker in a way that left him feeling as if he'd left his backbone in the chopper.

'Alright, *I'll* search him,' Trasker relented with a sigh. 'You go check out the truck.'

Randall tried not to look as relieved as he felt. Inside the settlement, he wouldn't hesitate in picking off a troll without reason and frisking him down. What caused him to stall here was the glint in the trucker's eye, as if he couldn't wait for one of them to attempt to pat him down. Given how unhinged he looked, Randall decided that opening up the back of the lorry was the preferable option.

'What are you hauling here?' he asked the brute, like it mattered. Still, Randall liked to sound as if he was in full control of this situation.

'We're not here for his cargo,' said Trasker irritably. 'Just look for the runaways.'

'Affirmative.' The Governor grimaced to himself as he scurried wide around the trucker. What he really needed to do, he decided, was get a grip. The young suit might consider himself a hotshot, but at such a tender age he'd surely buckle under further pressure. Randall figured he'd need to be ready to react if required, and right now a little space might give him that advantage. On reaching the rear of the lorry, Randall looked one way and then the other before grasping the lock handle. If a troll and his two partners in crime were cowering inside then they were about to be confronted by a wild dog in human form. With Trasker engaged around the side of the truck, and out of eyeshot from the chopper, the Governor was free to knock some heads together to remind himself, as much as the fugitives, just who deserved the most respect around here.

'Come out, come out!' he yelled, hoisting the shutter high. 'Wherever you are . . .'

Had Randall given further consideration to what the trucker might be transporting, nappies would've been low down on the list. Still, that's what he found himself facing. Not just a few boxes rattling around in the back, but pallets stacked from floor to ceiling. He took a step back, considering the solid wall of super-absorbent baby product, and figured his quarry had to be hiding out in the cab. Unwilling to face Trasker without a troll for a trophy, Randall hurried around the vehicle's passenger side. As soon as the chopper came into view, right there in the road with the blades bowed now they'd ceased rotating, he spotted Bonnie in the cockpit. In a bid to make amends and show her who was running this operation, he gave her the double thumbs up. Immediately, she stopped filming with her phone and looked at him like such a gesture had been outlawed several decades earlier. At that moment, Randall didn't care. He just hoped she would resume filming when he pressed his back to the truck's front wheel arch and hammered the side of his fist against the door.

'I'm counting to three,' he called out, and couldn't resist a confident grin for his daughter. 'If I get to four, there will be tears.'

Randall paused for a moment, hoping the fugitives might register his presence and surrender on camera. When that didn't happen, he began to count, bellowing each digit like the build up to a detonation. He hesitated on reaching three, and dropped the volume on four. This was followed by a silent curse, then the Governor abandoned any sense of caution and just hauled open the passenger door. With his feet on the rungs, he peered inside and hurriedly entered the cab. On finding only an empty bench, he grabbed the curtain and snapped it back, saw nothing but the bunk, and pinched the bridge of his nose in frustration.

'Where are you?' he muttered, only to snap his eyes sideways on hearing something slump to the roadside. With his skin prickling, Randall noticed that the driver's door was ajar. 'Kyle?' he called out quietly. 'Sir?'

Just then, with a gentle breeze over the fens, Governor Randall Shores' instinct was to hold still inside the cab and hope his presence would go undetected. As soon as he had encountered the trucker, he knew the guy was trouble. Now it seemed that the government apprentice really had paid a price for thinking he could handle it. Still, with Bonita filming again from the chopper, seemingly unaware that something had just happened between the verge and the truck, he realised with a heavy heart that there was only one option available to him. Tentatively, he clambered across the cab and peered through the gap in the door.

'Mr Trasker?' He had expected to see a body on the ground. The noise had been unmistakeable. He just didn't anticipate seeing the trucker lying spread-eagled on his back. The sight filled him with relief as much as surprise, and prompted him to climb out without hesitation. 'For a kid, you know how to take care of yourself,' he said, scrambling down the steps, 'You should've told me. I can show you some moves.'

Randall planted his feet on the ground, and then turned to look for the young man with the sculpted hair and the shooter. He figured Kyle Trasker would be examining the grip of his pistol, having presumably used it to cosh the man when he resisted. Instead, and it took a moment to process, he was sprawled on the verge nearby. Struggling to make sense of the situation, the Governor detected a presence close in behind him. He had time to look up and gasp, just as a hand reached around and pressed a cloth to his face. Randall attempted to grab it, aware of an intoxicating smell, and then promptly lost consciousness before his backside hit the ground.

*

'My dad is such a douche,' said Bonita Shores, still reeling from the gesture he had made before climbing into the truck. After the mortifying thing with the thumbs, which she planned to pixilate, her father had clambered through the cab like an infant at a playground. She'd lost sight of him now. Even Trasker was nowhere to be seen, but this was still an opportunity she just had to capture on film. Footage of the troll when they finally located him had to be worth some money, she decided, still training her camera phone through the side glass of the helicopter's cockpit. It would certainly pay for her to get wasted with Benny and Ryan. 'What's taking him so long?'

'Miss Shores, just sit nicely and let Mr Trasker do his job.'

Seated beside her, leafing through his operations manual, the pilot looked pointedly at her foot, which she'd just rested on the edge of her seat for comfort. Bonita rolled her eyes, placing it back on the floor of the cockpit like it hurt to do so. In his dark glasses and short-sleeved shirt with the epaulette bars, she had already marked him down as the kind of man who locked himself away on his home computer and flew helicopter simulators for fun. Then she glanced at the pages open on his lap, and smiled to herself.

'That's a big joystick.' Still recording video footage on her phone, she trained the lens on the diagram he had been reviewing. 'Maybe you could show me how it works?'

The pilot looked across at his passenger, a note of irritation in his expression, and suggested that she remain quiet until her father returned. Exhaling pointedly, Bonita reached for her seat belt and prepared to bolt from the cockpit before the pilot could react. Whatever was going on out there, Bonita needed to be on hand. She grasped the door release, only to let go smartly when the pilot swore out loud.

'I wasn't doing anything!' she snapped, twisting in her seat to round on him. 'Give me a break or I'll say you put your hand inside my top!'

It took a second for Bonita Shores to register that the pilot wasn't at all concerned by her, and another to realise that the truck's engine had just gunned into life. She turned to see the vehicle lurch towards them, shrieking as it appeared to grow in size. Like the man beside her, all she could do was adopt the brace position before the thundering lorry clipped the tail rotor and spun the chopper to face the rising sun.

27

It had been a time of troubling firsts for Candy Lau.

Looking back, finding herself suspended from a job was the least of her worries. The same went for the loss of her hatchback to arson and idiocy. Just then, as she wrestled with the wheel of the truck, which was in itself not something the social worker had ever attempted before, she wondered what kind of prison sentence she could be looking at for her crimes over the last forty-eight hours. Despite no previous convictions, Candy was now facing a potential charge sheet that ran from aiding and abetting a wanted troll to the assault of a settlement governor and his pistol-packing sidekick, as well as wilful damage to a police helicopter. Just then, however, her central concern was the trucker slumped on the seat between Maurice and Wretch. Given the restraining equipment the trio had discovered in the secret compartment, and the conclusions they had drawn, Candy struggled to focus on the road.

'He's coming round,' said the boy anxiously when she glanced at him again. The little troll watched Maurice fumbling in his bid to bind The Bulge's wrists with the rope they had found. 'Did you really have to drug him, too?'

Earlier, from their hiding place under the bunk, Candy had been aghast to spot the tyre iron peeping from the back of The Bulge's jeans. Alerting Maurice to the hidden weapon, they had watched helplessly as the guy with the silver-screen hairstyle and the pistol approached him to carry out a search. Wretch, meanwhile, had continued to pluck troubling objects from the dark reaches of the space. Everything from the plastic restraining ties to the discarded items of uniform had left Candy in no doubt that the trucker had a penchant for preying on law enforcers. It was Maurice who had been first to act. Without word, and pausing only to snatch the chloroform used to soak the cloth as Wretch attempted to take a sniff, he had clambered back out into the cab. The little troll had followed close behind. He appeared to relish the moment, which had worried Candy greatly and left her with no option but to follow them into the daylight.

On reaching the open driver's side door, her first thought was that Maurice must have acted fast. Her second, in view of the two figures collapsed on the roadside, was that panic might've caused the boy to overreact. She had just assumed that he would take out the guy with the gun to spare him from kidnap and worse. There had been no opportunity for her to discuss the wisdom of also disabling the troll with the keys to the truck. Instead, with the sound of Governor Shores clambering into the cab from the passenger side, the trio could only slip out and hide under the truck until Maurice was in a position to spring at him as well. Once he had done so, creeping up on Randall with the pungent rag in hand, the trio turned their attention to the sedated trucker. It had taken them several minutes to manhandle Byron back into the cab. Unlike the Governor and his wingman, The Bulge hadn't been rendered completely senseless by the drug. Instead, he'd groaned and moaned as Maurice pushed him onto the bench, before his head lolled back when Candy gunned the vehicle at the tail of the chopper and embarked upon their getaway.

'Byron's going to be mad with you,' warned Wretch just then, as the boy finished binding the trucker's wrists. 'You wait until his head clears.'

'I was facing a killer!' Maurice glared defensively at the little troll. 'What else could I have done? This is the lunatic who has been snatching police officers that are never seen again. We're lucky to be alive!'

'We don't know that he intended to harm anyone back there,' said Candy, who was trained to diffuse conflict in a conversation. 'Then again,' she told Wretch, 'Maurice was only being cautious.'

'I don't think Byron will see it that way.' Wretch faced the trucker as he stirred once more. 'Brother, you're going to need an elephant tranquilliser to keep him at bay.'

Concentrating on keeping the truck steady as they barrelled along, Candy sensed Maurice reach for the floor where he had dumped the rag. Still soaked in chloroform, which filled the cab with a dangerously pungent aroma, her first move on starting the truck engine had been to wind down the windows.

'Give him some air,' she said. 'Let him come to his senses.'

'What?' Maurice shrank from the trucker's reach as he opened his eyes and looked around groggily. 'But he might murder *me*.'

'We still need his help,' she reminded him. 'Byron is the only one who knows where we're heading.'

'That's if he's telling the truth about helping Wretch get home,' Maurice pointed out. 'Can we trust a cop slayer? I'm really not sure that we can.'

With a grunt, The Bulge surfaced to discover his wrists bound, raised both hands up and snapped them outwards. The rope binding proved to be as effective as a ribbon around a birthday present.

'Let's not go crazy,' Candy pleaded with the trucker as he blinked to focus and growled. 'Maurice only did what he thought was right.'

With a groan, Byron sat forward and wedged his hands to his temples.

'You're lucky I don't break you into little bits,' he grunted, sounding horribly casual with his threat. 'But the truth is we share the same outlook. Doing the right thing is the only way to live with a clear conscience.'

Maurice glanced over the trucker at Wretch, who appeared equally baffled.

'With respect,' the boy replied in a small voice, 'I'm not sure killing cops would help me sleep at night.'

'*Killing* cops?' Byron turned his head, frowning at the boy. 'You want to go easy with the accusations, son.'

'But the . . . the hiding space under the bunk.' Immediately, Maurice looked at Candy for support. With her foot on the truck's accelerator, she grimaced at his sense of timing. 'It looked kind of . . . specialist,' he pressed on. 'Like you might've kept an officer of the law or two in there against their will.'

259

'Maybe,' said Byron, like he'd just admitted to nothing more than collecting butterflies, and chuckled dismissively. 'But I don't kill them.'

'Well, that's good to hear.' The boy cleared his throat. 'But I suppose what I mean is that depriving them of their liberty is hardly a public service.'

'It is when they're trolls,' said the trucker, who belched just then and thumped his chest with the side of his fist. 'Someone has to look out for the rogue elements.'

Candy kept her eyes on the road. What Byron had told them about his own background was still fresh in her mind. Slowly, she came to understand just who he was tracking down here.

'The ones who slipped through adolescence without being found out?'

The Bulge made a noise that might've been to confirm Candy's observation or the chemical hangover was really causing his head to pound. She couldn't be sure, but then keeping the truck steady was her priority.

'Not all of us who make it into adulthood above ground choose the right career paths,' he said. 'In my job, all I need to watch out for is my road rage. The trouble is some trolls have found themselves in positions of responsibility. If they fail to keep their natural instincts under control, it can have . . . consequences.'

'Rogue cops,' said Maurice, nodding to himself.

'Taking bribes. Planting evidence. You know the kind of thing.'

'So, you've been doing us all a favour.'

'No troll in your society is beyond the law,' he said. 'Even the ones that got into the banking sector.'

'Banking?' Candy caught her breath. All of a sudden, world events took on an entirely new complexion. 'Trolls caused the global recession?'

'Those guys were reckless,' agreed Byron, 'but I've taken care of them and now I'm tackling the cops. After that, the ticket touts and estate agents will need to start looking over their shoulders.'

'Perfect cover for trolls,' agreed Candy.

'It's never too late to challenge unacceptable behaviour,' he stressed. 'We're all in this life together, after all.'

'Sounds like some of our kind could learn a thing or two from you,' muttered Maurice.

'So, you're a bit like a bounty hunter,' said Candy. 'Rounding up the main offenders –'

'– and escorting them home,' he said to finish, puffing out his considerable chest.

'*Home!*' Wretch reacted as if he'd been searching for the word for a lifetime. 'So, are we nearly there yet?' he asked.

The Bulge studied the road ahead, bunching his lips together. By now, the strengthening sun had begun to burn through the mist. It was shaping up to be a dazzling day.

'I think you know the answer to that,' he said with a nod.

Wretch punched the air in delight.

'Well, I don't know the answer.' Maurice sounded baffled. Candy sensed him looking across at her. 'Do you?'

Clutching the wheel with both hands, feeling more comfortable in the driving seat with every minute that passed, Candy shifted up a gear.

'It's a troll thing,' she assured him, relishing the fact that Wretch was bouncing up and down like he'd just enjoyed the ultimate sugar rush. 'For all our sakes, let's just hope there's a welcome when we arrive.'

*

As the water splashed over his face, Governor Randall Shores gasped and snapped open his eyes. It took a moment for the flaring sun to settle around a silhouette of a young woman looming over him.

'I thought you were dead,' said Bonita with a plastic bottle in one hand and her camera phone in the other.

There was a distinct lack of relief in his daughter's voice, Randall noted, as he hauled himself off the ground, and then sank onto all fours when his head threatened to send him back into a chemically induced unconsciousness.

'I'll survive,' he muttered, collecting his hat and dusting it off. 'What just happened?'

'You got totally owned,' she told him simply. 'Which is obviously not that difficult.'

Randall looked up, squinting in the strengthening sunlight, and immediately showed Bonita the palm of one hand when he realised she was filming.

'Will you cut that out?' he demanded angrily. 'Make yourself useful and help me onto my feet!'

A protracted groan drew their attention to the verge just then. Kyle Trasker appeared to have broken from a call on his mobile to vomit into the grass. He looked deathly pale and very shaken.

'The schoolkid must've jumped you, too,' said Trasker weakly. 'According to your daughter, he and the troll took off with the trucker propped up between them and the social worker behind the wheel. For an ex-employee of yours,' he added, pausing only to spit, 'that woman is kind of disgruntled.'

'You can rest assured we'll have Miss Lau tested,' said Randall. 'The same goes for the schoolboy.'

'You guys should really keep all this between yourselves.' Bonita shook her head disapprovingly, her camera focused on the man from the government now. 'Especially the part where you both got taken down by a four-eyed teenager in a school blazer.'

Kyle Trasker wiped his mouth on his sleeve, the pistol still in his grasp. He held his phone in the other hand. Randall could hear a voice through the speaker faintly repeating Kyle's surname in a bid to get his attention.

'Backup will be here shortly,' Trasker assured the pair, before turning away to resume his communication.

On the fenland road some way behind him, the pilot could be seen on his mobile phone, presumably arranging for a low loader to collect his stricken chopper. As he spoke, he dipped down to collect a mangled panel from the tail. Randall watched him pause to inspect it in closer detail before hurling it to the ground in anger. It was nothing compared to his own mood, however. Clambering to his feet, a surge of outrage and indignation coursed through the Governor's system that proved far more overwhelming than the chloroform.

'I'll handle this.' Marching over to Trasker, Randall snatched the phone from him and pressed it to his ear. 'Cancel whatever reinforcements your boy here has just requested,' he said, having identified himself with a sense of great authority. 'All he needs is a medic. I have the wider situation under control.'

'*What?*' Kyle Trasker spread his hands. Even Bonita looked up from her camera phone as if to check she had heard her father correctly. For a moment, with his rage barely contained, Randall felt intensely aware of his surroundings. Here they were on a tranquil road with nothing to break the horizon all around. The truck had only recently taken off, and though it was out of sight now, it wouldn't take long to hunt down if they hurried. As the rumble of a tractor approached from behind him, most likely a farmer drawn by the drama, Randall had no intention of waiting for backup before resuming the chase. Nor did he have any inclination to follow orders from Trasker. The guy had comprehensively failed in his bid to capture Wretch and his friends since they left the confines of the settlement. What's more, Randall was now prepared to go beyond the law to bring the trio to task.

'You really don't want to join me,' he told Trasker before stepping into the road with his hand held high as the tractor approached. 'From this moment on,' he added, tossing the phone back, 'we play by my rules.'

Kyle Trasker rose up to catch his mobile. With a sickly sweat beading across his brow, he quickly dropped into a crouch to prevent himself from keeling over. Bonita watched him go down, and then stood before her father.

'I have a problem with your rules, Daddy. Do I need to share it?'

The way she addressed him with a barb in her voice, Randall knew exactly what she was threatening here. Ever since that unfortunate day outside his office when she overheard just how he kept his trolls in order, it had come to serve as the unspoken flashpoint in their relationship. It was ironic, he thought, that Bonita should now choose to align herself with low life rights. After everything he had done to keep her on the straight and narrow on her journey from a babe in his arms to becoming a responsible young adult, this was how she repaid him. For a moment, both father and daughter glared at one another. Trasker meanwhile, had turned away once more to dry heave into the weeds.

'You and I are flesh and blood,' Randall reminded her, his fury temporarily at bay, before switching away to commandeer the startled farmer's vehicle. 'I like to think we're on the same side.'

PART THREE

28

The moment Wretch fell silent, Maurice figured they had arrived. As soon as Candy steered the truck onto a track between fields, following a nod from Byron, the little troll quit voicing his string of unanswered questions about what life was like underground. Did trolls keep pets, he had wanted to know, put the clocks back by an hour or suffer from the opposite of vertigo? What about birthdays, drying the washing, stargazing and trench foot? Instead, clutching the dashboard as if to brace himself, he pressed his face to the windscreen and pretty much his eyeballs too.

'Is this really it?' Maurice looked around. A flock of birds sprayed from a treeline as the vehicle rumbled on, but he saw nothing to suggest this was anything other than remote agricultural land.

'What were you expecting?' The Bulge sat between Maurice and the little troll. 'The Emerald City?'

While the effects of the chloroform wore off, Byron had insisted that Candy remain at the wheel of his truck. He had even expressed admiration at her abilities to handle a vehicle of this size. Maurice struggled to feel so upbeat. Even if they delivered the little troll into the arms of his true family, he had reflected, where did that leave him? After all his parents' efforts to protect him from the big, bad world, their son was not so little any more. When they learned the lengths he had gone to assist a member of the gang who had kidnapped him, the boy figured their heartache would turn to crushing disappointment. What's more, he'd need legal representation so expensive it could ruin them.

'When Dorothy returns to Kansas,' Maurice said a moment later, 'everyone is pleased to see her.'

'There's no place like home,' agreed Candy. 'Wherever that might be for us now.'

As the truck crawled on, Wretch began muttering animatedly under his breath. Maurice couldn't make out what he was saying this time, but when a rickety farm gate took shape through the mist, a sense of awe silenced the little troll. Beyond, the boy made out a static caravan with two plastic crates for steps and planks laid out like a path. A cattle shed loomed in the background. With hangar-like doors open wide, the run-down structure appeared to be used for nothing more than sheltering an old flatbed pick-up. Judging by the rusting remains of agricultural machinery, and the nettles and brambles that encroached on the concrete loading area, it looked like a farm that had gone to seed some time ago.

Then three patrol dogs prowled out from behind the caravan, causing Maurice to bristle in his seat.

'There's no need to worry,' The Bulge assured him. 'They're expecting us.'

'Really?'

The trucker gestured at the CB radio mounted under the dashboard.

'I like to call ahead before bringing a troll in from the wild.'

Having picked up on the approaching truck, the dogs began to bark and switch back and forth behind the gate.

'Do they come here willingly?' asked Maurice.

'Having travelled gagged and bound?' The trucker scoffed at the question. 'Most arrive kicking and screaming, but they soon calm down when they realise what they've been missing.'

'But isn't life underground just dark, damp and dingy?' Maurice persisted.

Byron shrugged like he couldn't argue with him.

'Let's just say that lately we've started learning to be thankful for what we have.'

Maurice frowned to himself, just as Candy pulled up in front of the gate, and focused on the caravan once more. The transmitter mast certainly suggested that The Bulge might have been in communication with the occupant, but the windows were so grubby it was impossible to see inside. Maurice glanced warily at Candy, who shrugged as if reversing wasn't an option.

'Before we go any further,' he asked Byron, 'do you mind if I check a small issue on my mind? You haven't lured us out here just so you can murder us or anything? Because obviously if you have I'd like to leave if that's alright with you.'

The trucker looked taken aback, but only for a moment because that's when Wretch bounced in his seat and hooted. Maurice followed his line of sight to see the door to the caravan had just flapped open. It framed a grizzled figure in a dark beanie and donkey jacket. The most striking thing about him was the fleece-like white beard that appeared to hook over his ears.

271

'Santa's fallen on hard times,' observed Maurice under his breath, but the comment was lost to the little troll's joy on seeing the figure negotiate the plastic crates and the planks.

'I can't believe what I'm seeing!' Wretch declared. 'I heard stories in the settlement, but never thought he could exist for real.'

Maurice looked side on at Wretch.

'Uh . . . I was joking about the Santa thing.'

'I know that.' Just for a second, Wretch faced Maurice in a way that left him feeling like *he* was the one who needed to stop fooling around. 'So, is it really him?' the little troll asked the trucker.

The Bulge nodded, pressing himself into his seat as Wretch scrambled across him to exit the truck.

'This guy is our saviour?' Even Candy sounded surprised and uncertain. 'Are you sure we've come to the right place?'

Maurice peered at the pensioner, relieved nonetheless that the dogs fell obediently behind him.

'I don't mean to be rude,' he said, 'but he looks like one of those hoarders you sometimes see on the telly.'

'Well, he's certainly taken in plenty of trolls over the years.' The Bulge invited Maurice and Candy to climb out of the truck. 'Say hello to Pearly Gates Pete.'

*

Following the party along the planks towards the caravan, across mud that could well have been slurry, Candy Lau was beyond caring about her shoes. Without a doubt, this was the last place on earth she imagined Wretch had in mind when he spoke of heading home to get help. Despite their surroundings, the old guy seemed to know all about the little troll. He had greeted him by clasping his face with both hands and looking searchingly into his eyes. Then, nodding to himself, as if satisfied by what he saw, Pete had opened the gate so that Candy could pull the truck into the cattle shed. Candy had offered to hand the task to Byron, but the trucker simply stood back with a grin on his face and the promise that she had a whole new career on the road ahead of her if social work was no longer an option.

'You're the first to return from a settlement,' she heard Pete tell Wretch, as they crossed the threshold into the caravan. 'Now tell me the truth about life inside those walls.'

Candy followed close behind, unable to make out much from Wretch's mumbling. She looked up and around. A kettle had just come to the boil, filling the place with steam. She tried hard not to express any response whatsoever to the fact that Maurice had been right about the hoarding. Just one glimpse around the interior told her this was someone who couldn't bear to lose things.

'I used to think of the settlements as a sanctuary,' she said, in a bid to focus on something other than the shelves stacked with everything from tins of beans to toilet rolls and mouse traps. Even Wretch looked taken aback by the collection of empty condiment bottles that covered the kitchenette surface, and retreated into his hoodie. 'A place where changelings could expect protection and support.'

'When the walls went up we shared the same belief,' said Pete, who began picking off cups from a shelf and wiping each rim clean with his finger. 'Now, who's for tea?'

'That's kind, but we'll pass,' said Maurice, who got in before Candy could decline the offer. Even Wretch raised the palm of his hand when Pete looked in his direction. 'We probably don't have long before this place is crawling with police.'

Pearly Gates Pete shrugged like it was no big deal, and poured a cup for himself and The Bulge.

'Three sugars, please,' the trucker added, and then addressed Candy and Maurice as the old man reached for the spoon. 'Pete knows I like my tea like my rogue cops and bankers.'

'Sweet?' asked the schoolboy, ignoring Candy's puzzled face and a snigger from the little troll. Even Maurice looked unconvinced by his own suggestion. More so when The Bulge scowled at him.

'I mean all cooled off,' he said, like it was obvious. 'The sugar is just for taste.'

Candy took a step away, feeling the need for some fresh air, only to back into Pete's bunk. She believed the trucker's claim that he served as some kind of rogue troll recovery enforcer. Even so, Byron's mood could switch in a blink, and she really didn't want to get on his bad side.

'So,' she said in a bid to change the subject, 'where would Wretch find the rest of your family?'

'Hey, I'm not family.' Pearly Gates Pete finished stirring the sugar into Byron's tea, but not before pausing to consider Candy's question. 'Are you saying I look like a troll?' he asked, and turned to face her.

Candy took one look at the gruff expression on the old man's face, his wiry brows so compressed they touched in the middle, and immediately looked to her feet. At the same time, after everything she'd learned lately, she reminded herself not to leap to conclusions.

'Sir,' said Maurice, 'we've come a long way to bring Wretch here. We just want to make sure he's in good hands.'

Pete locked his gaze on the schoolboy for a moment before breaking off to sip at his tea. He took another mouthful, sluiced it between his cheeks, and then grimaced as if he'd fixed a bad brew.

'Then we shouldn't keep them waiting,' he said, and gestured through a window coated in condensation. 'They saw you coming, after all.'

*

The tractor cab was a squeeze for Randall. It also took some persuasion before his daughter could be coaxed into joining him. They were perched on either side of the farmer, with their backs to the windows. Unshaven, with a grubby sweatshirt emblazoned with a logo for a chicken feed manufacturer, the man behind the wheel didn't look like he had washed that morning, or possibly all week. The smell wasn't an issue for the governor of a troll settlement, whose nose had long since become accustomed to stale sweat. It was Bonita who looked visibly troubled. As the tractor buzzed along, nearly half an hour after leaving Trasker sitting on the verge with his head between his knees and a helicopter pilot who looked like an angel with his wings plucked to quills, she repeatedly poked a finger in her mouth and pretended to gag.

'Manners,' he hissed behind the farmer's back. 'Anyone would think you've been raised by wolves!'

Bonita's mouth tightened into a pout. It had become such a familiar response, her father brooded to himself, that it was beginning to look like the default expression for her face. The farmer seemed not to notice. Then again, he hadn't spoken a word since Randall flashed his canteen pass and commandeered the vehicle. The Governor was grateful to the man for not objecting, though he suspected such drama would serve as the high point of his year. As they rolled along, he just wished the guy lived in a world where time was a bit more precious.

'How long do we have to travel with this soap dodger?' asked Bonita with a sigh. 'Are we nearly there yet?'

The nerve endings sparked in Randall's rear molars. Now, the pain just made him all the more determined to bring the troll and his friends to task. He focused on the road, concentrating hard for several minutes, and then clasped the farmer by the shoulder.

'See that!' he said, and pointed at a track between two fields. 'Those tyre marks look fresh!'

As the tractor slowed to a halt, Bonita followed his line of sight.

'We're looking for a troll, Daddy, not hunting big game.'

'There are similarities.'

Randall rose from his perch, straining to see what lay at the end of the pass. Despite the sun, the mist still clung to the earth, making it impossible to see anything more than the faint trace of an industrial shed of some sort.

'Take us up there,' he commanded the farmer, who shook his head in response.

'I'd prefer not to.'

His voice came as quite a surprise to Randall. Not only were these the first words he had uttered since they climbed on board, the reluctance in his response told the Governor that something had spooked this guy.

'Got a problem?' he asked, still making every effort to determine where the track led.

With one hand on the steering wheel, the farmer looked back at Randall.

'Around here,' he said, 'everyone knows each other's business.'

'That's the countryside.' Randall shot a grin at Bonita. 'Who needs social media, eh?'

'Except for this place.' The farmer jabbed a thumb over his shoulder. 'Whatever's been going on behind those gates lately, they don't want people knowing.'

Randall beamed at him.

'My friend,' he said, and prepared to climb out of the cab, 'may all your crops flourish this season.'

Bonita rolled her eyes as she followed her father onto the road.

'I'm sorry you had to hear that nonsense,' she told the farmer on her way out. 'Imagine being me!'

Randall was midway along the track when Bonita caught up with him.

'If you were a troll,' he asked, 'why would you hide in a place like this?'

By now, the gate had taken shape through the mist as well as the caravan behind it.

'Maybe it's a weed farm,' she suggested, sounding suspiciously interested to her father's ear. 'If I'd been on the run from the settlement for this long, by now I'd want to get *seriously* stoned.'

Randall paused for a moment, waiting for his daughter to face him.

'I want you to stay outside when I go in, OK?'

Bonita was just drawing her expression into a scowl when a long, protracted growl drew their attention. Randall looked up the track, saw the three patrol dogs charging up to the other side of the gate, and fought the urge to swallow.

'They don't scare me,' he said with some hesitation in his voice. 'Bonbon, for once in your life please do as I ask.'

'Hey, no problem!' Gazing warily at the dogs, Bonita raised her hands to signal that she had every intention of obeying his instructions. 'I can stay here and keep a lookout.'

'That's my girl.'

Randall offered her a long, genuine smile. Bonita seemed to relish it, and then looked to her feet as if seeking the right way to ask him the question that followed.

'If you do find some dope,' she suggested quietly, 'I'd be happy to carry it back for you as evidence.'

29

Maurice was relieved to be out of the caravan, only to feel some tension as they made their way around the cattle shed. Wretch walked alongside the old man, chattering animatedly. He had also brushed the hood off his shoulders for once. With his hands out of his pockets, and the sun bathing his face, he appeared to be relishing the moment. Such a show of confidence from the little troll left the boy feeling increasingly wary.

'Are you sure about this?' Maurice whispered to Candy, and gestured at The Bulge who was following close behind. 'If we try to run, he's got us covered.'

'Why would we run?' she asked. 'This could be the moment Wretch has been longing for.'

'Which is what, exactly?' Maurice pushed his glasses into place and glanced around. Ever since Pete declared that their arrival had been noted, he felt as if eyes were upon him from every direction. 'Candy, nobody has ever witnessed a troll emerge from underground. If this is some kind of secret gateway, do you really think they'll be happy that we know the location?'

'You're right. Wretch has forced them to break cover. They won't like that one bit.'

The response, coming from behind the pair, caused Maurice to catch his breath. He switched around, walking backwards for a moment, and addressed The Bulge directly.

'What does that mean?'

'It means you need to relax,' he said. 'I'm just fooling with you, Maurice, but all this fretting is a waste of energy. Don't be the one who reflects on his life and wishes he'd been a bit bolder.'

Candy nodded in agreement.

'I always said we could learn a lot from the trolls.'

'Arson isn't hard to master,' grumbled Maurice.

'But at least they're not afraid to express themselves,' she insisted. 'You see nothing but troublemakers. In the right environment, I see free spirits.'

With the cattle shed behind them, the group followed Pete and Wretch across a fallow field. The surface was dry and punctured by hoof marks. Looking around, through mist that hung like slashed veils, the field seemed to stretch out for ever. It should've left Maurice feeling both isolated and exposed. Instead, with Candy's words in mind, the boy instructed himself not to worry.

'I guess even being here is an achievement for me,' he told her. 'The old Maurice would've turned around long ago.'

'Whatever happens now,' said Candy, and placed a hand between his shoulders, 'we did the right thing.'

Maurice glanced across at her and grinned.

'Most people will believe we did the *wrong* thing,' he said. 'But I think we had good reasons for the choices we made.'

Carefully, Candy continued to pick her way over the rutted terrain.

'I always wanted to help people less fortunate than myself,' she said after a moment. 'Sometimes, that means making sacrifices.'

'Your boyfriend?' asked Maurice, and then immediately wished that he hadn't.

'I meant my career,' she said, smiling despite herself. 'Greg and I were just holding each other back.'

Just then, without word, Pearly Gates Pete stopped in his tracks with one hand raised. Wretch glanced at Maurice. A sense of unease had crept into his manner, the boy noted, on seeing his gaze flit to Candy, The Bulge and then back to the old man.

'What's up, boss?' asked the little troll.

'They're here,' said Pete solemnly, his gaze fixed directly ahead.

Maurice looked around, his heart rate rising. A whisper of a breeze caused the mist to shred and shift. If there was a presence out there, it was impossible to determine. He looked across at Candy, and saw her eyes widen. It was a shuffling sound some way beyond Wretch and Pete that seized his attention. As the breeze continued to thin the mist, several shapes became visible ahead of the pair. Not figures, he realised, but standing stones. The kind of ancient and mysterious arrangement that might once have drawn a school geography trip until the sinkholes took over the syllabus.

'They're just rocks,' he said, with some relief, and that's when the first figure emerged from behind them.

'Let's not leap to conclusions,' said Candy, as several more emerged into the light and began to assemble in front of them. 'Show you have an open mind.'

All of a sudden, as Maurice squinted into the glare of the sun at the scene unfolding before him, the purpose of the stones didn't seem like such an age-old mystery.

'Wait until Mr Wallace marks my next paper,' he muttered to himself.

They lacked the lope and swagger everyone came to expect from trolls. That was the next thing Maurice registered. Instead, as the numbers continued to grow, male, female, young and old, he sensed they shared his air of caution. Silhouetted by the sun, they seemed to huddle close to one another, as if expecting Maurice and his friends to attack. Some of them wore hoodies, just like Wretch, but most sported an odd combination of formal and casual clothing. He saw one troll in a suit jacket, with a scruffy T-shirt, braces and cargo pants. Another wore a puffball dress, shredded to rags at the hem, but with sequins stitched into the shoulders that glittered brightly. As his composure settled, Maurice's first impression was that this band of underground dwellers had access to a plentiful source of jumble. He just didn't like to put that into words.

'Should we have brought gifts or something?' he asked Candy under his breath.

Maurice was sure he hadn't been overheard, but then Pete stepped forward with his hands spread wide. In response, a slender-looking troll in a casual tracksuit and straw trilby mirrored his move. Both grunted happily as they fell into an embrace.

'It's been a while,' said Pete, pulling back to take a good look at him. 'How is life down under?'

The troll responded with a loud but incoherent mumble. Still, it was enough to cause a ripple of laughter to spread through the gathering behind him. Even Wretch giggled nervously, scuffing his feet in turn.

'What did he say?' asked Maurice.

'No idea.' Wretch shrugged, his eyes locked on the slender troll still. 'But just hearing that voice feels good.'

As the pair continued to chatter, in a way that sounded totally familiar to Maurice and yet entirely incomprehensible, his attention was drawn for a moment by the sound of dogs barking and baying in the distance. He glanced over his shoulder, following the noise, and found The Bulge was also looking towards the cattle shed.

'Something's upset them,' he said.

'Should we check it out?'

The trucker faced Maurice.

'They're big dogs,' he said. 'No doubt they can take care of trespassers.'

Maurice focused on the noise for a moment longer, and then wheeled around when an anguished cry rose up from one of the trolls. It was enough to break off the conversation between Pete and the figure in the tracksuit and trilby, and caused everyone to face the shrieking individual.

Having just emerged from behind the stones, she stood with her hands to her mouth and her eyes locked on Wretch. In her shawl and pleated skirt, she appeared to have made some effort to dress up for the occasion. As she fell in and out of words, great tears snaked down her cheeks. Wretch tipped his head to one side, and glanced warily at Maurice and Candy. Then he looked back at the sobbing figure, blinking into the strengthening sun.

'Mum?' he asked quietly, and again when she pushed her way into the clearing between the two parties.

Maurice watched Wretch step forward and stop in front of her. All of a sudden, her composure had returned. Despite being a little shorter than Wretch, she looked oddly formidable in her jackboots and striped stockings. She placed her hands on his shoulder, and then his cheeks. For a moment, they looked deep into each other's eyes. Just then, it seemed to Maurice that everyone had ceased to breathe, only to gasp in surprise when she raised one hand and slapped the little troll across the cheek. If this was an expression of her displeasure at his conduct above ground, another maternal instinct quickly kicked in. Before Wretch could react, she threw her arms around him, weeping once again, and clung on as if he might vanish should he ever let go.

With a tightening in his throat, Maurice turned to find Candy smiling at the pair. Her eyes shone brightly. The boy fought to hold back his own tears.

'We did the right thing,' he said again, and grinned to himself when a firm hand came to rest on his shoulder from behind.

'Most people wouldn't dream of going this far for Wretch,' said Byron. 'I guess that means I no longer have to squash you for that stunt you pulled with the chloroform.'

*

The patrol dogs stalked around Randall Shores in a tight, menacing ring. With teeth bared and ears flattened, all three braced to throw themselves upon him.

'Bonbon,' he said, struggling to stay calm, 'would you fetch help, please?'

'Are you serious?' Having watched her father clamber over the gate towards the caravan, Bonita Shores crinkled her nose as though his request came with a bad smell. 'Help from where?'

Randall was ready to rip out his back molars just then, had it not been for the giant dogs now threatening to cause him even greater pain.

'Use this.' Making no sudden movements, he collected his mobile phone from a top pocket. 'Just do the right thing, Bonnie, for once in your life!'

Randall tossed the phone towards her. It connected with the upper bar of the gate and bounced back into the slurry. Bonnie watched the device drop and folded her arms.

'That went well,' she observed.

'Can you reach it?'

'I'm not putting my hands in *that*,' she objected. 'Do you want me to die of mad cow disease?'

At that precise moment, Governor Shores was more concerned about not dying from a savaging by three ferocious canines. A minute earlier, he had clambered over the gate with complete confidence. All dogs look for leadership and authority, he had told his daughter. They're pack animals, much like a troll. As soon as they saw who was in charge, they would shrink from his path.

Sure enough, when Randall planted his feet on the other side of the gate, resisting the urge to curse when his polished shoes sunk into the slop, the dogs had kept their distance. They barked and snapped, but behaved as if an invisible force field protected him. That force field was created from pure confidence, as he told his daughter, and began to pick his way in the direction of the planks leading to the caravan.

Then the first dog had crept forward and found the force field to be non-existent. Within seconds Randall was surrounded.

'Go fetch Trasker,' he said, his voice pitched over the snarling pack. 'If medics are with him then bring them as a precaution.'

'That's miles back,' Bonnie pointed out. 'I don't have the right shoes.'

One of the dogs went for him just then, succeeding only in ripping at his shirt sleeve.

'Do you want me to die?' he shrieked.

'I want you to calm down and ask nicely.'

A lunge from a second dog and then the third prompted Randall to wail.

'Please!' he begged his daughter. 'Do it for Daddy.'

Bonita grasped the gate, her eyes narrowing.

'I want the car at weekends just as soon as it's fixed,' she said calmly. 'No curfews.'

If he made a break for it, Randall figured he could reach the caravan door. What stopped him was the possibility that he would find it locked.

'Have I ever told you what a selfish, rude and unpleasant individual you can be?' he snapped at Bonita, no longer able to restrain his anger and rage. 'I'm ashamed to be your father.'

'Fine.' Bonnie let go of the gate and took a step backwards. 'Good luck with the dogs, Dad. Let me know how that works out for you.'

'Where are you going?'

'Home,' she said, quite calmly, before her face clouded over. 'Far away from *you*!

30

Candy Lau looked on in wonder. As Wretch was introduced to trolls who could well have been his brothers and sisters, she clasped her hands together and beamed. They crowded around him, exchanging hugs and high fives. In all her time at the settlement, working hard to encourage the residents to take some pride in themselves, she had never seen one smile so broadly.

'That's quite a welcome,' observed Maurice. 'Just how big is his family?'

'Impossible to say.' Pearly Gates Pete turned to face the pair. 'Underground, everyone lives under the same roof.'

'A collective,' said Candy, still watching the welcome. Though each member of the group was dressed in the same mismatched fashion, a thought crossed her mind that quickly gathered in conviction. 'Some of these trolls,' she observed, and switched her attention to Pete, 'they're not trolls, are they?'

The old man held her gaze, and then nodded to confirm what she was thinking.

'When we swapped our babies at birth it broke hearts below ground as much as above,' he said. 'It was a sacrifice, in the belief that our offspring might thrive, but the ones we spirited away weren't neglected. Far from it. You might not think we have much of an existence where the sun can't reach us. Nor did we until recently. But what we do have is each other, and that bond is unbreakable.' He paused to look at the group with Wretch. 'Those kids are free to leave at any time, but you know what? They take one look at the outside world, see all the things we hoped would benefit our kind, and without exception decide that life is better below the surface. Now that Wretch has brought home some truths about what's been going on up here lately, we can see that they were right.'

'What *is* down there?' asked Maurice.

It was a question that had been asked so many times since the trolls had been exposed. Both Maurice and Candy waited expectantly for the old man to answer. Instead, Pete turned his eyes to the trucker looming behind them, and then nodded as if to grant his consent.

Byron slipped a hand inside his flannelled shirt to scratch at an armpit.

'Only love,' he offered, as if it was obvious. 'Maybe that's all any of us need'

Candy smiled to herself.

'It sounds like you guys have got it all worked out.'

'Well, let's not get carried away here.' Pete gestured at Byron as if to illustrate his point. 'Trolls act from the heart first and foremost. It can make them a handful when they're growing up, but with the right guidance that spirit can become a positive force.'

'I quite agree,' said Candy.

Pearly Gates Pete looked unimpressed.

'The mistake we made, Miss Lau, was to assume you people would know how to handle it. Instead, you responded by turning them into outcasts.'

'The settlements,' said Maurice, aware that the volume of their conversation had dropped enough for them to hear the dogs in the distance once again.

'When they came into existence we had to accept it was in everybody's best interests,' said Pete, his voice rising once more. 'Of course, we heard the rumours about life inside the perimeter.' He glanced around at Wretch once more, smiling to himself on seeing him fooling about with a group of young trolls. 'I guess our faith in human nature meant none of us could believe it. Until now.'

Candy cleared her throat.

'What happened to Wretch has come as a shock to us all,' she told him. 'It's why we're here.'

'From what he told me just now,' said Pete, gesturing at the path they had trodden across the field, 'he's not the only one to be mistreated.'

Candy said nothing. It simply confirmed what she had learned about Governor Shores.

'So, what can we do?' asked Maurice. 'There are thousands of trolls inside those walls.'

'And many more of us underground,' said The Bulge, with a cursory stamp of his foot. 'What do you reckon?' he asked the old man in the donkey jacket, who stood with his back to the stones. 'It has to be worth a shot, no?'

For a moment, Pearly Gates Pete seemed lost in thought. He was oblivious to the trolls chattering behind him, and the baying of the dogs on the other side of the cowshed. Finally, pushing back his beanie, he sunk a hand inside a pocket and held out an ignition key. It dangled from a plastic fob shaped like a pair of angel wings.

'Take my old flatbed and head back to the settlement,' he told Candy and Maurice. 'Nobody will be on the look out for you in that.' Before either of them could draw breath in surprise, Pete spun around to summon Wretch's attention. 'What's central there?' he asked the little troll.

Wretch shrugged. 'The park in front of the old mayor's office?' he suggested, and then lifted his chin while pulling his shoulders upright. 'You'll find my tag on every bench.'

The old man from the caravan turned back around full circle.

'Go there and wait for further instruction,' he told the pair.

In response, Candy swapped a glance with Maurice.

'Why?' she asked.

Pete gestured for Wretch to stand alongside him.

'Did you trust these two to get you here safely?'

'I guess so.' Wretch shrugged, eyeing Maurice and then nodding as if to strengthen his statement.

Seemingly satisfied by his response, Pete addressed Candy and Maurice once more.

'They say you can't trust a troll,' he said. 'It would be an honour for us all if you proved that to be wrong. All you have to do is make your presence known in the park –'

'But that's just asking for trouble!' Maurice interrupted with a voice pitched several octaves higher than usual. 'It'll just draw everyone out!'

'– and have faith in us to do the right thing.'

Pearly Gates Pete completed the brief with his brow pulled tight into a scowl.

'So, you want us to break back *into* the settlement?' Maurice asked after a moment. 'That's the last place we should be.'

'Exactly.' Pete tossed the key into the air before gesturing towards the group in front of the standing stones. 'The same goes for Wretch and these guys.'

Instinctively, Candy reached out and caught the key by the fob. Byron nodded in approval.

'You're in good hands with her,' he told the schoolboy. 'Don't talk too much on the journey. If Candy switches on the radio, that's your cue to shut up.'

'What about you?' asked Candy.

'Every squad car in the country will be looking out for my wagon,' the trucker told her, before crossing to join the other trolls. 'I'd prefer to take the scenic route.'

'The tunnels?' Maurice voiced precisely what Candy was thinking. 'On foot?'

'It won't take them as long as you think,' assured Pete, who gestured for the trolls to get going. 'They know all the shortcuts.'

Candy watched the trolls gravitate behind the stones. She wondered what kind of underground access was hidden back there, but then Wretch glanced around and she realised that only one thing mattered. Breaking off from the others, he faced his former social worker and the schoolboy.

'I just want to say something,' he mumbled, his hands plunged into the pouch of his hoodie, and then promptly looked to the ground. A grimace crossed his face, as if the words inside him were literally struggling to get out.

'Once upon a time,' she said, 'you found that *sorry* was the hardest word.'

Candy glanced across at Maurice, who was also trying hard not to smile.

'OK, I'll go first.' The schoolboy took a moment to compose himself. He shot his wrists from the cuffs of his blazer and then looked Wretch in the eye. 'I want to *thank* you.'

Wretch looked at him in astonishment.

'For what?'

'For everything,' Maurice said simply. 'But above all for having faith in me even after I'd marked you down as a dim-witted hooligan.' He took a step forward, opening his arms like this was a moment of honesty he just had to share. 'After everything we've been through, I realise I was half wrong.'

Wretch blinked in response, grinned as the schoolboy beamed at him, and then appeared to review what he'd just heard.

'What half?' he asked, and promptly received a hug in response.

The little troll seemed frozen in time when Maurice stepped back. Then he twitched his nose, as if thawing from the shock of what had just happened, and promptly peeled off his hoodie.

'As parting gifts I can think of better,' said Maurice, who was forced to throw out his hands when Wretch flung the garment at him. 'Really, there's no need.'

'Take it, brother,' said the little troll. 'You're going to need all the protection you can get.'

'What about you?' asked Maurice after a moment. 'Returning to the settlement isn't safe for you either.'

'I'll watch your back,' said Wretch. 'You watch mine.'

His daughter certainly knew how to flounce. Randall Shores had to give her credit for that. Watching Bonita make her way back down the farm track, he wondered if she could stomp her feet any more dramatically. Even the dogs picked up on her departure as they continued to circle the beleaguered settlement governor.

'Let's be reasonable.' He showed his palms to the slavering pack, only to snatch them away when one of them snapped at his fingers. 'Bonita!'

'*Mister, can I give you some advice?*'

Randall grabbed a breath and froze. The voice from behind him sounded worn, like it belonged to an old guy. What it lacked was any surprise on finding a stranger surrounded by killer hounds.

'Do these beasts belong to you?' he asked, too scared to turn around for fear of being torn to shreds.

'*Doesn't matter who they belong to right now. They're just doing their job. Serving a purpose. Same as all of us, I guess.*' To Randall's ear, the guy sounded like he should be sitting on a mountaintop being philosophical. That was all very well, he thought bitterly, but an enlightened way of looking at life was really not what he needed right now. A tranquilliser gun would be far more effective.

'Can you help me?' he pleaded, and slowly clasped his hands in the prayer position to keep them from harm's way.

From up ahead somewhere – in the cowshed, perhaps – the sound of a starter motor turning joined the snarls and growling of the dogs. It failed to catch on the first attempt, and then sputtered into life with a throaty roar.

'*Just don't move a muscle*,' the old guy said, raising his voice a little to be heard over the engine. '*Close your eyes so they're certain you're no threat.*'

Randall followed instructions. It did little to calm the dogs, however. If anything, as he heard the vehicle pulling towards the gate, it just sounded like slavering zombies surrounded him.

'I need assistance here!' he bellowed, in the hope that the driver of what sounded like some old rust bucket had stopped for him. Instead, Randall was forced to listen to the gate creaking open and then closing once the vehicle had passed through.

'*I told you to stay still*,' the old man said, from in front of him this time. '*Don't give them any reason to think you're a threat.*'

'Do I look like a threat?' asked Randall.

'*This is private property*,' said the man. '*You're definitely a threat.*'

Randall gritted his teeth and grimaced to the sound of the vehicle trundling down the track.

'I know what you're hiding!' he yelled, struggling to contain himself despite the dogs. 'Harbouring a loose troll is a criminal offence!'

'*Wretch has gone to earth*,' the old man replied, silencing the Governor. The guy was freely admitting that his quarry was present, and yet remained coolly unconcerned about the consequences. '*He's back where he belongs*,' he added.

With his eyes still closed, Randall's mind raced to make sense of what he had just heard.

'There's a way underground here?' he asked, stunned by this revelation, and not unaware of the reputation this might earn him for making such a discovery.

'*Not any more*,' said the old man, who sounded like he was tiring of this conversation. '*Like any subterranean dweller, from foxes to rabbits and meerkats, we're quick to move on when danger closes in.*'

This time, Randall Shores snapped open his eyes.

'You're a troll!' he declared under his breath, which the patrol dogs didn't like one bit. 'Hey!' he said, no longer caring about his safety, and wheeled around. On finding nothing but the caravan, he continued to turn in vain for a sign of the figure who'd just been talking to him. 'Hello?'

The slurry underfoot sucked back on his feet as he moved. It took Randall a moment to realise that the silence that descended was down to the fact that the dogs had also melted away. Even so, he didn't move for another minute. Only when he had convinced himself that he was completely alone on an abandoned farm did he straighten his hat and begin to pick his way towards the gate. It was a long walk back to the site of the grounded chopper, but he figured that some kind of search for him had to be underway. He had hoped to return to Trasker with the troll and his two friends in his custody. Instead, as he steered towards the verge in a bid to wipe down his shoes, Randall Shores had already started to summon a story that would avoid him looking like a total fool.

31

Maurice had resigned himself to not knowing his home phone number. Still, as Candy steered the old flatbed truck through suburban streets with cars parked on either side, he had no trouble remembering where he lived. After hours on the road, and following his request for a brief detour before they reached the settlement, the boy was close to returning at last.

'It's been a long journey,' he said, having directed Candy into his street.

'And a testing one.' She exhaled deeply, and looked up into the rear-view mirror. 'How are you doing back there, Miss Shores?'

'Still cramped!' Bonita scowled back at her. 'Are we nearly there yet?'

They had come across the young lady on reaching the end of the farm track. Bonita Shores had heard the flatbed approach, stepped aside and then held out her thumb in the hope of a lift. Candy and Maurice had recognised her immediately. When Candy stopped for her Maurice hadn't protested. From what he'd seen of the girl, tagging behind her father in his attempt to track them down, she looked like just another innocent caught up in the crisis.

Within twenty minutes of their journey, both Candy and Maurice had revised their opinion. The hitchhiker in the back seat might've shared their desire to get away from the Governor, but in their view she was no more related to him than they were.

'*Troll*,' Maurice had mouthed at Candy, the second time Bonita opened up the window to let a sweet wrapper whip into the vehicle's slipstream.

'Please don't litter,' Candy had asked, only for the young lady in the back to respond with a sigh like she expected better from the former social worker.

'If you can't focus on the road then let me drive,' she had added, digging her knees into Maurice's seat as she sat back to fiddle with her phone. A moment later, she cursed out loud and tossed the device to one side. 'Are either of you carrying a charger?'

It came as a relief to Maurice when Candy pulled up outside his house, but not for the reasons he had imagined. He wound down the window, noting that his mother hadn't failed to tend to the window boxes in his absence. Since Wretch had sprung into his life, there had been times when he feared he might never see the place again. Now he was home, and yet strikingly the desire to rush for the front door was just not there. Yes, he had an urge to get out of the flatbed, if only to give his back a rest from Bonnie's persistent kicking. What stopped him was the thought that if he did so, things might just return to normal.

'As soon as I walk through that front door,' he said, turning to Candy, 'I'm pretty sure my parents will never let me leave the house again.'

'A prisoner in your own home, eh?' Candy relaxed into the head rest for a moment. 'I dare say the food will be nicer than it is in a young offender's unit.'

Maurice smiled, ignoring the loud tut from the back seat. He and Candy had put up with moaning and complaints all the way here. Several times, he'd had to ask Bonita to stop making obscene gestures at passing cars simply because she didn't like the look of the occupants. A reckless disregard for other road users was a known troll signifier, particularly among the younger generation, as Candy had whispered to him. Given that Bonita wasn't even behind the wheel spoke volumes to the pair. At any other time, Maurice would've been glad to get out of the car. Just then, with his mum and dad in mind, he found a pencil stub and an old invoice for fertiliser among the clutter in the door storage pocket. Without word, he began to scribble a note on the back.

'Can you please take me back to my place?' whined Bonita. 'If I don't get some juice for my phone soon I'm going to die of boredom. I have a string of video clips to upload and some party time with my boys to arrange.'

'Just give me a moment,' said Maurice, before climbing out.

The note, which he was careful not to push all the way through the letterbox in case the flap sprung back against the door, was brief but sincere. When he rejoined the others, Bonita openly wondered whether he'd just issued some kind of blackmail initiative. Maurice chose not to answer, and figured Candy knew what it contained. For he had addressed them from the heart, assuring his parents he was fine and asking them to be patient. Knowing his mum and dad, they would never agree to let him take something like a gap year. It was too dangerous, they would argue, and a distraction from his studies. In a way, all Maurice was proposing here was a chance to find himself over a shorter time span.

'I was thinking about leaving a note for Greg as well,' said Candy as they pulled up at the junction at the end of the street. 'Just to let him know I'm safe and well.'

'We don't have time,' Bonnie cut in, leaning between the front seats. 'My phone won't charge itself.'

'How would he respond?'

Maurice looked across at Candy, doing his level best to ignore their hitchhiker. A space appeared in the traffic. Candy eased the flatbed out on the road.

'Well, first he'd complain about my handwriting,' she said, and shifted up a gear. 'And for that reason I won't give him the satisfaction.'

Maurice chuckled, aware that Bonita was switching her attention between them.

'Does that mean you'll take me home now?'

Candy glanced in her mirror.

'We did just that for Wretch,' she told her. 'It's only fair we do the same for you.'

*

Governor Randall Shores had come to seriously regret returning to the settlement in the passenger seat of the squad car. Had Bonita not stomped off, no doubt she would've insisted on riding up front and that would've been just fine under the circumstances. Even with the light bar flashing, it was too late to swap seats with the guy in the back. Kyle Trasker didn't seem so cool any more, Randall noted with a wary glance over his shoulder at the crumpled-looking figure bent over a paper bag. His hair was no longer swept into a perfectly sculpted lick, but dangled over his brow like seaweed.

'Are we nearly there yet?' he croaked, before making yet another gurgling noise that caused the Governor to grimace.

Ever since the perimeter wall loomed into view on the horizon, Randall had hoped that Trasker would hold on to the contents of his gut.

'You should've stayed with the medics,' he told Trasker, noting him wipe his mouth on his shirt sleeve. 'Let me know if you need another bag.'

They'd both been taken out by a cloth soaked in chloroform, but only Trasker seemed to have experienced serious ill effects. Despite feeling the occasional fleck of vomit hit the back of his neck and ear, Randall hadn't suffered at all. It was a measure of iron in the blood, he decided. Just because the young man was packing a piece, he simply wasn't cut out to lead this operation.

Not that the hunt for Wretch and his co-conspirators had worked out so well, the Governor reminded himself bitterly.

'I'll have to file a report.' Trasker sounded thoroughly defeated. 'It isn't going to look good for either of us.'

'Speak for yourself,' said Randall, as the main gates to the settlement swung into view. 'We may have lost one troll, but there's a horde here that will pay the price.'

'You're going to punish them all?'

Randall smiled to himself. The guy from the government had no idea what they were dealing with here.

'A lesson must be learned,' he told Trasker as they waited for the barrier to lift. 'Once I'm finished, we could leave the gates wide open and not a single troll would dare to leave.'

As he spoke, the security guard rapped on the driver's window. The cop behind the wheel, who had escorted them back in silence without once breaking the speed limit, lowered the glass by a few centimetres.

'I need to see some badges,' said the guard, peering in at Randall and Trasker. 'This settlement is in lockdown. Access is restricted to police and personnel only.'

Governor Randall Shores recognised the man straight away. Jeffrey was his name, the silver-haired senior who looked like he'd played down his age to avoid retirement.

'Lift the barrier,' Randall asked him calmly. 'Or say goodbye to your pension.'

Jeffrey met his glowering stare with some poise and calmness.

'Just doing my job,' he reminded the Governor.

'It was me who ordered the lockdown,' Randall reminded him, bitterly aware that he had also drawn up the settlement's access protocol at times of heightened security. 'You really need to make an exception here.'

'Not without seeing your badge.' Jeffrey tapped the lanyard hanging around his neck. 'You do have a badge you can show me, don't you, sir?'

Randall Shores pressed his fingertips to one side of his jaw. The jolt served to distract him from all thoughts of stepping out of the car and shoving the stupid lanyard down the guard's throat. Had he not left his own badge on his desk inside the settlement compound, the Governor would've made him chew on that as well.

'Here,' said Trasker, and slipped him a government card from a fancy leather holder. 'At least let me in so I can lie down for a while.'

Jeffrey returned his attention to Randall, who quickly flashed his canteen pass.

'That'll get you lunch,' Jeffrey told him. 'I need ID from every one of you.'

Randall eyeballed the man for a moment, quietly knifing him in his imagination.

'For your information I had to skip lunch today,' he said, quietly but with some menace. 'I've been a bit busy trying to track down a troll.'

Jeffrey cast his eye towards the space beside Trasker.

'So, the little guy made it?' he said, as if to himself, and with what looked like a twinkle in his eye.

'Lift the damn barrier!'

Randall faced the front, inhaling and exhaling through his nostrils as the security guy finally submitted to his request. As the squad car headed towards the compound, the Governor was already planning the briefing he intended to issue to those journalists who would no doubt be awaiting his return. Just as soon as he'd picked up his painkillers from his office, and once he'd summoned his head of security to stand behind him so it looked like he meant business, he would outline the shock tactics he pledged to deploy in order to instil discipline across the settlement. Waiting for the cop to reverse into a narrow parking space, abandon the procedure and find a bigger gap, Randall made a note to collect his identity badge as well as the pills, just so there was no misunderstanding as to who laid down the law around here.

32

'Let me do the talking,' said Candy, as she pulled up in front of the security gate. 'Jeffrey and I go back a long way.'

'Is this sensible?' Beside her, Maurice dug his fingers into the edge of his seat, as if braced for a sudden stop.

'No, it isn't,' said Candy. 'But we're doing this for Wretch.'

'So, now the troll's more important than the Governor's daughter?' Bonita sat in the back with her arms tightly folded. 'This doesn't look like home to me. You guys are as lame as my dad.'

Candy lowered the window, well aware that Jeffrey had already scoped out the schoolboy.

'Do you trust me?' she asked quickly, and prayed the senior security guard wouldn't reach for his walkie-talkie. 'If it had been anyone but you, I would've turned around and driven off,' she added.

'So, this is the kid who helped the troll break free?' Jeffrey looked across and nodded. 'Son, you're in a lot of trouble.'

'Things couldn't get any worse for us,' said Candy before Maurice had a chance to answer.

'Things are about to get *really* bad in there.' Jeffrey gestured towards the towering perimeter wall. 'The Governor just returned.'

'Daddy is back?' Bonita sighed and cursed to herself. 'I'd better stay out of his way.'

'That goes for all of us,' said Candy, who continued to face Jeffrey. 'You have to believe we're not the bad guys here.'

'I think I just learned that for myself.' Jeffrey stood back, adjusting his belt with the handcuffs attached. 'Mr Shores was steaming mad. Kind of rude with it.'

'Please,' added Candy, which drew a slow smile from the guard.

'You know I've probably lost my job already,' he told her. 'How can I turn you away since you asked so nicely?'

Watching Jeffrey return to the booth, Candy swapped a grin with Maurice.

'Did you hear that?' he said to Bonita, just as the barrier began to rise. 'Good manners go a long way.'

*

With his identity lanyard slung around his neck at last, and several painkillers dissolving in his stomach, Governor Randall Shores drew breath to make his address.

'We are no longer in the business of settlement security,' he began, with one eye on the journalists hovering at the back of the crowded room. Randall faced a full house, having ordered every single guard to attend or face instant dismissal. 'With a troll on the loose, no doubt many others will be looking at the perimeter wall with a view to joining him. That makes us *pest* controllers, my friends. And it falls to us to halt this outbreak now.' For dramatic effect, Randall swapped his attention from one flank to the other. He was glad to have his security chief alongside him, despite the man's reservations at what he had to say. That Kyle Trasker had flopped into a plastic chair in the corner only increased his sense of authority over the situation. Once the guy had stopped spinning out, he could write all he wanted in his report. Only Randall had refused to be defeated by a dirty little low life and his friend with the chloroform cloth. Lifting his chin, he focused on his audience once more. 'It is time to reclaim the streets,' he told them, in an attempt to sound as presidential as possible, 'and I will be leading the charge.'

A hand went up towards the back.

'Sir, since the kidnapping and the escape, the trolls have been kind of subdued.'

'The calm before the storm.'

Randall looked around as if hoping to draw some sense that his staff were looking to him for leadership. Instead, he faced a sea of solemn faces. 'We head out in a show of strength,' he continued, hardening his voice. 'Any troll who squares up to us will find themselves crushed like a bug beneath our boot heels, and we will not rest until every last low life has remembered why they're here!' Governor Shores delivered his final point like an orchestra conductor. It was only when he fell silent, to the flash from a photographer's camera, that he realised he had finished with an unfortunate upswing of one outstretched arm. Hurriedly, Randall stood back and glanced across at his chief of security in the hope that he would wrap things up. All of a sudden, the guy looked as if he'd developed an allergy to his uniform.

'You heard the boss,' he said after a moment, having cleared his throat several times. 'Let's go to work.'

After everything he had been through, Maurice was determined not to be beaten by a simple walk. That the route took him through the streets towards the place where he had been snatched from a school coach didn't make it easy.

'It's too quiet,' he whispered to Candy, looking around at the buildings on each side. 'We've barely seen any sign of life since we got here, and yet I get this feeling everyone is watching us.'

On the school trip, Maurice remembered every corner had been teeming with trolls. Now, they passed abandoned plastic chairs around the charred remains of fires that had once been burned for warmth. From the next street, a flock of pigeons took wing, as if something had disturbed then. Shadows crept across their path, stretching out at the tail end of a long day on the road for Maurice, Candy and the hitchhiker he was beginning to wish they had left back on the farm track.

'Hey, maybe there's been a viral outbreak!' Bonita picked up the pace as she said this, moving ahead and then switching around to address them. 'Guys, we could be heading into a zombie troll *apocalypse*!' For once, Maurice thought, she seemed all fired up with enthusiasm, rather than bored and abrupt, only for the light to leave her expression with a frown. 'OK, so how am I going to survive this without power in my phone?'

In response, Maurice reached for the hood of the top that Wretch had given him, and pulled it low over his brow. As soon as he did so, he understood why the little troll had wanted him to wear it. Returning to the settlement was suicidal in his view. He had barely escaped from the place with his life. Coming back here just seemed crazy, but with his face obscured,

307

Maurice at least felt some sense of comfort. Walking alongside him, Candy toyed with the staff pass around her neck as if it was a protective amulet.

'It's only natural to be nervous,' she said.

'Bonnie doesn't seem bothered.' Maurice wished the girl would stop rattling the shutters of every makeshift store they passed as if hoping to find one unlocked.

'Maybe that's because she's not an outsider,' whispered Candy.

Maurice grinned to himself, and then pulled up with a sigh as Bonita noisily tested another grill.

'Please stop that,' he hissed. 'The trolls won't be happy if they think you're here to shoplift.'

'What trolls?' Bonita threw out her arms, her voice raised horribly loudly. 'Everyone knows low lives are lazy. Maybe they just haven't got out of bed yet.'

It was a thought that Maurice wished could be true as they ventured deeper into the settlement. Things hadn't been right ever since they'd left the flatbed outside the perimeter fence. Creeping through a side entrance to the compound, to find the desks and guard stations empty, the muffled speech Maurice had heard made him think every last member of staff must have gathered to hear some kind of briefing. It meant they had been free to slip through the corridors. Even so, with every step it had felt like he was leaving his confidence behind. The cracks in his composure had spread even further once Candy used her pass to swipe open the gate into the settlement suburbs. Maurice had expected some attention, but instead the first trolls they encountered took one look at the visitors and melted away.

*

From there on out, as they had progressed through empty thoroughfares and squares, Maurice couldn't shake the thought that somehow *he* was the threat. By the time the roads had opened into broad avenues, with civic buildings on each side, he was convinced that every last resident was aware of their presence. It was only as they passed the pillars of the old theatre just then that Maurice picked up on some movement. It came from behind the broken window of the box office, as if someone had seen them and pulled back into the gloom. He looked up with a start, but saw no sign of life.

'I feel like the troublemaker at school who's on a final warning,' he whispered. 'Nobody wants to be seen with us.'

'Are we nearly there yet?'

Maurice turned to see that Bonita had stopped dead. She glared at him, her arms hanging loose like she'd lost the will to stand straight.

'You probably shouldn't fall behind,' he told her. 'It isn't safe.'

Bonita reacted like he'd cracked a joke.

'If a troll hits on me they'll be sorry,' she said. 'Just like you'll be sorry when my old man finds out you're here.'

With Candy waiting up ahead and unwilling to hang around, Maurice jogged back and took Bonita by the wrist.

'I feel like we're responsible for you now,' he hissed. 'I'd be in more trouble with your dad if something bad happened.'

'Something bad happened when you failed to drop me off at home.' Bonita Shores stood firm with her mouth drawn tight. 'I don't belong in this *zoo*!'

In no mood to suggest otherwise, and well aware of further movement in the shadows between buildings, Maurice tightened his grip and tugged the girl onwards. Bonita protested loudly, but fell into step on spotting several hunched figures emerge from a passage across the avenue. For the first time, the trolls didn't retreat on seeing them. Instead, joined by others from behind, they spread out into the low light with their gaze fixed in particular on the boy. Maurice picked up the pace, just as another appeared from a doorway opposite. This one tipped back the bill of his baseball cap and grinned. Immediately, Maurice felt as if the dwindling sun was taking any last sense of security with it. He glanced over his shoulder, drawn by the sound of a tin can rolling. Some distance behind them, trolls were now fanning into the open. They sauntered out with little urgency but a shared focus, as if Maurice and his friends had nowhere to hide.

'Unless we're nearly there for real,' he said, catching up with Candy and hurrying onwards with Bonita in tow, 'then we're dead.'

'We stood by Wretch all the way,' Candy said to remind him, though the anxiety in her voice spoke volumes. 'We can only hope he does the same for us.'

33

Governor Randall Shores was first through the gate into the settlement suburbs. From his steel-capped boots to the stab jacket and helmet, he was ready for action, as were the security squads and the journalists who filed onto the streets behind him in similar attire. No doubt the media would witness some combative scenes, but if that's what it took to assert authority over the trolls then the nation would only be grateful for his leadership. At the same time, Randall quietly reminded himself not to be within sight of a camera when he personally deployed his baton. Tipping his chin towards the buildings far off in the central district, he inhaled long and hard, as if to assess the threat level.

'It's quiet,' observed Kyle Trasker, which served to disrupt Randall's focus.

'Shouldn't you be in the medical bay?' he asked irritably. 'Or doing your homework?'

'I need the fresh air.' Kyle continued to break sweat, despite looking like his core body temperature was several degrees below normal. 'Anyway, before I can write my report,' he added pointedly, 'I want to be sure that the loss of one settlement resident won't lead to another.'

'Wretch was the first and last.' The Governor felt a renewed sense of power now he was back on familiar ground. With his show of strength assembled, and the media primed to record the moment, he set off at a stride. 'Right now, I should imagine that miserable low life will be crouched in some cramped and forsaken tunnel wondering what possessed him to leave this place behind.' Kyle Trasker broke into a trot to keep up. Randall noted him looking around at the neglected, tumbledown buildings, and waited in vain for him to agree. 'If you can find some chin then you ought to buckle up that strap,' he suggested, and fanned one hand at the helmet on his head. 'This could get ugly.'

The dull patter of dozens of boots marked the next few minutes of their march towards the centre of the settlement. Randall scanned ahead throughout, looking for any sign of troll activity.

'It's like everyone left,' observed Trasker, who had hauled down the knot of his tie.

'Oh, they're here alright.' Randall smiled to himself at the personal schooling the government guy was about to receive. 'You see that crisp packet?' he drew Trasker's attention to the bag in the breeze as it skittered the last of its contents across their path. 'Freshly dropped,' he said, and promptly pointed to a couple of screwed-up gum stick wrappers. 'These litter louts can't help themselves!'

Trasker nodded, seemingly impressed, and then turned as if searching for something.

'Do you provide bins on these streets?'

Randall resisted the urge to ask the man if he'd like to oversee the settlement and its unruly inhabitants. Instead, with the painkillers doing little for his molars, he called out for his security chief to join him.

'What's with the ghost town?' he asked under his breath. 'This whole show is useless without some low lives to scare.'

'Sir, I have to consider the safety of my staff here. We should return to the compound and gather intelligence before taking them deeper.'

The guy was carrying a rifle, just like every squad member. Each weapon was locked and loaded with a clip of rubber bullets guaranteed to sting a troll into submission. Randall had seen the marks they could leave, and it wasn't pretty. Much like his methods when he'd been forced to use a belt strap on the worst offending low lives, Randall had instructed his team to strike at the torso. With the press among them, he was well aware that any visible bruising wouldn't play well with the public. Before leaving the briefing room, he'd even made a big song and dance about not drawing weapons unless lives depended on it. That kind of caution would cover him, he had decided, in case it all kicked off.

'Son,' said Randall just then, despite being chest high to the former prison warden, 'leave the intelligence to me. You're the brawn in this operation, and that means following my orders. Is that clear?'

'My vote is to return to base,' said Kyle Trasker.

With his root canals flowing with what felt like molten lava, Governor Randall Shores spun around to glare at Trasker.

'If you want to run away then go ahead,' he added. 'I am king of these streets. 'Nobody orders me around. *Nobody!*'

Stunned silence followed Randall's outburst, just as his mobile phone sounded into life. He didn't need to check the screen to see who was calling. Nor did he have to question who had fiddled with his ringtones and assigned his wife's number with the hee haw of a donkey.

When Bonita finally came back to the family fold, he told himself, she would learn the value of respect.

'What have you got?' he asked on taking the call, hoping to make out that it was coming from a command centre and not his kitchen at home. 'She threw a strop and took off,' he said in response, and tried in vain to turn away from the sea of faces as his other half pressed him about their daughter's whereabouts. 'I was a little stuck at the time, *surrounded by killer dogs*!' Flecks of spittle smacked against the mouthpiece of his phone as the Governor attempted to restrain his temper. When his wife failed to respond, clearly stung by his outburst, Randall grimaced and started again. 'Bonbon will be fine,' he promised her. 'Our daughter's just going through a testing phase right now, but it's not in her nature to get into serious trouble. Just you wait and see.'

Oblivious to the distant cries that rose up from the centre of the settlement just then, Governor Randall Shores killed the call before his wife could challenge him. He really needed to establish some ground rules about ringing him during working hours. It was all about boundaries. He just hoped that despite her occasional diversions on the road to adulthood, Bonita also understood where to draw the line.

'*Sir?*'

'What now?'

314

Randall turned to face his chief of security, stepping back a pace at the same time in case this was a warning that Trasker was about to be sick again. As he did so, the mounting cries in the background caught Randall's attention. It sounded like an army on the warpath, he thought, and bristled on seeing that his guy had turned as pale as the man from the government.

'Something's happening,' he told Randall, as the teams behind him shuffled nervously on the spot. 'A block or two away at most.'

Randall cocked his head. He then took a sharp intake of breath as a lone female voice rose above the din and curdled the air with cursing. With his face set in shock, Bonita Shores' father faced Kyle Trasker, as if seeking permission from him to blink.

'She's here,' he said in all but a whisper.

*

The park, when Candy Lau hurried through the gates, seemed an oddly tranquil place to be under the circumstances. The late sun spread across the scrubby patches of grass and uneven pathways, dragging shadows out of bushes and benches. Panting hard, just like her two companions, she came to a standstill in the middle and wished they had arrived inside a protective bubble.

'They're everywhere!' said Maurice, turning on the spot as countless trolls emerged from the surrounding avenues and buildings to press against the railings. One in particular caught his attention just then. He was the first to climb over the top, and stood out from the others on account of the bandage wrapped around his head. It was the shape of his skull that struck Candy, for it looked as if it had been squeezed, though the way the troll glowered across the grass at Maurice was all that mattered just then. In response, the boy dropped his hood away, abandoning any hope of remaining incognito, and sighed to himself. 'If they take me,' he said quietly, 'maybe that means they'll spare you.'

'No way!' Candy grasped him by the shoulder. 'We agreed to come here together.'

'Well, I didn't!' Bonita stepped forward, whistling at the troll with the bandage as if he was a dog who needed bringing to heel. 'Oi, Migraine! Can you show me the way out of this dump?'

'His name is Long Skull,' said Maurice. 'At least, that's how I knew him when he snatched me from the coach.'

Candy snapped her attention from the boy back to the troll. He was still focused on Maurice, with his head dipped like a bull. Slowly, one side of his mouth curled upwards. It could've been a smile. It might've been a snarl. Either way, she didn't like it one bit.

'Tell your girlfriend to shut up,' he growled, with a cursory nod towards Bonita.

'Girlfriend?' Bonita pressed a hand to her chest as if she'd just been gravely wounded. 'Do I look like someone who dates a virgin?'

'Thanks,' muttered Maurice. 'Maybe now is not the time to go into this?'

In response, Long Skull took a step forward and threw out his hands.

'So, you came back?' he said, addressing the boy like an old friend. Behind him, several trolls began climbing over the railings. Maurice recognised some from the kidnap gang, including the pair who looked like they might chew gum in their sleep. 'Unfinished business, eh?'

'This has nothing to do with you.' Maurice shifted from one foot to the other. 'We're here for Wretch.'

'Wretch?' Long Skull repeated the name out loud as if trying it out for size. The trolls beside him glanced at one another in amusement. 'Do you have any idea what he's done for us?'

'He has a good heart.' Candy spoke up on such an impulse that it came as a surprise to find attention turn to her. 'You all do,' she went on, addressing not just the troll with the dressing around his head but the masses now surrounding them.

'You're the social worker, right?' Long Skull sounded scornful.

'I tried to bring out the best in him.'

'By encouraging him to think for himself?' All of a sudden, Candy felt deeply intimidated by the violence present in the troll's voice. 'We didn't kidnap Maurice for fun,' he continued. 'We did it because there was no other way to make ourselves heard! This place is hell on earth, but nobody listens to a troll. Not until they snatch a schoolboy off the streets. Then it's time to talk. Only we didn't get that far because Wretch helped him to escape!'

'We helped each other.' Maurice took a step forward, holding his head high before Long Skull. 'I'm sorry you got hurt, but I tried to help you, too.'

Long Skull considered the boy, simmering for a moment. Then, much to Candy's surprise as well as Maurice's, he stepped towards him with his hand outstretched.

'I'm grateful for what you did,' he said, and waited for Maurice to accept the gesture. Candy watched him grasp the troll's hand. Despite everything, she felt her heart swell, and then contract with a sharp intake of breath when Long Skull yanked the boy towards him and brought his great brow into the bridge of his nose. At once a roar went up around them, which drowned out her appeal to Maurice as he crumpled. Long Skull took a step away, drawing his foot back to strike, and then froze when a figure rushed towards him and climbed into his face.

'Leave him alone!' cried Bonita, and shoved the troll backwards with both hands and a barrage of bad language. 'I once did nothing when someone took a beating, and it haunted me. I'll not make the same mistake again!'

'Stay out of this.' Long Skull's glare slowly turned to a sneer. 'Or there'll be tears.'

'You don't want to mess with Bonnie,' warned Candy. 'Believe me when I say she can handle herself.'

On the ground, his upper lip glistening with blood, Maurice rolled onto his back and groaned.

'Don't milk it,' Bonnie told the boy, glancing down briefly. 'He didn't hit you that hard.'

Long Skull turned his attention to Candy.

'You have one chance to explain why you've come back,' he growled. 'Then I'll decide on the right thing to do.'

Aware that yet more trolls were making their way over the railings and through the gates to the park, far outnumbering them now, Candy stepped back so she could be heard by them all.

'Do you want the truth?' she asked out loud. 'The truth is we're here for Wretch and those who care for him. We didn't ask questions.'

'Why not?' asked Long Skull, playing to those behind him as Maurice clambered to his feet. 'You can't trust a troll.'

'Yes, we can.' Candy stepped forward, commanding his attention. At the same time, she extended her hand. 'Without trust and understanding, what hope do we have of getting along?'

'Oh, please!' Bonita rolled her eyes. 'Spare us the low life love-in.'

'Candy, be careful.' Maurice spoke up through the sleeve of his hoodie, which he had used to staunch the flow of blood. 'Take it from me, it's going to leave you with a headache if you're wrong about him.'

'It's the only way forward,' said Candy, without taking her eyes off the figure in front of her.

As she awaited Long Skull's response, it seemed as if his confidence began to waver. He glanced at her hand, then to those looking on from behind as if seeking support, before flicking his gaze back to hers. Then, with a pained sigh, he reached out and accepted her handshake. She sensed him attempt to let go, but with their hands wrapped she held firm and squeezed. His eyes pinched in shock and surprise, and then relaxed as he abandoned any last sense of menace.

'This doesn't mean I trust you,' he told her. 'Yet.'

For the first time since they had returned to the settlement, Candy breathed in without any sense of tension or fear. Despite the air of hostility that had closed in on them with the trolls, it genuinely felt as if she could count on one who carried some influence.

'We promised to see Wretch home safely,' she told Long Skull. 'We didn't let him down.'

319

As she spoke, a rumble like distant thunder drew her attention. Others looked around with her as the sound began to build. At first it appeared to be coming from behind the buildings on one side of the park, only to spread around to the other side. By the time Candy realised she was listening to footfalls, the first wave of figures in full riot gear thundered into view.

Long Skull snapped his attention back to Candy.

'You set us up!'

'This has nothing to do with us.' She raised her hands, facing Maurice for support.

'You have to believe her,' he said, as many of the trolls around them began to scatter. 'Wretch swore he would watch my back.'

'So, where is he?'

Long Skull looked set to run. He spun around, but even Candy could see that the avenues on either side of the park were rapidly filling with figures brandishing shields and batons.

'Daddy?' This was Bonita. With her gaze fixed on a figure among the security detail who had just swept around the corner, she groaned like this was a party and he'd shown up early to collect her. 'Why do you always have to spoil *everything*?'

A hand took Candy's elbow just then.

'We need to get out of here,' said Maurice. 'Right now!'

By now, with trolls rushing to melt away and the security squads closing in, an air of chaos presided over the square. Such was the volume of shouting and screaming that it took Candy a moment to register that the rumbling noise underneath it all had turned to a tremor. One she could feel beneath her feet. Candy looked down, as did Long Skull, who stepped back smartly when a patch of scrub between them suddenly sank away. Before the former social worker could react, the troll threw himself upon her. She gasped as he dragged her off balance, just as the tremor turned to a quake. With shrieks and cries amid the thunderous rumble, the ground where they'd been standing just fell away. In desperation, sensing herself begin to slide with it, Candy pushed her heels into the avalanche of soil.

'Help!' she cried out, clawing in vain at the earth. 'Help me!'

'*Hold on!*'

She heard Maurice under the roar of falling bedrock, bushes and benches, and called his name as a hand grasped her wrist. Then another grabbed her collar at the moment that her feet lost all purchase. The noise by now was intense, as if the world was draining in on itself. And then it faded. Just dwindled with the sound of tumbling debris. A moment later, after Maurice had hauled her onto firmer ground, and with Bonita standing over them looking dumbstruck, Candy turned to find herself at the edge of a vast sinkhole. As the dust settled, she looked up and realised it had practically swallowed the park.

'Way to spoil a good top,' said Bonita, brushing her clothing.

An eerie silence had settled over the settlement, broken only by the tentative approach of trolls and security personnel. As they came close to the edge, and Candy climbed to her feet, she noticed movement in the gloom that pooled inside the massive crater. Long Skull appeared alongside her, having spotted the same thing.

'Now that's an entrance,' he cooed, and lit up with a smile as the first figures scrambled up the sloping walls.

34

Like so many people, Governor Randall Shores had often been inconvenienced by underground troll activity. Many times, sitting in traffic jams because the road ahead had caved in, he had punched his car horn and cursed their very existence, but this was a new experience. Standing at the gates to the park, rooted to the spot, he had watched in astonishment as the biggest sinkhole ever opened up before him.

'Everybody stay calm!' he yelled when the earth finally stopped behaving like a failed soufflé. Glancing around, just as the security squad behind him retreated by several steps, he sensed his indignation mount. 'Stay calm and stand your ground!'

Beside him, Randall's security chief struggled to take in the unfolding scene. If Kyle Trasker had regained some colour on the sortie into the settlement, it was rapidly draining away. Without taking his eyes off the chasm that had swallowed the park, he grabbed his mobile from his pocket.

'Let me summon the chopper to get us out of here!' he said, before seemingly freezing. Then, with a blink, having apparently reminded himself that the helicopter was grounded, he looked helplessly at Randall.

'Son,' said the man who had instructed his people to be

prepared, 'put your fancy phone away, forget your toys and be ready to fight like a man.'

'This fight is too big for us.' The security guy wasn't even looking at the Governor when he said this. Randall followed his line of sight, turning on the spot to face the ruins of the park once more. 'Sir, this is serious.'

Randall barely registered the man. Through the settling dust and debris, his attention locked on to the first wave of figures to scuttle out of the sinkhole. They arrived in the open air as if on a mission, squaring up to his security squads and urging the scattering trolls to join them. Most looked like low lives to his eye. Randall could smell trouble, and this mob reeked. Even so, one or two stood out from the others. Despite contributing to what was shaping up to sound like a battle cry, they seemed more at ease with the natural light, and altogether more *human*.

'Who is responsible for this?' he asked, stepping back smartly as a clutch of invaders barrelled over the crater rim. As they charged by, hell bent on confrontation, it seemed, Randall's focus fell upon an individual that caused his eyes to widen. On the far side of the giant sinkhole, a familiar little low life was close to reaching the ridge of the crater. The Governor recognised him in a heartbeat, having once been pushed into such a rage by the runt that his face was now imprinted on his memory. Compared to those around him who emerged into the late sun, Wretch seemed to move in slow motion. It was as if he'd already found what he was looking for. Randall lifted his attention to a figure who approached the edge of the sinkhole just then. With those glasses, the hoodie was fooling nobody. The kid was obviously wearing a school uniform underneath as well. It would've earned him an instant detention back in the Governor's day, but that was a minor distraction to the fact that Randall knew that at last he had a visual on his quarry.

It had to be Maurice, the kid he held responsible for the break out, and who was undeniably involved in all this.

'You,' the Governor growled to himself, and closed his hand around the riot stick he had slotted into his duty belt before leaving the compound, 'will *pay!*'

Standing quite still amid the growing pandemonium, he watched Maurice help Wretch to his feet. Both grinned broadly, exchanging a fist bump as they faced one another. Seeing this, after everything he had been through in a bid to hunt them down, Randall drew the stick from his belt and ordered some backup to follow him.

*

Every time, Maurice thought to himself, no matter what was kicking off, the damn troll found something to snigger about.

'What now?' he asked, as Wretch looked him up and down with an air of barely restrained amusement. Maurice noted how his knees, palms and fingernails were covered in mud from his travels underground.

'The hoodie suits you,' he told the boy. 'You don't look like such a victim.'

'Thanks.' Maurice gestured at the sinkhole. 'You guys move fast.'

As he addressed the troll, he spotted Pearly Gates Pete make his way up the bank of earth in front of the mayor's building, helped by the formidable figure of the troll trucker with the belly, plaits and the bandit moustache. Still more underground dwellers clawed their way up the steep, unstable slope. When one slipped and sank back down, Candy rushed to the edge to offer her hand, while Bonita simply turned in circles with an air of elation at the bedlam that had broken out around her. By now, those who surfaced first had forced the security teams into a slight retreat. Others had caught up with pockets of settlement trolls and were engaged in some kind of urgent appeal. In the chaos it was impossible for Maurice to hear properly, but whatever they said served to stop anyone from melting away. He drew breath to ask Wretch for an explanation, only to find him staring bug eyed at the figure with the bandaged head.

The one with his hand around the little troll's throat.

'You betrayed me,' snarled Long Skull, as Wretch's toes left the ground.

'He saved you!' Maurice grabbed at the assailant's arms only to be shoved away with considerable force. 'All this,' he begged him. 'It isn't some random tunnel collapse. They're here to get you out because of Wretch!'

Long Skull snapped his gaze towards Maurice, his eyes reduced to slits.

'Talk to me,' he grunted.

'There's nothing more to say.' Maurice threw out his hand, urging him to register what was going on around them. 'You need to seize this moment before it's too late!'

Slowly, Long Skull looked around, lowering the little troll back onto his feet as if he no longer mattered. When he released his grip, Wretch fell to his knees, gasping for breath.

'We can leave?' the troll asked Maurice, the menace gone from his voice.

The boy nodded.

'Go,' he said, with one eye on the security detail now holding their ground on a street corner. '*Now!*'

Long Skull took in his surroundings one more time. A smell of burning had crept into the air. He looked towards the mayoral building, where flames now flickered from a ground-floor window. Then, with a victorious grin, he threw his head back and cried out to the skies. The roar turned heads, rising above the din. It was an expression of such elemental joy that all Maurice could do was stand aside as the troll then turned and threw himself into the abyss with his arms spread wide. It was the kind of swallow dive that Maurice would've never dared perform from the side of a pool, let alone into a sinkhole with no bottom in sight, but he figured the troll was on familiar ground. When others flocked to follow, the boy began to smile. It was as if the departure of one figurehead had served as a trigger for everyone else. He glanced at Wretch. Through the exodus, which quickly became a blur, he watched the little troll rise to his feet and relish the moment.

'We did it,' Wretch declared, his voice hoarse from the assault. 'We only went and did it!'

'You *started* it,' said Maurice, as if to correct him. 'It was me who got you this far.'

Wretch furrowed his brow for a moment, and then grinned.

'Your kind reckon you're so smart, but it took a troll to make this happen!'

Maurice chuckled to himself, the settlement residents still pouring towards the sinkhole, and told Wretch they should consider it a joint success. When Wretch responded with a gasp, it took a moment for Maurice to register the shadow falling

326

over him from behind. He spun around, and then promptly stumbled backwards as the little troll hauled him clear from the arc of a riot stick. On his back, Maurice looked up in horror at Governor Randall Shores as he prepared to strike.

'You've made me very angry!' yelled Randall. 'Did Wretch not warn you what happens when I'm angry?'

All Maurice could do was twist to one side, gasping in shock as the stick came down where his head had been. As he braced himself for a second assault, a figure appeared out of nowhere and threw herself on the man.

'Don't you dare!' yelled Bonita, and snatched the stick from her father's grasp. Before he could respond, she braced herself to hit him with it. 'There's no way you're going to get away with this again!'

'Bonbon –'

'Don't even go there!' she screamed, clutching the stick as if braced to knock a ball into the bleachers. 'I'm not five years old any more, Daddy. You have to learn to treat people properly, and not just the trolls,' she added, with a glance at Maurice. 'Even no-marks like him deserve respect.'

Randall seemed taken aback, but only for a second. With a nod at the presence looming behind Bonita, Maurice watched helplessly as the bald-headed security guy plucked the riot stick from her grasp.

'Take them out,' Governor Shores instructed the man, with a dismissive gesture towards Maurice and the little troll. 'It's a shame the only bullets we have are rubber.'

The security guy held the stick aloft, away from Bonita as she fought to grab it, but didn't act as directed.

'Sir, physical violence won't resolve this.'

'Take them *out*!'

Maurice watched the Governor attempt to snatch the baton, as if to seize the lead, only for the beefy, bald guy to turn on him.

'Now, that's *enough*!' he snapped at Randall, in a way that sounded like it had been a long time coming.

'He beats them,' said Bonita, glaring balefully at her father. 'Badly. Behind closed doors.'

Maurice hauled himself back a little, sensing trouble.

'Is that true?' asked the security guy.

This time, it was Wretch who responded. He stepped up beside Maurice and hoisted his shirt to show the man his ribs. From where the boy was standing, the welts that striped his lower back looked even worse.

'He was asking for it!' The Governor registered his protest in a voice tight with panic. 'Someone has to set an example around here.'

By now, the numbers in the avenues surrounding the sinkhole had begun to thin. Trolls continued to rush by the gathering, hurling themselves into the abyss, while the fire inside the mayoral building had found teeth. Maurice attempted to look invisible when the suit crossed to join them. Having earlier assaulted him with a rag soaked in chloroform, he felt sure he wasn't about to receive a congratulatory clap on the back. Before he could look to his feet, however, the guy flashed the kind of identity badge that left him thinking he was about to be read his rights.

'Kyle Trasker from the Social Order Programme.' He addressed Maurice with his eyes fixed on the Governor.

Although Wretch hurried to cover his scars, the boy was in no doubt that the man had just witnessed their exchange. Then Maurice found himself the subject of Trasker's full attention, and shrunk inside his hoodie. 'You've been causing me some problems.'

Just then, after everything they had been through, as he stood in the eye of a storm of anarchy, Maurice experienced a sense of profound resignation. The feeling didn't weigh heavily on his shoulders, however. If anything, it came as a release.

'I won't give you any trouble,' he said.

Hanging his head, Maurice turned his wrists outwards.

If Kyle Trasker was carrying cuffs, he made no attempt to reach for them. Instead, he waited for Maurice to look up at him before speaking.

'Do you know how much paperwork your exploits have created?' Trasker invited the boy to take in his surroundings, and then allowed a moment for him to digest what he was hinting at here. 'Maurice, if I take you into custody I'm looking at even more forms to fill. Right now I'm feeling sick to my core, no thanks to you. Pushing pens is the last thing I want to do.'

'*What?*' Governor Randall Shores had turned so red in the face it looked like something had gone awry with his internal thermostat. 'So a little headache is stopping you from carrying out your duties? That's the trouble with graduates like you. One sniffle and you're signed off sick for a month! Under my watch, the perpetrators would be severely punished.'

'Your watch,' said Trasker with a sigh, as if he'd just been reminded of the work ahead of him, 'will form a large part of my report.'

'Fine!' Incandescent now, the Governor turned to his security chief, slapping the gorilla in the groin with the back of his hand to momentarily disable him. 'If nobody wants to detain them I'll do it myself!!'

Despite the winding, which would've floored Maurice, the security guy still found the presence to grab Randall by the wrist as he attempted to reclaim the riot stick. Then, in a manoeuvre that showed some skill in restraint procedures, the man twisted Randall's arm until he howled.

'Sir, you need to calm down.'

In response, Governor Shores cursed and fought to wriggle free, only for the security guy to tighten his grip.

'Take a breath,' the government suit advised him. 'It's a basic principle of anger management. I learned that in my training year,' he added with a barely concealed smile, and then appeared to consider a further point. 'You know, a refresher course might be useful to you, in fact. No doubt you'll have plenty of opportunity to embrace that in jail.'

Wild-eyed and snarling, Governor Randall Shores spat squarely in Trasker's face.

'Are you going to let these animals run wild?' he bellowed. 'Look around you, man!'

Without even a glance at the ongoing skirmishes, Kyle Trasker unfolded a handkerchief from his pocket. From where Maurice was standing, it looked as if it had been ironed.

'It's a little too late to shut the cage door,' said Trasker, sounding strikingly calm as he wiped himself down. Then he nodded at the security guy, who responded by rotating Randall's forearm by a further degree. 'Tell your teams to hold their fire and retreat when safe. Without doubt, we're going to have to take a long, hard look at our handling of this whole situation, but at least I can say we've captured the primary troublemaker.'

It was Wretch who gasped at this. With his eyes fixed on Trasker, he appeared to have some trouble exhaling. Maurice glanced across at him, hoping the little troll would remember his manners. He flexed his eyebrows in a bid to prompt him, which simply caused Wretch to adopt a pleading expression.

'For crying out loud!' Exasperated at the troll, Maurice turned to address Trasker. 'Sir, my friend here would like to say thanks. Only he has a little difficulty with that word, so I'm speaking on his behalf. And can I just add how sorry I am for all the trouble we've caused.'

'Maurice!' This was Candy, who clasped him by the shoulder and stepped forward to take over. 'He has no further comment,' she said. 'Not without a lawyer present.'

Kyle Trasker nodded, appreciating her position and possibly also admiring it, if Maurice had read him correctly. Picking up on the apparent closure between the pair, Governor Randall Shores exploded.

'You're worse than the low lives!' he yelled at Trasker, fighting in vain to free himself from his security chief. 'They need putting down, frankly, and so do you!'

'What a fine example you're setting,' said Candy.

Kyle Trasker smiled despite himself, and then stepped back smartly when a snarling, scowling young lady shouldered him out of the way and squared up to her father.

'When will you stop humiliating me?' Bonita demanded to know, and promptly kicked Randall in the shin. 'All these trolls have done here is show that they have feelings! I'm not surprised they're rising up after the *appalling* way you've treated them!'

'They had everything they needed here! It's just they chose to trash it!'

'Because you deprived them of the one thing they needed more than anything else!' Candy Lau sounded surprised by the sound of her own voice. Maurice watched her take a breath, and then look around on registering that everyone was facing her. 'All they really wanted,' she said, quieter now, 'was hope.'

For a moment, with his arm still locked behind him, Randall simply stared at her. Slowly, he switched his attention to everyone else in turn. When he reached Bonita, the fight had left him.

'How can you stand by and let them do this to me?' he asked, his voice ragged now. 'My own flesh and blood?'

Maurice exchanged a glance with Candy. Just one look told him she was thinking exactly the same thing.

'There's something you should know,' he said, and cleared his throat. 'Governor, it seems Bonita isn't your daughter.'

'Let's just say she has more in common with Wretch than she does with you.' This time, Candy spoke with some confidence. 'Even so, she still deserves your respect.'

Governor Randall Shores absorbed her words with widening eyes, while Bonita simply lost all control of her jaw hinges.

'*What?*' she asked, sounding shocked and strained. 'Are you insane?'

Randall blinked and appeared to surface from his thoughts. Then he raised his eyes to the sky and thanked some greater presence.

'That explains everything,' he declared, as if a huge weight had just left his shoulders. 'At least some good will come from this!'

'Daddy!' Bonita's mouth began to tighten. 'You can't just walk away from me!'

'Why not?' snarled Randall. 'It all makes sense to me now. Just like those two boys you've been so desperate to impress lately.'

'Benny and Ryan?' Bonita's lower lip had begun to tremble. 'No way.'

'The test results came in,' he spat back at her. 'In view of what your friends have just shared, no doubt you'll prove positive, too. It's obvious, in fact, after everything you've put me through. You're a troll. A dirty low life!'

Bonita screamed at the accusation, as if it had just stung her, and then drew breath to wail.

'*She's not a troll.*'

Maurice, along with everyone else, turned to Wretch. Even Bonita fell silent. Wretch looked around, surprised by the attention.

'How can you say that?' asked Maurice, before addressing him under his breath. 'Look at her! The girl's a nightmare.'

'You must be mistaken,' said Randall, making no attempt to hide the desperation in his voice. 'Somewhere underground, there's a sweet, well-mannered girl who needs to be reunited with her true family!'

Wretch stepped up to Bonita, grasped her gently by the arms and sniffed her behind the ear. 'I'm telling you for sure, she's not one of ours.'

It was Candy who rested a reassuring hand on Bonita's back.

'It's not too late to bring out the best in you,' she said sympathetically, and hardened her gaze at Randall. 'Your father might be a bad apple, but that doesn't mean you have to be like him.'

Governor Shores looked both stunned and enraged. Maurice braced himself for an outpouring of abuse, only for the man to grasp his own jaw with tears in his eyes.

'I can't handle this pain any more!' he wailed.

'Are you talking about me?' Bonnie asked with barely concealed disdain. 'The guilt you carry around for mistreating the trolls? Or your manky, rotten back teeth?'

'I dare say we can have a dentist check him out at the station.' Trasker sounded like he had reached the limits of his patience. 'Take him away,' he told the security guy. 'Have him charged with assault, neglect, dereliction of duty, whatever. I'm just sorry we can't add being a poor father to the charge sheet.' Turning to leave as the Governor found himself dragged towards the gates, he paused and came back around. 'This place is going to be crawling with reinforcements at any moment. You guys would do well to get as far from here as possible.'

Maurice took a moment to consider this. By now, the crackle of flames from the burning buildings filled the air, along with cries of rage and also elation as some of the trolls who had squared up to the guards broke off for the sinkhole. Several rushed past, but Maurice didn't even blink.

'So, we're free to leave?' he asked. 'Despite everything?'

By now, some colour had returned to Trasker's cheeks.

'You're free to go *because* of everything.' He invited Maurice to look around. 'This place isn't fit for purpose,' he added, as yet more trolls surged over the park railings. 'Having seen the lengths you went for the sake of these people, I'm thinking they deserve a break.'

'Won't you get in trouble?' asked Maurice.

From a back street, the sound of breaking glass punctured the din. Kyle Trasker heard it loud and clear. Blowing the air from his cheeks, he lifted his arms away from his side.

'It can't get much worse, can it?'

Maurice smiled to himself.

'But it feels like the right thing to do,' he offered, and shared a smile with Candy.

Trasker levelled his gaze with Maurice, holding it steady for a second without expression. Then he nodded, as if he'd just thought it through for himself.

'Go,' he said next, and took a step away. 'Before my conscience deserts me.'

Maurice watched the guy from the government leave. Even from behind, as he moved against the stream of trolls heading for the sinkhole, he looked like someone who just wanted to be curled up in bed. A moment later, the boy heard someone calling for his attention.

'Help!' Wretch appealed to him quietly but urgently as Bonita held his face in her hands and gazed into his eyes.

'So, you're the bad boy who drove my old man over the edge?' she asked, squeezing his cheeks at the same time until his mouth went mushy. 'That makes me feel all funny inside. In a good way.'

Wretch switched his attention to Maurice, repeating his plea for assistance.

'She likes you,' said the boy. 'You should be flattered!'

The little troll squeaked as Bonita released his face, only for her to grasp one hand and cling on tight.

'Do you want to have some fun together?' she asked.

Wretch shook his head furiously from side to side.

'Oh, come on.' Candy stepped up beside Maurice. She folded her arms and chuckled. 'Show the girl a good time!'

'I have to go,' he squeaked, and gestured frantically at the sinkhole.

'Take me,' she said.

'*What?*'

'Take me with you.'

Wretch opened his mouth to protest, and then appeared to reconsider.

'You want to go underground?' he asked to clarify.

'Why not? My dad isn't around to spoil the fun any more. I can do as I please!'

Once again, Wretch turned to Maurice.

'Go for it,' said the boy, and invited him to look around. 'Right now, life down there looks more appealing than it does at ground level.'

'For a wet blanket, your mate speaks a lot of sense,' Bonita added, and began to tug at the little troll's hand. '*Please!*' she added in a whiny voice. 'Bonny wants to party!'

'What have you got to lose?' Candy asked.

Just then, Wretch reminded Maurice of someone who had found a stray dog and was just coming round to the realisation that nobody was around to claim it.

'It's a simple life down there,' he said, making it sound like a warning. 'Can you survive without the internet, text messaging and TV?'

Bonita grimaced at each potential sacrifice.

'What about vodka shots?' she asked with some concern.

Maurice pressed his lips together and shrugged.

'Who needs that when you have family?'

All of a sudden, Bonita didn't look so keen.

'He's talking about love.' This was Candy, who waited for everyone to look at her and then beamed. 'Something every home should have.'

Wretch nodded, confirming her interpretation, and then appeared to remind himself what this could mean.

'It's also really gloomy,' he said hurriedly. 'Lots of tight spaces, too.'

If the little troll had hoped to persuade Bonita to rethink, the significant upswing in her spirit told him that he had in fact just sealed his own fate.

'So, what are we waiting for? If Dad's going to jail, then Mum will just blame me. And if Ryan and Benny are on their way down then there's no reason for me to stay. C'mon! Take me to your leaders!'

A sense of resignation had settled across Wretch's face, which he seemed to find less uncomfortable as she pleaded with him.

'OK,' he said eventually. 'Just promise me you won't keep talking.'

337

Bonita squealed, practically yanking Wretch off balance as she turned for the sinkhole. He looked at Candy, the uncertainty leaving his eyes now, and then stopped in his tracks.

'One thing,' he said, and fished around inside his pocket. 'You probably should have this back.'

Maurice recognised Candy's phone as he handed it to her.

'I left this in the glove compartment of the hire car,' she said. 'Switched off so nobody could track us.'

'I was just looking after it for you.' Wretch looked to the ground, unconvinced by his own story. 'You know? In case someone stole it.'

Candy examined the phone, and hit the button to power it up. As she did so, Bonita lost patience with her new companion.

'Mobiles are for mugs!' she snapped, as yet more trolls rushed for the sinkhole. 'If I have to queue to get in there'll be trouble!'

Helplessly, Wretch caught Maurice's eye.

'You'll be OK,' the boy assured him.

'That's easy for you to say.'

'With your guidance, she'll settle in just fine.' Maurice swallowed hotly. 'Good luck,' he said, 'my brother.'

Wretch nodded, blinking hard all of a sudden, which only caused Maurice to draw breath. Just then, it struck him that they might not see each other again. For someone who had only just come into his life, and promptly turned it upside down, he was going to miss his unpredictable, hyperactive and flame-happy friend. The little troll sniggered, but this time it didn't last. Slowly, a calm, almost solemn expression emerged in its place. Then he nodded, just once, before succumbing to a tug at his arm from Bonita.

Smiling to himself, Maurice watched the pair head down the slope. Part of him wanted Wretch to look around. Part of him was glad that he didn't.

He cleared his throat, looking away to make things easier on himself. It took a moment for the boy to register that his surroundings were still in chaos. The number of trolls still present had diminished significantly, and yet those who remained showed no sign of standing down. The security squads that Maurice could see had contracted into tight groups. They were taking steps backwards wherever possible, and frankly looked like they were itching to just turn tail. It was Candy's phone that drew him from his thoughts, signalling the presence of a waiting message. Maurice watched her respond to it with some hesitation.

'Greg,' she reported with a glimpse at the screen. It took her a moment to read the text. Then, nodding reflectively, Candy shut down her phone once more.

'Bad news?' asked Maurice.

Candy blinked and faced him. Then she smiled and shook her head.

'I was expecting nothing else,' she told him. 'At least now I'm free to move on with my life.'

'Where will you go?' he asked, raising his voice as a cheer marked the moment that the roof of the city hall caved under the blaze. 'Back to the flat?'

Candy swatted away the suggestion, looking genuinely liberated.

'Apparently the locks have been changed,' she told him. 'And my stuff is by the bins.'

'So, not really what you'd call a keeper.' Maurice tried and failed to sound convincingly upbeat. 'You deserve better,' he added simply.

Candy nodded, lost in thought for a second.

'How about your plans?' she asked, and strengthened her composure. 'Isn't this the moment you wake up in Kansas with friends and family around your bedside?'

Maurice smiled thinly. It struck him that he hadn't given his home life a moment's thought since slipping the note under the front door.

'Everything goes back to boring black and white when Dorothy goes home,' he pointed out.

'You mean sepia,' said Candy. '*The Wizard of* Oz starts and ends in sepia. Not quite as dull, but equally plain and simple.'

Maurice took a moment to register this, and another to realise she was playing with him.

'Either way, I'm kind of used to having lots of colour in my life now.'

'What about your mum and dad?' she asked, smiling openly now. 'They'd be thrilled to have you back, no?'

'Maybe,' he said with a shrug. 'Though I'm always going to be their baby boy.'

'After everything you've done?' Candy's voice held a note of surprise. 'You might be a few years younger than me, Maurice, but you've proven you can take care of yourself . . . and those less fortunate,' she said on reflection. 'Personally, you've shown me how to dig deep when times get tough.'

Listening to this left Maurice with a warm sensation in his cheeks. With the sun on the cusp of setting, and light from the fires flickering across the buildings around the park, he turned his attention to the sinkhole. Across from them he caught sight of the trucker, Byron, and the old man from the caravan. The pair were assessing the scene. They looked mightily satisfied. Still more trolls continued to break for the abyss, throwing themselves in with great glee. When Maurice pointed them out to Candy, he found it had already earned her full attention.

'Looks like fun,' he said, as yet another one appeared to hop, skip and jump over the edge.

Watching the figure hoot joyfully on diving into the gloom, he sensed a hand find his, and squeeze it tightly. With a gasp, he looked around. Candy was entirely focused on the sinkhole.

'How about we find out for ourselves?' she asked.

Just considering this left Maurice feeling giddy. Instinctively, he wondered how much trouble it would earn them. Then he cast the thought aside. For having come to the end of one journey, embarking on a bigger one suddenly struck him as the most natural thing in the world. Just then, the sound of sirens rose up from the settlement outskirts. It prompted the remaining knots of trolls to break towards the sinkhole. Taking a slow, deep breath, Maurice faced the abyss once more and squeezed Candy's hand.

'It looks like a long way down,' he observed.

Candy appeared set to respond, only to be distracted by the sight of yet more figures somersaulting into the heart of a great unknown.

'There's a troll inside us all,' she said. 'You know that now, don't you?'

341

Well aware that she was inviting him to join her in a leap of faith, Maurice began to nod; hesitantly at first but then with some conviction.

'I do,' he said, as the pair stood serene amid such chaos. 'And now is the time to set it free.'

Acknowledgements

This book has been some while in the making. I've worked on the story over several years – not just in West Sussex but Lagos and Mexico City. Since I started writing BAD APPLE, sink holes have become a news staple all over the world. As yet, no trolls have been spotted in the wild – but give it time. I've enjoyed this long journey, from a fleeting idea to the book in your hands, and I have many people to thank who have helped me on the way: my editor, Naomi Colthurst, her trusty sidekicks, Monique Meledje and Georgia Murray, as well as everyone in the Hot Key family. Then there's my agent and literary wife, Philippa Milnes Smith and my real other half, Emma Whyman, with thanks also to Emily Thomas and Sarah Odedina, Elizabeth Briggs and Daphne Lao Tonge for their much-valued support.

Matt Whyman

Matt Whyman is the author of several critically aclaimed novels, including *The Savages*, *American Savage* and *Boy Kills Man*, as well as two comic memoirs, *Pig in the Middle* and *Walking with Sausage Dogs*. He is married and lives with his family in West Sussex.